O N C

(A RILEY PAIGE MYSTERY—BOOK 6)

BLAKE PIERCE

BOOKS BY BLAKE PIERCE

RILEY PAIGE MYSTERY SERIES
ONCE GONE (Book #1)
ONCE TAKEN (Book #2)
ONCE CRAVED (Book #3)
ONCE LURED (Book #4)
ONCE HUNTED (Book #5)
ONCE PINED (Book #6)

MACKENZIE WHITE MYSTERY SERIES
BEFORE HE KILLS (Book #1)
BEFORE HE SEES (Book #2)
BEFORE HE COVETS (Book #3)

AVERY BLACK MYSTERY SERIES
CAUSE TO KILL (Book #1)
CAUSE TO RUN (Book #2)
CAUSE TO HIDE (Book #3)

KERI LOCKE MYSTERY SERIES
A TRACE OF DEATH (Book #1)

PROLOGUE

The physical therapist smiled kindly at her patient, Cody Woods, as she turned off the machine.

"I think that's enough CPM for the day," she told him as his leg gradually stopped moving.

The machine had been slowly and passively moving his leg for a couple of hours now, helping him recover from his knee replacement surgery.

"I'd almost forgotten it was on, Hallie," Cody said with a slight chuckle.

She felt a bittersweet pang. She liked that name—Hallie. It was the name she'd used whenever she'd worked here at the Signet Rehabilitation Center as a freelance physical therapist.

It seemed to her rather a shame that Hallie Stillians was going to disappear tomorrow, as if she'd never existed.

Still, that was the way things had to be.

And besides, she had other names that she liked just as well.

Hallie took the continuous passive motion machine off the bed and set it on the floor. She gently straightened Cody's leg and arranged the covers around him.

Finally she stroked Cody's hair—an intimate gesture that she knew most therapists would avoid. But she often did little things like that, and she'd never had a patient who minded. She knew that she projected a certain warmth and empathy—and most of all, complete sincerity. A little innocent touching was perfectly appropriate, coming from her. No one ever misunderstood.

"How's the pain?" she asked.

Cody had been having some unusual swelling and inflammation after the operation. That was why he'd stayed here an extra three days and hadn't gone home yet. That was also why Hallie had been brought in to work her special healing magic. The staff here at the center knew Hallie's work well. The staff liked her, and patients liked her, so she often got called in for situations like this.

"The pain?" Cody said. "I'd almost forgotten about it. Your voice made it go away."

Hallie felt flattered but not surprised. She'd been reading a book to him while he'd been on the CPM machine—an espionage thriller. She knew her voice had a calming effect—almost like an anesthetic. It didn't matter whether she was reading Dickens or

1

some pulp novel or the newspaper. Patients didn't need much pain medication when they were under her care; the sound of her voice was often enough.

"So is it true that I can go home tomorrow?" Cody asked.

Hallie hesitated just a split second. She couldn't be entirely truthful. She wasn't sure how her patient would be feeling by tomorrow.

"That's what they tell me," she said. "How does it feel to know that?"

A sad expression crossed Cody's face.

"I don't know," he said. "In just three weeks, they're doing my other knee. But you won't be here to help me through it."

Hallie took hold of his hand and held it gently. She was sorry that he felt this way. Since he'd been under her care, she'd told him a long story about her supposed life—a rather boring story, she'd thought, but he'd seemed enchanted by it.

Finally, she'd explained to him that her husband, Rupert, was about to retire from his career as a CPA. Her younger son, James, was down in Hollywood trying to make it as a screenwriter. Her older son, Wendell, was right here in Seattle teaching linguistics at the University of Washington. Now that the kids were grown and out of the house, she and Rupert were moving to a lovely colonial village in Mexico, where they planned to spend the rest of their lives. They were leaving tomorrow.

It was a beautiful story, she thought.

And yet none of it was true.

She lived at home, alone.

Utterly alone.

"Oh look, your tea has gotten cold," she said. "I'll just heat it up for you."

Cody smiled and said, "Yes, please. That would be nice. And have some yourself. The teapot is right there on the counter."

Hallie smiled and said, "Of course," just as she did every time they repeated this routine. She got up from her chair, picked up Cody's mug of lukewarm tea, and took it to the counter.

But this time, she reached into her purse beside the microwave. She took out a small plastic medicine container and emptied the contents of the container into Cody's tea. She did it quickly, stealthily, a practiced move she had down, and she felt certain he had not seen her. Even so, her heart beat just a little bit faster.

She then poured her own tea and put both mugs into the microwave.

I've got to keep these straight, she reminded herself. *The yellow mug for Cody, blue for me.*

While the microwave hummed, she sat down beside Cody again and looked at him without saying anything.

He had a nice face, she thought. But he'd told her about his own life, and she knew that he was sad. He had been sad for a long time. He'd been a prize-winning athlete when he was in high school. But he'd injured his knees playing football, ending his hopes for an athletic career. Those same injuries at long last led to his need for knee replacements.

His life ever since had been marked by tragedy. His first wife had died of a car wreck, and his second wife left him for another man. He had two grown children, but they didn't speak to him anymore. He'd also had a heart attack just a few years ago.

She admired the fact that he didn't seem the least bit bitter. In fact, he seemed full of hope and optimism about the future.

She thought he was sweet, but naive.

She knew that his life wasn't going to take a turn for the better.

It was too late for that.

The bell from the microwave snapped her out of her little reverie. Cody was looking up at her with kindly, expectant eyes.

She patted his hand, got up, and walked over to the microwave. She took out the mugs, which were now hot to the touch.

She reminded herself yet again.

Yellow for Cody, blue for me.

It was important not to mix them up.

They both sipped their tea without saying much. Hallie liked to think of these moments as times of quiet companionship. It made her a little sad to realize that there would be no more of them. After just a few days, this patient would no longer need her.

Soon Cody was nodding off to sleep. She had mixed the powder with just enough sleeping medicine to make sure he did.

Hallie got up and gathered her belongings to leave.

And then she began to sing softly, a song she'd known for as long as she could remember:

Far from home,
So far from home—
This little baby's far from home.
You pine away
From day to day
Too sad to laugh, too sad to play.

3

No need to weep,
Dream long and deep.
Give yourself to slumber's sweep.
No more sighs,
Just close your eyes
And you will go home in your sleep.

His eyes closed, she stroked his hair from his face lovingly.

Then, with a gentle kiss on the forehead, she stood and walked away.

CHAPTER ONE

FBI Agent Riley Paige worried as she walked through the jetway at Phoenix Sky Harbor International Airport. She'd been anxious all during the flight from Reagan Washington International. She'd come here in a hurry because she'd heard that a teenage girl was missing—Jilly—a girl Riley felt especially protective toward. She was determined to help the girl and was even thinking about trying to adopt her.

As Riley stepped through the exit gate, walking hurriedly, she looked up and was shocked to see the very girl herself standing there, FBI agent Garrett Holbrook from the Phoenix field office beside her.

Thirteen-year-old Jilly Scarlatti stood next to Garrett, blinking back, clearly waiting for her.

Riley was confused. It was Garrett who had called to tell her that Jilly had run away and was nowhere to be found.

Before Riley could ask any questions, though, Jilly rushed forward and threw herself into her arms, sobbing.

"Oh, Riley, I'm sorry. I'm so, so sorry. I'll never do it again."

Riley hugged Jilly comfortingly, looking at Garrett for an explanation. Garrett's sister, Bonnie Flaxman, had tried to take Jilly in as a foster child. But Jilly had rebelled and run away.

Garrett smiled a little—an unusual expression from a normally taciturn man.

"She called Bonnie shortly after you left Fredericksburg," he said. "She said she just wanted to say goodbye once and for all. But then Bonnie told her that you were on your way here to take her home with you. She got really excited and told us where to pick her up."

He looked at Riley.

"Your flying all the way here saved her," he concluded.

Riley just stood there for a moment, Jilly sobbing in her arms, feeling oddly clumsy and helpless.

Jilly whispered something that Riley couldn't hear.

"What?" Riley asked.

Jilly drew her face back and looked into Riley's eyes, her own earnest brown eyes filled with tears.

"Mom?" she said in a choked, shy voice. "Can I call you Mom?"

Riley hugged her close again, overwhelmed by a confusing

onslaught of emotions.

"Of course," Riley said.

Then she turned to Garrett. "Thank you so much for everything you've done."

"I'm glad I could help, at least a little," he replied. "Do you need a place to stay while you're here?"

"No. Now that she's been found, there's no point. We'll catch the next flight back."

Garrett shook her hand. "I hope this works out for both of you." Then he left.

Riley looked down at the teenager who was still clinging to her. She was struck with an odd mix of elation to have found her and concern for what the future might hold for them both.

"Let's go grab a burger," she said to Jilly.

*

It was snowing lightly during the drive home from Reagan Washington International Airport. Jilly sat staring silently out the window as Riley drove. Her silence was a big change after the more than four-hour flight from Phoenix. Then, Jilly hadn't been able to stop talking. She'd never been on a plane before and was curious about absolutely everything.

Why is she so quiet now? Riley wondered.

It occurred to her that snow must be an unusual sight for a girl who had lived all her life in Arizona.

"Have you ever seen snow before?" Riley asked.

"Only on TV."

"Do you like it?" Riley said.

Jilly didn't reply, which made Riley feel uneasy. She remembered the first time she had seen Jilly. The girl had run away from an abusive father. In sheer desperation, she had decided to become a prostitute. She'd gone to a truck stop that was notorious as a pickup place for prostitutes—"lot lizards," they were called, because they were especially down-and-out.

Riley had gone there investigating a series of murders of prostitutes. She'd happened to find Jilly hidden away in the cab of a truck, waiting to sell herself to the driver whenever he came back.

Riley had gotten Jilly into Child Protective Services and had stayed in touch with her. Garrett's sister had taken Jilly in as a foster child, but eventually Jilly had run away again.

It was then that Riley had decided to take Jilly home herself.

But now she was starting to wonder if she'd made a mistake. She already had her own fifteen-year-old daughter, April, to take care of. April alone could be a handful. They had been through some traumatic experiences together since Riley's marriage had broken up.

And what did she really know about Jilly? Did Riley have any idea how deeply scarred the girl might be? Was she the least bit prepared to deal with the challenges Jilly might present? And although April had approved of her bringing Jilly home, how would the two teenagers get along?

Suddenly, Jilly spoke.

"Where am I going to sleep?"

Riley felt relieved to hear Jilly's voice.

"You'll have your own room," she said. "It's small, but I think it's just right for you."

Jilly fell silent for another moment.

Then she said, "Was it somebody else's room?"

Jilly sounded worried now.

"Not since I've lived there," Riley said. "I tried using it as an office, but it was too big. So I moved my office into my bedroom. April and I bought you a bed and a dresser, but when we have time, you can pick out some posters and a bedspread that you like."

"My own room," Jilly said.

Riley thought she sounded more apprehensive than happy.

"Where does April sleep?" Jilly asked.

Riley more than half wanted to tell Jilly to just wait until they got home, and then she'd see everything for herself. But the girl sounded like she needed reassurance right this minute.

"April has her own room," Riley said. "You and April will share a bathroom, though. I've got my own bathroom."

"Who cleans? Who cooks?" Jilly asked. Then she added anxiously, "I'm not a good enough cook."

"Our housekeeper, Gabriela, takes care of all that. She's from Guatemala. She lives with us, in her own apartment downstairs. You'll meet her soon. She'll take care of you when I have to be away."

Another silence fell.

Then Jilly asked, "Will Gabriela beat me?"

Riley was stunned by the question.

"No. Of course not. Why would you think that?"

Jilly didn't reply. Riley tried to comprehend what she meant.

She tried to tell herself that she shouldn't be surprised. She remembered what Jilly had said when she'd found her in the truck cab and told her that she needed to go home.

"I'm not going home. My dad will beat me up if I go back."

Social services in Phoenix had already removed Jilly from her father's custody. Riley knew that Jilly's mother had gone missing long ago. Jilly had a brother somewhere, but nobody had heard from him in a while.

It broke Riley's heart to realize that Jilly might be expecting similar treatment in her new home. It seemed that the poor girl could barely imagine anything better in life.

"Nobody's going to beat you, Jilly," Riley said, her voice shaking a little with emotion. "Never again. We're going to take good care of you. Do you understand?"

Again, Jilly didn't reply. Riley wished she would just say that she *did* understand, and that she believed what Riley was saying. Instead, Jilly changed the subject.

"I like your car," she said. "Can I learn to drive?"

"When you're older, sure," Riley said. "Right now let's get you settled into your new life."

*

A little snow was still falling when Riley parked in front of her townhouse and she and Jilly got out of the car. Jilly's face twitched a little as snowflakes struck her skin. She didn't seem to like this new sensation. And she shivered all over from the cold.

We've got to get her some warmer clothes right away, Riley thought.

Halfway between the car and the front door, Jilly froze in her tracks. She stared at the house.

"I can't do this," Jilly said.

"Why not?"

Jilly said nothing for a moment. She looked like a frightened animal. Riley suspected that the thought of living in such a nice place overwhelmed her.

"I'll be getting in April's way, won't I?" Jilly said. "I mean it's her bathroom."

She seemed to be looking for excuses, grasping for reasons why this whole thing wouldn't work.

"You won't get in April's way," Riley said. "Now come on in."

Riley opened the door. Waiting inside were April and Riley's ex-husband, Ryan. Their faces were smiling and welcoming.

8

April rushed toward Jilly right away and gave her a big hug.

"I'm April," she said. "I'm so glad you came. You'll really like it here."

Riley was startled by the difference between the two girls. She'd always considered April to be rather thin and gangly. But she appeared positively robust next to Jilly, who looked skinny by comparison. Riley guessed that Jilly had gone hungry from time to time during her life.

So many things I still don't know, Riley thought.

Jilly smiled nervously as Ryan introduced himself and hugged her.

Suddenly Gabriela came rushing in from downstairs, introducing herself with a huge smile.

"Welcome to the family!" Gabriela exclaimed, giving Jilly a hug.

Riley noticed that the stout Guatemalan woman's skin was only slightly darker than Jilly's olive complexion.

"Vente!" Gabriela said, taking Jilly by the hand. "Let's go upstairs. I will show you your room!"

But Jilly pulled her hand away and stood there trembling. Tears began to stream down her face. She sat down on the stairs and cried. April sat down beside her and put her arm around her shoulders.

"Jilly, what's wrong?" April asked.

Jilly shook her head miserably.

"I don't know," she sobbed. "It's just … I don't know. It's all so much."

April smiled sweetly and patted her gently on the back.

"I know, I know," she said. "Come on upstairs. You'll feel at home in no time."

Jilly obediently got up and followed April upstairs. Riley was pleased by how graciously her daughter was handling the situation. Of course, April had always said that she wanted a younger sister. But April had been through some difficult years herself, and had been severely traumatized by criminals eager to get even with Riley.

Maybe, Riley thought hopefully, *April will be able to understand Jilly better than I can.*

Gabriela gazed sympathetically after the two girls.

"¡Pobrecita!" she said. "I hope she will be all right."

Gabriela went back downstairs, leaving Riley and Ryan alone. Ryan stood staring up the stairs, looking somewhat dazed.

I hope he's not having second thoughts, Riley thought. *I'm going to need his support.*

A lot had gone on between her and Ryan. During the last years of their marriage he'd been an unfaithful husband and an absent father. They'd been separated and divorced. But Ryan had seemed like a changed man lately and they were cautiously spending more time together.

They'd talked about the challenge of bringing Jilly into their lives. Ryan had seemed enthusiastic about the idea.

"Are you still OK with this?" Riley asked him.

Ryan looked at her and said, "Yeah. I can see that it's going to be tough, though."

Riley nodded. Then came an awkward pause.

"I think maybe I'd better go," Ryan said.

Riley felt relieved. She kissed him lightly, and he put on his coat and left. Riley fixed a drink for herself and sat down alone in the living room.

What have I gotten us all into? she wondered.

She hoped that her good intentions weren't going to tear her family apart all over again.

CHAPTER TWO

Riley woke up the next morning with a heart full of apprehension. This was going to be the first day of Jilly's life in her home. They had a lot to do today and Riley hoped that no trouble was in store.

Last night she had realized that Jilly's transition to her new life would mean hard work for all of them. But April had pitched in and helped Jilly get settled. They had picked out clothes for Jilly to wear today—not from the meager possessions she'd brought along in a grocery bag but from new things that Riley and April had bought for her.

Jilly and April had finally gone to bed.

Riley had too, but her sleep had been troubled and restless.

Now she got up and dressed, and headed straight to the kitchen, where April was helping Gabriela get breakfast ready.

"Where's Jilly?" Riley asked.

"She hasn't gotten up yet," April said.

Riley's worry mounted.

She went to the base of the stairs and called out, "Jilly, it's time to get up."

She heard no reply. She was seized by a wave of panic. Had Jilly run off during the night?

"Jilly, did you hear me?" she called out. "We've got to register you at school this morning."

"I'm coming," Jilly yelled back.

Riley breathed a sigh of relief. Jilly's tone was sullen, but at least she was here and being cooperative.

In recent years, Riley had often heard that sullen tone from April. Now April seemed to have gotten past it, but she still had lapses from time to time. Riley wondered if she was really up to the job of raising another teenager.

Just then there was a knock at the front door. When Riley answered it, her townhouse neighbor, Blaine Hildreth, was standing outside.

Riley was surprised to see him, but hardly displeased. He was a couple of years younger than she was, a charming and attractive man who owned an upscale restaurant in town. In fact, she had felt an unmistakable mutual attraction with him that definitely confused the issue of possibly reconnecting with Ryan. Most importantly, Blaine was a wonderful neighbor and their daughters were best friends.

"Hi, Riley," he said. "I hope it's not too early."

"Not at all," Riley said. "What's up?"

Blaine shrugged with a rather sad smile.

"I just thought I'd stop by to say goodbye," he said.

Riley gaped with surprise.

"What do you mean?" she asked.

He hesitated, and before he could answer, Riley saw a huge truck parked in front of his townhouse. Movers were carrying furniture from Blaine's home into the truck.

Riley gasped.

"You're moving?" she asked.

"It seemed like a good idea," Blaine said.

Riley almost blurted out, *"Why?"*

But it was easy to guess why. Living next door to Riley had proved to be dangerous and terrifying, both to Blaine and his daughter, Crystal. The bandage that was still on his face was a harsh reminder. Blaine had been badly injured when he'd tried to protect April from a killer's attack.

"It's not what you probably think," Blaine said.

But Riley could tell by his expression—it was exactly what she thought.

He continued, "It has turned out that this place just isn't convenient. It's too far away from the restaurant. I've found a nice place that's much closer. I'm sure you understand."

Riley felt too confused and upset to reply. Memories of the whole terrible incident came flooding back to her.

She'd been in Upstate New York working on a case when she'd learned that a brutal killer was at large. His name was Orin Rhodes. Sixteen years earlier, Riley had killed his girlfriend in a gunfight and sent him to prison. When Rhodes was finally released from Sing Sing, he was bent on revenge against Riley and everyone she loved.

Before Riley could get home, Rhodes had invaded her home and attacked both April and Gabriela. Next door, Blaine had heard the struggle, so he came over to help. He'd probably saved April's life. But he'd gotten badly hurt in the attempt.

Riley had seen him twice in the hospital. The first time had been devastating. He'd been unconscious from his injuries, with an IV in each arm and an oxygen mask. Riley had blamed herself bitterly for what had happened to him.

But the next time she'd seen him had been more heartening.

He'd been alert and cheerful, and had joked a bit proudly about his foolhardiness.

Most of all, she remembered what he'd said to her then …

"There isn't much I wouldn't do for you and April."

Clearly he'd had second thoughts. The danger of living next door to Riley had proven too much for him and now he was going away. She didn't know whether to feel hurt or guilty. She definitely felt disappointed.

Riley's thoughts were interrupted by April's voice behind her.

"Oh my God! Blaine, are you and Crystal moving? Is Crystal still there?"

Blaine nodded.

"I've got to go over and say goodbye," April said.

April dashed out the door and headed next door.

Riley was still grappling with her emotions.

"I'm sorry," she said.

"Sorry for what?" Blaine asked.

"You know."

Blaine nodded. "It wasn't your fault, Riley," he said in a gentle voice.

Riley and Blaine stood gazing at each other for a moment. Finally, Blaine forced a smile.

"Hey, it's not like we're leaving town," he said. "We can get together whenever we like. So can the girls. And they'll still be in the same high school. It'll be like nothing has changed."

A bitter taste rose up in Riley's mouth.

That's not true, she thought. *Everything has changed.*

Disappointment was starting to give way to anger. Riley knew that it was wrong to feel angry. She had no right. She didn't even know why she felt that way. All she knew was that she couldn't help it.

And what were they supposed to do right now?

Hug? Shake hands?

She sensed that Blaine felt the same awkwardness and indecision.

They managed to exchange terse goodbyes. Blaine went back home, and Riley went back inside. She found Jilly eating breakfast in the kitchen. Gabriela had put Riley's own breakfast on the table, so she sat down to eat with Jilly.

"So are you excited about today?"

Riley's question was out before she could realize how lame and clumsy it sounded.

13

"I guess," Jilly said, poking her pancakes with a fork. She didn't even look up at Riley.

*

A while later, Riley and Jilly walked through the entrance to Brody Middle School. The building was attractive, with brightly colored locker doors lining the hallway and student artwork hanging everywhere.

A pleasant and polite student offered her help and directed them toward the main office. Riley thanked her and continued down the hall, clutching Jilly's registration papers in one hand and holding Jilly's hand with the other.

Earlier, they had gone through registration at the central school office. They'd taken along the materials that Phoenix Social Services had put together—records of vaccination, school transcripts, Jilly's birth certificate, and a statement that Riley was Jilly's appointed guardian. Jilly had been removed from her father's custody, although he had threatened to challenge that decision. Riley knew that the path to finalizing and legalizing an adoption wouldn't be quick or easy.

Jilly squeezed Riley's hand tightly. Riley sensed that the girl felt extremely ill at ease. It wasn't hard to imagine why. As rough as life in Phoenix had been, it was the only place that Jilly had ever lived.

"Why can't I go to school with April?" Jilly asked.

"Next year you'll be in the same high school," Riley said. "First you've got to finish eighth grade."

They found the main office and Riley showed the papers to the receptionist.

"We'd like to see someone about enrolling Jilly in school," Riley said.

"You need to see a guidance counselor," the receptionist said with a smile. "Come right this way."

Both of us could use some guidance, Riley thought.

The counselor was a woman in her thirties with a mop of curly brown hair. Her name was Wanda Lewis, and her smile was as warm as a smile could be. Riley found herself thinking that she could be a real help. Surely a woman in a job like this had dealt with other students from rough backgrounds.

Ms. Lewis took them on a tour of the school. The library was neat, orderly, and well stocked with both computers and books. In the gym, girls were happily playing basketball. The cafeteria was clean and sparkling. Everything looked absolutely lovely to Riley.

All the while, Ms. Lewis cheerfully asked Jilly lots of questions about where she'd gone to school before, and about her interests. But Jilly said almost nothing in reply to Ms. Lewis's questions and asked none of her own. Her curiosity seemed to perk up a little when she got a look at the art room. But as soon as they moved on, she became quiet and withdrawn all over again.

Riley wondered what might be going on in the girl's head. She knew that her recent grades had been poor, but they had been surprisingly good in earlier years. But the truth was, Riley knew almost nothing about Jilly's past school experience.

Maybe she even hated school.

This new one must be daunting, where Jilly knew absolutely nobody. And of course, it wasn't going to be easy to get caught up in her studies, with only a couple of weeks left before end of the term.

At the end of the tour, Riley managed to coax Jilly into thanking Ms. Lewis for showing her around. They agreed that Jilly would start classes tomorrow. Then Riley and Jilly walked out into the bite of the cold January air. A thin layer of yesterday's snow lay all around the parking lot.

"So what do you think of your new school?" Riley asked.

"It's OK," Jilly said.

Riley couldn't tell if Jilly was being sullen or was simply dazed by all the changes she was facing. As they approached the car, she noticed that Jilly was shivering deeply and her teeth were chattering. She was wearing a heavy jacket of April's, but the cold was really bothering her.

They got into the car, and Riley switched on the ignition and the heater. Even as the car got warmer, Jilly was still shivering.

Riley kept the car parked. It was time to find out what was bothering this child in her care.

"What's wrong?" she asked. "Is there something about school that upsets you?"

"It's not the school," Jilly said, her voice shaking now. "It's the cold."

"I guess it doesn't get cold in Phoenix," Riley said. "This must be strange to you."

Jilly's eyes filled up with tears.

"It does get cold sometimes," she said. "Especially at night."

"Please tell me what's wrong," Riley said.

Tears started to pour down Jilly's cheeks. She spoke in a small, choked voice.

"The cold makes me remember …"

Jilly fell silent. Riley waited patiently for her to gone.

"My dad always blamed me for everything," Jilly said. "He blamed me for my mom going away, and my brother too, and he even blamed me because he kept getting fired from whatever jobs he could get. Anything that was wrong was always my fault."

Jilly was sobbing quietly now.

"Go on," Riley said.

"One night he told me he wanted me gone," Jilly said. "He said I was a dead weight, that I was keeping him down, and he'd had enough of me and he was through with me. He kicked me out of the house. He locked the doors and I couldn't get back in."

Jilly gulped hard at the memory.

"I've never felt so cold in my life," she said. "Not even now, in this weather. I found a big drainpipe in a ditch, and it was big enough for me to crawl into, so that was where I spent that night. It was so scary. Sometimes people were walking around near me, but I didn't want them to find me. They didn't sound like anybody who would help me."

Riley closed her eyes, picturing the girl hiding in the dark drainpipe. She whispered, "And what happened then?"

Jilly continued, "I just scrunched down and stayed there all night. I didn't really sleep. The next morning I went back home and knocked on the door and called for Dad and begged him to let me in. He ignored me, like I wasn't even there. That's when I went to the truck stop. It was warm there, and there was food. Some of the women were nice to me and I figured I'd do whatever I had to do to stay there. And that night is when you found me."

Jilly had grown calmer as she'd told her story. She seemed relieved to let it out. But now Riley was crying. She could hardly believe what this poor girl had gone through. She put her arm around Jilly and hugged her tight.

"Never again," Riley said through her sobs. "Jilly, I promise you, you'll never feel like that ever again."

It was a huge promise, and Riley was feeling small, weak, and fragile herself right now. She hoped that she could keep it.

CHAPTER THREE

The woman kept thinking about poor Cody Woods. She was sure that he was dead by now. She'd find out for sure from the morning newspaper.

As much as she was enjoying her hot tea and granola, waiting for the news was making her grumpy.

When is that paper going to get here? she wondered, looking at the kitchen clock.

The delivery seemed to be getting later and later these days. Of course, she wouldn't have this trouble with a digital subscription. But she didn't like to read the news on her computer. She liked to settle down in a comfortable chair and enjoy the old-fashioned feel of a newspaper in her hands. She even liked the way the newsprint sometimes stuck to her fingers.

But the paper was already a quarter of an hour late. If things got much worse, she'd have to call in and complain. She hated to do that. It always left a bad taste in her mouth.

Anyway, the newspaper was really the only way she had of finding out about Cody. She couldn't very well call the Signet Rehabilitation Center to ask about him. That would cause too much suspicion. Besides, as far as the staff there was concerned, she was already in Mexico with her husband, with no plans ever to return.

Or rather, Hallie Stillians was in Mexico. It felt a bit sad that she'd never get to be Hallie Stillians ever again. She'd gotten rather attached to that particular alias. It had been sweet of the staff at Signet Rehab to surprise her with a cake on her last day there.

She smiled as she remembered. The cake had been colorfully decorated with sombreros and a message:

Buen Viaje, Hallie and Rupert!

Rupert had been the name of her imaginary husband. She was going to miss talking so fondly about him.

She finished her granola and kept sipping her delicious homemade tea, made from an old family recipe—a different recipe from the one she'd shared with Cody, and of course minus the special ingredients she'd added for him.

She idly began to sing …

Far from home,

17

So far from home—
This little baby's far from home.
You pine away
From day to day
Too sad to laugh, too sad to play.

How Cody had loved that song! So had all the other patients. And many more patients in the future were sure to love it just as much. That thought warmed her heart.

Just then she heard a thump at the front door. She hurried to open it and look outside. Lying on the cold stoop was the morning newspaper. Trembling with excitement, she picked up the paper, rushed back to the kitchen, and opened it to the death notices.

Sure enough, there it was:

*SEATTLE — **Cody Woods**, 49, of Seattle ...*

She stopped for a moment right there. That was odd. She could have sworn that he'd told her he was fifty. Then she read the rest ...

... at the South Hills Hospital, Seattle, Wash.; Sutton-Brinks Funeral Home and Cremation Services, Seattle.

That was all. It was terse, even for a simple death notice.

She hoped that there would be a nice obituary in the next few days. But she was worried that maybe there wouldn't be. Who was going to write it, after all?

He'd been all alone in the world, at least as far as she knew. One wife was dead, another had left him, and his two children wouldn't speak to him. He'd said barely a word to her about anybody else—friends, relatives, business colleagues.

Who cares? she wondered.

She felt a familiar bitter rage rising in her throat.

Rage against all the people in Cody Woods' life who didn't care whether he lived or died.

Rage against the smiling staff at Signet Rehab, pretending that they liked and would miss Hallie Stillians.

Rage against people everywhere, with their lies and secrets and meanness.

As she often did, she imagined herself soaring over the world upon black wings, wreaking death and destruction upon the wicked.

And everybody was wicked.

Everybody deserved to die.

Even Cody Woods himself had been wicked and deserved to die.

Because what kind of man had he been, really, to leave the world with no one to love him?

A terrible man, surely.

Terrible and hateful.

"Serves him right," she growled.

Then she snapped out of her anger. She felt ashamed to have said such a thing aloud. She didn't mean it, after all. She reminded herself that she felt nothing but love and goodwill toward absolutely everybody.

Besides, it was almost time to go to work. Today she was going to be Judy Brubaker.

Looking in the mirror, she carefully made sure that the auburn wig was properly aligned and that the soft bangs hung naturally over her forehead. It was an expensive wig and no one had ever caught on that it wasn't her own hair. Beneath the wig, Hallie Stillians' short blond hair had been dyed dark brown and trimmed into a different style.

No sign of Hallie remained, not in her wardrobe and not in her mannerisms.

She picked up a pair of stylish reading glasses and hung them on a sparkly cord around her neck.

She smiled with satisfaction. It was smart to invest in the proper accessories, and Judy Brubaker deserved the best.

Everybody loved Judy Brubaker.

And everybody loved that song that Judy Brubaker often sang—a song she sang aloud as she dressed for work ...

No need to weep,
Dream long and deep.
Give yourself to slumber's sweep.
No more sighs,
Just close your eyes
And you will go home in your sleep.

She was overflowing with peace, enough peace to share with all the world. She'd given peace to Cody Woods.

And soon she'd give peace to someone else who needed it.

CHAPTER FOUR

Riley's heart pounded and her lungs burned from breathing hard and fast. A familiar tune was stuck in her head.

"Follow the yellow brick road ... "

As tired and winded as she was, Riley couldn't help but be amused. It was a cold early morning, and she was running the six-mile outdoor obstacle course at Quantico. The course was nicknamed, of all things, the Yellow Brick Road.

It had been called that by the US Marines who had built it. The Marines had placed yellow bricks to mark every mile. FBI trainees who survived the course were given a yellow brick as their reward.

Riley had won her yellow brick years ago. But every now and then, she ran the course again, just to make sure that she was still up to it. After the emotional stress of the last couple of days, Riley needed some full-on physical exertion to clear her head.

So far, she had overcome a series of daunting obstacles and had passed three yellow bricks along the way. She had climbed over makeshift walls, pulled herself over hurdles, and leaped through simulated windows. Just a moment ago she had pulled herself up a sheer rock face by a rope, and now she was lowering herself back down again.

When she hit the ground, she looked up and saw Lucy Vargas, a bright young agent she enjoyed working and training with. Lucy had been glad to be Riley's workout partner this morning. She stood panting at the top of the rock face, looking down at Riley.

Riley called up to her, "Can't keep up with an old fart like me?"

Lucy laughed. "I'm taking it slow. I don't want you to overdo it—not at your age."

"Hey, don't hold back on my account," Riley yelled back. "Give it all you've got."

Riley was forty, but she had never let her physical training lapse. Being able to move fast and strike hard could be crucial when battling human monsters. Sheer physical force had saved lives, including her own, more than once.

Even so, she wasn't happy when she looked ahead and saw the next obstacle—a shallow pool of freezing cold, muddy water with barbed wire hanging over it.

Things were about to get tough.

She was well bundled for winter weather and was wearing a

waterproof parka. But even so, the crawl through the mud was going to leave her soaked and freezing.

Here goes nothing, she thought.

She threw herself forward into the mud. The icy water sent a severe shock through her whole body. Still, she forced herself to start crawling, and she flattened herself as she felt the barbed wire scrape her back slightly.

A gnawing numbness kicked in, triggering an unwanted memory.

Riley was in a pitch-dark crawlspace under a house. She had just escaped a cage where she had been held and tormented by a psychopath with a propane torch. In the darkness, she'd lost track of how long she'd been in captivity.

But she'd managed to force the cage door open, and now she was crawling blindly in search of a way out. It had rained recently, and the mud underneath her was sticky, cold, and deep.

As her body grew ever more numb from the cold, a deep despair crept through her. She was weak from sleeplessness and hunger.

I can't make it, she thought.

She had to force such ideas out of her mind. She had to keep crawling and searching. If she didn't get out, he'd eventually kill her—just as he'd killed his other victims.

"Riley, are you OK?"

Lucy's voice snapped Riley out of her memory of one of her most harrowing cases. It was an ordeal that she would never forget, especially because her daughter later became a captive to the same psychopath. She wondered if she would ever be entirely free of the flashbacks.

And would April ever be free of those devastating memories?

Riley was back in the present again, and she realized that she'd crawled to a halt under the barbed wire. Lucy was right behind her, waiting her for her to finish this obstacle.

"I'm OK," Riley called back. "Sorry to hold you up."

She forced herself to start crawling again. At the water's edge, she scrambled to her feet and gathered her wits and her energy. Then she took off down the wooded trail, certain that Lucy wasn't far behind her. She knew that her next task would be to climb across a rough hanging cargo net. After that, she still had almost two miles to go, and more than a few really tough obstacles to overcome.

*

At the end of the six-mile course, Riley and Lucy stumbled along arm-in-arm, panting and laughing and congratulating each other over their triumph. Riley was surprised to find her longtime partner waiting for her where the trail ended. Bill Jeffreys was a strong, sturdy man of about Riley's age.

"Bill!" Riley said, still gasping for breath. "What are you doing here?"

"I came looking for you," he said. "They told me I could find you here. I hardly believed you wanted to do this—and in the dead of winter, too! What are you, some kind of masochist?"

Riley and Lucy both laughed.

Lucy said, "Maybe *I'm* the masochist. I hope I can run the Yellow Brick Road like Riley can when I'm her ripe old age."

Teasingly, Riley said to Bill, "Hey, I'm ready for another go at it. Want to join me?"

Bill shook his head and chuckled.

"Huh-uh," he said. "I've still got my old Yellow Brick at home, and I use it as a doorstop. One's enough for me. I'm thinking about going for a Green Brick, though. Want to join me for that?"

Riley laughed again. The so-called "Green Brick" was a joke around the FBI—an award given to anyone who could smoke thirty-five cigars on thirty-five successive nights.

"I'll pass," she said.

Bill's expression suddenly turned serious.

"I'm on a new case, Riley," he said. "And I need you to work with me on it. I hope you're OK with this. I know it's really soon after our last case."

Bill was right. To Riley, it seemed like only yesterday when they'd apprehended Orin Rhodes.

"You know I've just brought Jilly home. I'm trying to get her settled into her new life. New school … new everything."

"How is she doing?" Bill asked.

"She's erratic, but she's really trying. She's so happy to be part of a family. I think she's going to need a lot of help."

"And April?"

"She's absolutely great. I'm still blown away by how fighting with Rhodes made her feel stronger. And she's already very fond of Jilly."

After a pause, she asked, "What kind of case have you got, Bill?"

Bill was silent for a moment.

"I'm on my way to meet with the chief about it," he said. "I really do need your help, Riley."

Riley looked directly at her friend and partner. His expression was one of deep distress. When he'd said he needed her help, he'd really meant it. Riley wondered why.

"Let me take a shower and get into some dry clothes," she said. "I'll meet you at headquarters right away."

CHAPTER FIVE

Team Chief Brent Meredith wasn't a man to waste time with niceties. Riley knew that from experience. So when she walked into his office after her run, she didn't expect small talk—no polite questions about health and home and family. He could be kindly and warm, but those moments were rare. Today, he was going to get right down to business, and his business was always urgent.

Bill had already arrived. He still looked extremely anxious. She hoped she would soon understand why.

As soon as Riley sat down, Meredith leaned over his desk toward her, his broad, angular African-American face as daunting as ever.

"First things first, Agent Paige," he said.

Riley waited for him to say something else—to ask a question or give an order. Instead, he simply stared at her.

It only took Riley a moment to understand what Meredith was getting at.

Meredith was taking care not to ask his question aloud. Riley appreciated his discretion. A killer was still on the loose, and his name was Shane Hatcher. He'd escaped from Sing Sing, and Riley's most recent assignment had been to bring Hatcher in.

She'd failed. Actually, she hadn't really tried, and now other FBI agents were assigned to apprehend Hatcher. So far they'd had no success.

Shane Hatcher was a criminal genius who had become a respected expert in criminology during his long years in prison. So Riley had sometimes visited him in prison to get advice on her cases. She knew him well enough to feel sure that he wasn't a danger to society right now. Hatcher had a weird but strict moral code. He'd killed one man since his escape—an old enemy who was himself a dangerous criminal. Riley felt certain that he wouldn't kill anybody else.

Right now, Riley understood that Meredith needed to know whether she'd heard from Hatcher. It was a high-profile case, and it seemed that Hatcher was quickly becoming something of an urban legend—a famed criminal mastermind capable of just about anything.

She appreciated Meredith's discretion in not asking his question out loud. But the simple truth was, Riley knew nothing about Hatcher's current activities or his whereabouts.

"There's nothing new, sir," she said in reply to Meredith's unspoken question.

Meredith nodded and seemed to relax a little.

"All right, then," Meredith said. "I'll get right to the point. I'm sending Agent Jeffreys to Seattle on a case. He wants you as a partner. I need to know whether you're available to go with him."

Riley needed to say no. She had so much to deal with in her life right now that taking on an assignment in a distant city seemed out of the question. She still had occasional returns of the PTSD she had suffered since being held captive by a sadistic criminal. Her daughter, April, had suffered at the same man's hands, and now April had her own demons to deal with. And now Riley had a new daughter who had been through her own terrible traumas.

If she could just stay put for a while and teach a few classes at the Academy, maybe she could get her life stabilized.

"I can't do it," Riley said. "Not right now."

She turned toward Bill.

"You know what I'm dealing with," she said.

"I know, I was just hoping ..." he said, with an imploring expression in his eyes.

It was time to find out what was the matter.

"What's the case?" Riley asked.

"There have been at least two poisonings in Seattle," Meredith said. "It appears to be a serial case."

At that moment, Riley understood why Bill was feeling shaken. When he was still a boy, his mother had been poisoned to death. Riley didn't know any of the details, but she did know that her murder had been one of the reasons he had become an FBI agent. It had haunted him for years. This case opened up old wounds for him.

So when he'd told her he needed her on the case, he'd really meant it.

Meredith continued, "So far, we know of two victims—a man and a woman. There may have been others, and there may be others still to come."

"Why are we being called in?" Riley asked. "There's an FBI field office right there in Seattle. Can't they handle it?"

Meredith shook his head.

"The situation there is pretty dysfunctional. It seems that the local FBI and the local police can't agree on anything about this case. That's why you're needed, whether you're wanted or not. Can I count on you, Agent Paige?"

Suddenly, Riley's decision seemed perfectly clear. In spite of her personal problems, she was really needed on this job.

"Count me in," she finally said.

Bill nodded and breathed an audible sigh of relief and gratitude.

"Good," Meredith said. "You'll both fly out to Seattle tomorrow morning."

Meredith drummed his fingers on the table for a moment.

"But don't expect a cozy welcome," he added. "Neither the cops nor the Feds will be happy to see you."

CHAPTER SIX

Riley dreaded taking Jilly to her first day at her new school almost as much as she'd dreaded some cases. The teenager was looking rather grim, and Riley wondered if she might even might make a scene at the last moment.

Is she ready for this? Riley kept asking herself. *Am I ready for this?*

Also, the timing seemed unfortunate. It worried Riley that she had to fly off to Seattle this morning. But Bill needed her help, and that decided the matter as far as she was concerned. Jilly had seemed all right when they had discussed the matter at home, but Riley really didn't know what to expect now.

Fortunately, she didn't have to take Jilly to school alone. Ryan had offered to drive, and Gabriela and April also came along to offer moral support.

When they all got out of the car in the school parking lot, April took Jilly by the hand and trotted along with her straight toward the building. The two slender girls were both wearing jeans and boots and warm jackets. Yesterday Riley had taken them shopping and let Jilly choose a new jacket, along with a bedspread, posters, and some pillows to personalize her bedroom.

Riley, Ryan, and Gabriela followed behind the girls, and Riley's heart warmed as she watched them. After years of sullenness and rebellion, April suddenly seemed incredibly mature. Riley wondered if maybe this was what April had needed all along—someone else to take care of.

"Look at them," Riley said to Ryan. "They're bonding."

"Wonderful, isn't it?" Ryan said. "They actually look kind of like sisters. Is that what drew you to her?"

It was an interesting question. When she'd first brought Jilly home, Riley had mostly been struck by how different the two girls were. But now she was becoming more and more aware of resemblances. True, April was the paler of the two, with hazel eyes like her mom, while Jilly had brown eyes and an olive complexion.

But right now, as the two heads of dark hair bounced along together, they did seem very much alike.

"Maybe so," she said, answering Ryan's question. "I didn't stop to think about it. All I knew was that she was in serious trouble, and maybe I could help."

"You may very well have saved her life," Ryan said.

Riley felt a lump in her throat. That possibility hadn't occurred to her and it was a humbling thought. She was both exhilarated and terrified by this feeling of newfound responsibility.

The whole family went straight to the guidance counselor's office. Warm and smiling as always, Wanda Lewis greeted Jilly with a map of the school.

"I'll take you straight to your homeroom," Ms. Lewis said.

"I can see this is a good place," Gabriela told Jilly. "You'll be fine here."

Now Jilly looked nervous but happy. She hugged them all, then followed Ms. Lewis down the hall.

"I like this school," Gabriela told Ryan, Riley, and April on the way back to the car.

"I'm glad you approve," Riley said.

She meant it sincerely. Gabriela was much more than a housekeeper. She was a true member of the family. It was important that she feel good about family decisions.

They all got into the car, and Ryan started the engine.

"Where to next?" Ryan asked cheerfully.

"I've got to get to school," April said.

"Then home right after that," Riley said. "I've got a plane to catch in Quantico."

"Got it," Ryan said, pulling out of the parking lot.

Riley watched Ryan's face as he drove. He looked really happy—happy to be a part of things, and happy to have a new member of the family. He hadn't been like this through most of their marriage. He really did seem like a changed man. And at moments like now, she felt grateful to him.

She turned and looked at her daughter, who was in the back seat.

"You're handling all of this really well," Riley said.

April looked surprised.

"I'm putting a lot into it," she said. "Glad you noticed."

For a moment Riley was taken aback. Had she been ignoring her daughter out of concern for getting their new family member settled in?

April was quiet for a moment, then said, "Mom, I'm still glad you brought her home. I guess it's all more complicated than I thought it would be, having a new sister. She's had an awful time and sometimes she isn't easy to talk to."

"I don't want to make this hard on you," Riley said.

April smiled weakly. "I was hard on you," she said. "I'm tough

28

enough to deal with Jilly's problems. And the truth is, I'm beginning to enjoy helping her. We'll be fine. Please don't worry about us."

It eased Riley's mind that she was leaving Jilly in the care of three people she felt sure she could trust—April, Gabriela, and Ryan. All the same, it bothered her that she had to be away right now. She hoped it wouldn't be for long.

*

The ground dropped away as Riley looked out the window of the small BAU jet. The jet climbed above the clouds for the flight to the Pacific Northwest—nearly six hours. In just a few minutes, Riley was watching the landscape rolling beneath them.

Bill was sitting next to her.

He said, "Flying across the country like this always makes me think of long ago, when people had to walk or ride horses or wagons."

Riley nodded and smiled. It was as if Bill had read her thoughts. She often had that feeling about him.

"The country must have seemed huge to people back then," she said. "It took settlers months to get across."

A familiar and comfortable silence settled between them. Over the years, she and Bill had had their share of disagreements and even quarrels, and at times their partnership had seemed to be over. But now she felt all the closer to him because of those hard times. She trusted him with her life, and she knew he trusted her with his.

At times like now, she was glad that she and Bill hadn't given in to their attraction to one another. They'd come perilously close at times.

It would have ruined everything, Riley thought.

They'd been smart to steer clear of it. The loss of their friendship would have been too hard for her to imagine. He was her best friend in the world.

After a few moments, Bill said, "Thanks for coming, Riley. I really need your help this time out. I don't think I could handle this case with any other partner. Not even Lucy."

Riley looked at him and said nothing. She didn't have to ask him what was on his mind. She knew he was finally going to tell her the truth about what had happened to his mother. Then she'd understand just how important and troubling this case really was to him.

He stared straight ahead, remembering.

"You already know about my family," he said. "I've told you that Dad was a high school math teacher, and my mom worked as a bank teller. With three kids, we were all comfortable without being especially well off. It was a pretty happy life for all of us. Until …"

Bill paused for a moment.

"It happened when I was nine years old," he continued. "Just before Christmas, the staff at Mom's bank threw their annual Christmas party, exchanging gifts and eating cake and all the usual office stuff. When Mom came home that afternoon, she sounded like she'd had fun and everything was fine. But as the evening wore on, she started behaving strangely."

Bill's face tightened at the grim memory.

"She got dizzy and confused, and her speech was slurred. It was almost like she was drunk. But Mom never drank much, and besides, no alcohol had been served at the party. None of us had any idea what was going on. Things rapidly got worse. She suffered from nausea and vomiting. Dad rushed her to the emergency room. We kids went along with them."

Bill fell quiet again. Riley could tell that it was becoming harder by the moment to tell her what had happened.

"By the time we got to the hospital, her heart was racing, and she was hyperventilating, and her blood pressure had gone through the roof. Then she slipped into a coma. Her kidneys started to fail, and she had congestive heart failure."

Bill's eyes were shut tight and his face was knotted with pain. Riley wondered if maybe it would be best for him not to tell the rest of his story. But she sensed that it would be wrong to tell him to stop.

Bill said, "By the next morning, the doctors figured out what was wrong. She was suffering from severe ethylene glycol poisoning."

Riley shook her head. That sounded familiar but she couldn't quite place it.

Bill quickly explained, "Her punch at the party had been spiked with antifreeze."

Riley gasped.

"My God!" she said. "How is that even possible? I mean, wouldn't the taste alone—?"

"The thing is, most antifreeze has a sweet taste," Bill explained. "It's easy to mix with sugary beverages without being noticed. It's awfully easy to use as a poison."

Riley was struggling to grasp what had she was hearing.

"But if the punch was spiked, weren't other people affected?" she said.

"That's just it," Bill said. "Nobody else was poisoned. It wasn't in the punch bowl. It was only in Mom's drinks. Somebody specifically targeted her."

He fell quiet again for a moment.

"By then, it was too late for anything," he said. "She stayed in a coma and died on New Year's Eve. We were all right there at her bedside."

Somehow, Bill managed not to break down in tears. Riley guessed that he'd done plenty of crying about it over the years.

"It didn't make sense," Bill said. "Everybody liked Mom. She didn't have an enemy in the world that anybody knew of. The police investigated, and it became clear that nobody who worked at the bank was responsible. But several co-workers remembered a strange man who came and went during the party. He'd seemed friendly, and everybody assumed that he was somebody's guest, a friend or a relative. He was gone before the party was over."

Bill shook his head bitterly.

"The case went cold. It's still cold. I guess it always will be. After so many years, it'll never be solved. It was terrible never to find out who did it, never bring him to justice. But the worst thing was never finding out *why*. It just seemed so pointlessly cruel. Why Mom? What did she do to make anybody want to do something so horrible? Or maybe she didn't do anything. Maybe it was just some sort of vicious joke. Not knowing was torture. It still is. And of course, that's one of the reasons I decided to—"

He didn't finish the thought. He didn't need to. Riley had long known that the unsolved mystery of his mother's death was why Bill had gone into a career in law enforcement.

"I'm so sorry," Riley said.

Bill shrugged feebly, as if a huge weight lay on his shoulders.

"It was a long time ago," he said. "Besides, you must know how it felt as well as anybody."

Bill's quiet words shook Riley. She knew exactly what he meant. And he was right. She'd told him all about it long ago, so there was no need to repeat it now. He knew already. But that didn't make the memory any less searing.

Riley was six years old, and Mommy had taken her to a candy store. Riley was excited and asking for all the candy she could see.

Sometimes Mommy would scold her for acting like that. But today Mommy was being sweet and spoiling her, buying her all the candy she wanted.

Just when they were in line at the cash register, a strange man walked toward them. He wore something on his face that flattened his nose and lips and cheeks and made him look funny and scary at the same time, sort of like a circus clown. It took little Riley a moment to realize that he was wearing a nylon stocking over his head, just like Mommy wore on her legs.

He was holding a gun. The gun looked huge. He was pointing it at Mommy.

"Give me your purse," he said.

But Mommy didn't do it. Riley didn't know why. All she knew was that Mommy was scared, maybe too scared to do what the man told her to do, and probably Riley should be scared too, and so she was.

He said some bad words to Mommy, but she still didn't give him her purse. She was shaking all over.

Then came a bang and a flash, and Mommy fell to the floor. The man said more bad words and ran away. Mommy's chest was bleeding, and she gasped and twisted for a moment before she fell completely still.

Little Riley started screaming. She didn't stop screaming for a long time.

The gentle touch of Bill's hand on hers brought Riley back to the present.

"I'm sorry," Bill said. "I didn't mean to bring it all back."

He'd obviously seen the tear trickling down her cheek. She squeezed his hand. She was grateful for his understanding and concern. But the truth was, Riley had never told Bill about a memory that troubled her even more.

Her father had been a colonel in the Marines—a stern, cruel, unfeeling, unloving, and unforgiving man. During all the years that followed, he'd blamed Riley for her mother's death. It didn't matter that she'd only been six years old.

"You might as well have shot her yourself, for all the good you did her," he'd said.

He'd died last year without ever forgiving her.

Riley wiped her cheek and looked out the window at the slowly crawling landscape miles below.

As she so often did, she realized how much she and Bill had in common, and how haunted they both were by past tragedy and injustice. During all the years that they'd been partners, they'd both been driven by similar demons, haunted by similar ghosts.

For all her worry about Jilly and life at home, Riley now knew that she'd been right to agree to join Bill on this case. Every time they worked together, their bond grew stronger and deeper. This time was going to be no exception.

They'd solve these murders, Riley was sure of it. But what would she and Bill gain or lose by it?

Maybe we'll both heal a little, Riley thought. *Or maybe our wounds will open and hurt more.*

She told herself it didn't really matter. They always worked together to get the job done, no matter how tough it was.

Now they could be facing a particularly ugly crime.

CHAPTER SEVEN

When the BAU plane landed at Sea-Tac, the Seattle-Tacoma International Airport, a heavy rain was streaking across the windows. Riley looked at her watch. It was about two in the afternoon at home now, but it was eleven in the morning here. That would give them time to get something done on this case today.

As she and Bill moved toward the exit, the pilot came out of his cabin and handed each of them an umbrella.

"You'll need these," he said with a grin. "Winter is the worse time to be in this corner of the country."

When they stood at the top of the stairs, Riley had to agree. She was glad they had umbrellas, but she wished she had dressed warmer. It was cold as well as rainy.

An SUV pulled up at the edge of the tarmac. Two men in raincoats hurried out of the vehicle toward their plane. They introduced themselves as Agents Havens and Trafford of the FBI field office in Seattle.

"We're taking you to the medical examiner's office," Agent Havens said. "The team leader on this investigation is waiting for you there."

Bill and Riley got into the car, and Agent Trafford started to drive through the drenching rain. Riley could make barely out the usual airport hotels along the way, and that was all. She knew there was a vital city out there, but it was practically invisible.

She wondered if she was ever going to see Seattle while she was here.

*

The minute Riley and Bill sat down in the conference room in Seattle's medical examiner's building, she sensed that trouble was brewing. She exchanged glances with Bill, and she could tell that he was feeling the tension too.

Team Leader Maynard Sanderson was a big-chested, big-jawed man with a presence that struck Riley as falling somewhere between a military officer and an evangelical preacher.

Sanderson was glowering at a portly man whose thick walrus mustache gave his face what seemed to be a permanent scowl. He had been introduced as Perry McCade, Seattle's Chief of Police.

The body language of the two men and the places they had

taken at the table spoke volumes to Riley. For whatever reason, the last thing they wanted was to be in the same room together. And she also felt sure that both men especially hated having Riley and Bill here.

She remembered what Brent Meredith had said before they left Quantico.

"Don't expect a cozy welcome. Neither the cops nor the Feds will be happy to see you."

Riley wondered what kind of minefield she and Bill had walked into.

A complex power struggle was going on, without a word being spoken. And in just a few minutes, she knew it was going to start getting verbal.

By contrast, Chief Medical Examiner Prisha Shankar looked comfortable and unconcerned. The dark-skinned, black-haired woman was about Riley's age and appeared to be stoic and imperturbable.

She's on her own turf, after all, Riley figured.

Agent Sanderson took the liberty of getting the meeting underway.

"Agents Paige and Jeffreys," he said to Riley and Bill, "I'm pleased that you could make it all the way from Quantico."

His icy voice told Riley that the opposite was true.

"Glad to be of service," Bill said, not sounding very sure of himself.

Riley just smiled and nodded.

"Gentlemen," Sanderson said, ignoring the presence of two women, "we're all here to investigate two murders. A serial killer might be getting started here in the Seattle area. It's up to us to stop him before he kills again."

Police Chief McCade growled audibly.

"Would you like to comment, McCade?" Sanderson asked dryly.

"It's not a serial," McCade grumbled. "And it's not an FBI case. My cops have got this under control."

Riley was starting to get the picture. She remembered how Meredith had said that the local authorities were floundering with this case. And now she could see why. Nobody was on the same page, and nobody agreed on anything.

Police Chief McCade was angry that the FBI was muscling in on a local murder case. And Sanderson was fuming that the FBI had sent Bill and Riley from Quantico to straighten everybody out.

The perfect storm, Riley thought.

Sanderson turned toward the chief medical examiner and said, "Dr. Shankar, perhaps you'd like to summarize what we currently know."

Seemingly aloof from the underlying tensions, Dr. Shankar clicked a remote to bring up an image on the wall screen. It was a driver's license photo of a rather plain-looking woman with straight hair of a dullish brown color.

Shankar said, "A month and a half ago, a woman named Margaret Jewell died at home in her sleep of what appeared to be a heart attack. She'd been complaining the day before of joint pains, but according to her spouse, that wasn't unusual. She suffered from fibromyalgia."

Shankar clicked the remote again and brought up another driver's license photo. It showed a middle-aged man with a kindly but melancholy face.

She said, "A couple of days ago, Cody Woods admitted himself to the South Hill Hospital, complaining of chest pains. He also complained of joint pain, but again that wasn't surprising. He'd had some arthritis, and he'd had knee replacement surgery a week before. Within hours of being admitted to the hospital, he, too, died of what appeared to be a heart attack."

"Totally unconnected deaths," McCade muttered.

"So now are you saying that neither one of these deaths was murder?" Sanderson said.

"Margaret Jewell, probably," McCade said. "Cody Woods, certainly not. We're letting him be a distraction. We're muddying the waters. If you'd just leave it to my boys and me, we'd solve this case in no time."

"You've had a month and a half on the Jewell case," Sanderson said.

Dr. Shankar smiled rather mysteriously as McCade and Sanderson continued to bicker. Then she clicked the remote again. Two more photos came up.

The room fell quiet, and Riley felt a jolt of surprise.

The men in both photos looked Middle Eastern. Riley didn't recognize one of them. But she sure did recognize the other.

It was Saddam Hussein.

CHAPTER EIGHT

Riley stared at the image on the wall screen. Where could the chief medical examiner possibly be going with a photo of Saddam Hussein? The deposed leader of Iraq had been executed in 2006 for crimes against humanity. What was his connection with a possible serial killer in Seattle?

After letting the effect of the photos settle in, Dr. Shankar spoke again.

"I'm sure we all recognize the man on the left. The man on the right was Majidi Jehad, a Shia dissident against Saddam's regime. In May 1980, Jehad was granted permission to travel to London. When he stopped at a Baghdad police station to pick up his passport, he was treated to a glass of orange juice. He left Iraq, apparently safe and sound. He died soon after he got to London."

Dr. Shankar brought up pictures of many more Middle Eastern faces.

"All of these men met similar fates. Saddam liquidated hundreds of dissidents in much the same way. When some of them were released from prison, they were offered congratulatory drinks to toast their freedom. None of them lived very long."

Chief McCade nodded with understanding.

"Thallium poisoning," he said.

"That's right," Dr. Shankar said. "Thallium is a chemical element that can be turned into a colorless, odorless, and tasteless soluble powder. It was Saddam Hussein's poison of choice. But he hardly invented the idea of assassinating his enemies with it. It is sometimes called the 'poisoner's poison' because it acts slowly and produces symptoms that can result in mistaken causes of death."

She clicked the remote, and a few more faces appeared, including that of Cuban dictator Fidel Castro.

She said, "In 1960, the French secret service used thallium to kill the Cameroon rebel leader Félix-Roland Moumié. And it is widely believed that the CIA tried to use thallium in one of its many failed attempts to assassinate Fidel Castro. The plan was to put thallium powder in Castro's shoes. If the CIA had succeeded in that particular method, Castro's death would have been humiliating as well as slow and painful. That iconic beard of his would have fallen out before he died."

She clicked the remote, and the faces of Margaret Jewell and Cody Woods appeared again.

"I'm telling you all this so that you'll understand that we're dealing with a very sophisticated murderer," Dr. Shankar said. "I found traces of thallium in the bodies of both Margaret Jewell and Cody Woods. There's no doubt in my mind that they were both poisoned to death by the same killer."

Dr. Shankar looked around at everybody in the room.

"Any comments so far?" she asked.

"Yeah," Chief McCade said. "I still don't think the deaths are connected."

Riley was startled by the comment. But Dr. Shankar didn't look surprised.

"Why not, Chief McCade?" she asked.

"Cody Woods was a plumber," McCade said. "Wouldn't it have been possible for him to have been exposed to thallium as an occupational hazard?"

"It's possible," Dr. Shankar said. "Plumbers have to be careful to avoid lots of hazardous substances, including asbestos and heavy metals such as arsenic and thallium. But I don't think this was what happened in Cody Woods' case."

Riley was becoming more and more intrigued.

"Why not?" she asked.

Dr. Shankar clicked the remote, and toxicology reports appeared.

"These killings seem to be thallium poisoning with a difference," she said. "Neither victim showed certain classic symptoms—hair loss, fever, vomiting, abdominal pain. As I said before, there was some joint pain, but little else. Death came quite suddenly, looking much like an ordinary heart attack. There was no lingering at all. If my staff hadn't been on their toes, they might not have even noticed that these were cases of thallium poisoning."

Bill seemed to be sharing Riley's fascination.

"So we're dealing with what—designer thallium?" he asked.

"Something like that," Dr. Shankar said. "My staff is still untangling the chemical makeup of the cocktail. But one of the ingredients is definitely potassium ferrocyanide—a chemical that you might be familiar with as the dye Prussian blue. That's strange, because Prussian blue happens to be the only known antidote to thallium poisoning."

Chief McCade's large mustache was twitching.

"That doesn't make sense," he growled. "Why would a poisoner administer an antidote along with the poison?"

Riley hazarded a guess.

"Might it have been to disguise the symptoms of thallium poisoning?"

Dr. Shankar nodded in agreement.

"That's my working theory. The other chemicals we found would have interacted with thallium in a complex way that we don't yet understand. But they probably helped control the nature of the symptoms. Whoever concocted the mixture knew what they were doing. They had a pretty keen knowledge of both pharmacology and chemistry."

Chief McCade was drumming his fingers on the table.

"I don't buy it," he said. "Your results for the second victim must have been skewed by your results for the first. You found what you were looking for."

For the first time, Dr. Shankar's face showed a trace of surprise. Riley, too, was taken aback by the police chief's audacity in questioning Shankar's expertise.

"What makes you say that?" Dr. Shankar asked.

"Because we have a surefire suspect for Margaret Jewell's killing," he said. "She was married to another woman, name of Barbara Bradley—calls herself Barb. The couple's friends and neighbors say the two were having problems, loud fights that woke up the neighbors. Bradley actually has a past record for criminal assault. Folks say she has a hair-trigger temper. She did it. We're all but sure of it."

"Why haven't you brought her in?" Agent Sanderson demanded.

Chief McCade's eyes darted about defensively.

"We've questioned her, at home," he said. "But she's a sly character, and we still haven't got enough evidence to bring her in. We're building a case. It's taking some time."

Agent Sanderson smirked and grunted.

He said, "Well, while you've been building your case, it seems that your 'surefire' suspect has gone right ahead and killed somebody else. You'd better pick up the pace. She might be getting ready to do it again right now."

Chief McCade's face was getting red with anger.

"You're dead wrong," he said. "I'm telling you, Margaret Jewell's killing was an isolated incident. Barb Bradley didn't have any motive to kill Cody Woods, or anybody else as far as we know."

"As far as you know," Sanderson added in a scoffing tone.

Riley could feel the underlying tensions coming to the surface.

She hoped the meeting would end without a knockdown, drag-out fight.

Meanwhile, her brain was clicking away, trying to make sense of what little she knew so far.

She asked Chief McCade, "How financially well off were Jewell and Bradley?"

"Not well off at all," he said. "Lower middle-class. In fact, we're thinking that financial strain might have been part of the motive."

"What does Barb Bradley do for a living?"

"She makes deliveries for a linen service," McCade said.

Riley felt a hunch forming in her mind. She thought that a killer who used poison was likely to be a woman. And as a delivery person, this one could have had access to various health facilities. This was definitely someone she'd like to talk to.

"I'd like to have Barb Bradley's home address," she said. "Agent Jeffreys and I should go and interview her."

Chief McCade looked at her as if she were out of her mind.

"I just told you, we've done that already," he said.

Not well enough, apparently, Riley thought.

But she stifled the urge to say so aloud.

Bill put in, "I agree with Agent Paige. We should go check Barb Bradley out for ourselves."

Chief McCade obviously felt insulted.

"I won't allow it," he said.

Riley knew that the FBI team leader, Agent Sanderson, could overrule McCade if he chose to. But when she looked to Sanderson for support, he was staring daggers at her.

Her heart sank. She instantly understood the situation. Although Sanderson and McCade hated each other, they were allies in their resentment of Riley and Bill. As far as both of them were concerned, agents from Quantico had no business being here on their turf. Whether they realized it or not, their egos were more important than the case itself.

How are Bill and I going to get anything done? she wondered.

By contrast, Dr. Shankar seemed as cool and collected as ever.

She said, "I'd like to know why it's such a bad idea for Jeffreys and Paige to interview Barb Bradley."

Riley was surprised at Dr. Shankar's audacity in speaking up. After all, even as the chief medical examiner, she was brazenly overstepping her bounds.

"Because I've got my own investigation going!" McCade said,

almost shouting now. "They're liable to make a mess of it!"

Dr. Shankar smiled that inscrutable smile of hers.

"Chief McCade, are you actually questioning the competence of two agents from Quantico?"

Then, turning toward the FBI team leader, she added, "Agent Sanderson, what do you have to say about this?"

McCade and Sanderson both stared at Dr. Shankar in open-mouthed silence.

Riley noticed that Dr. Shankar was smiling at her. Riley couldn't help smiling back at her in admiration. Here in her own building, Shankar knew how to project an authoritative presence. It didn't matter who else thought they were in charge. She was one tough customer.

Chief McCade shook his head with resignation.

"OK," he said. "If you want the address, you've got it."

Agent Sanderson quickly added, "But I want some of my people to go with you."

"That sounds fair," Riley said.

McCade scribbled down the address and handed it to Bill.

Sanderson called the meeting to a close.

"Jesus, did you ever see such a pair of arrogant jerks in your life?" Bill asked as Riley walked with him to their car. "How the hell are we going to get anything done?"

Riley didn't reply. The truth was, she didn't know. She sensed that this case was going to be tough enough without having to deal with local power politics. She and Bill had to get their job done quickly before anyone else died.

CHAPTER NINE

Today her name was Judy Brubaker.

She enjoyed being Judy Brubaker.

People liked Judy Brubaker.

She was moving briskly around the empty bed, straightening sheets and plumping the pillows. As she did so, she smiled at the woman who was sitting in the comfortable armchair.

Judy hadn't decided whether to kill her or not.

Time's running out, Judy thought. *I've got to make up my mind.*

The woman's name was Amanda Somers. Judy found her to be an odd, shy, and mousy little creature. She'd been under Judy's care since yesterday.

Continuing to make up the bed, Judy began to sing.

Far from home,
So far from home—
This little baby's far from home.

Amanda joined in with that small, reedy little voice of hers.

You pine away
From day to day
Too sad to laugh, too sad to play.

Judy was a bit surprised. Amanda Somers hadn't shown any real interest in the lullaby until just now.

"You like that song?" Judy Brubaker asked.

"I suppose so," Amanda said. "It's sad, and I guess it fits my mood."

"Why are you sad? Your treatment's over and you're going home. Most patients are happy to go home."

Amanda sighed and said nothing. She put her hands together in a prayer position. Keeping her fingers together, she moved her palms away from each other. She repeated the movement a couple of times. It was an exercise Judy had taught her to help the healing process after Amanda's carpal tunnel surgery.

"Am I doing this right?" Amanda asked.

"Almost," Judy said, crouching beside her and touching her hands to correct her movements. "You need to keep the fingers elongated, so they bow outward. Remember, your hands are

42

supposed to look like a spider doing pushups on a mirror."

Amanda was doing it correctly now. She smiled, looking rather proud of herself.

"I can really feel it helping," she said. "Thanks."

Judy watched Amanda continue to do the exercise. Judy really hated the short, ugly scar that extended along the lower part of Amanda's right hand.

Unnecessary surgery, Judy thought.

The doctors had taken advantage of Amanda's trust and credulity. She was sure that less drastic treatments would have worked as well or better. A splint maybe, or some corticosteroid injections. Judy had seen too many doctors insist on surgery, whether it was needed or not. It always made her angry.

But today, Judy wasn't upset just with the doctors. She felt impatient with the patient as well. She wasn't sure just why.

Hard to draw out, this one, Judy thought as she sat down on the edge of the bed.

During their whole time together, Amanda had let Judy do all the talking.

Judy Brubaker had plenty of interesting things to talk about, of course. Judy wasn't much like the now-vanished Hallie Stillians, who'd had the homey personality of a doting aunt.

Judy Brubaker was at once plainer and more flamboyant, and she usually wore a jogging suit instead of more conventional clothes. She loved to tell stories about her adventures—hang gliding, skydiving, scuba diving, mountain climbing, and the like. She'd hitchhiked across Europe and much of Asia.

Of course, none of those adventures had really happened. But they made for wonderful stories.

Most people liked Judy Brubaker. People who might find Hallie a bit cloying and sugary enjoyed Judy's more plainspoken personality.

Maybe Amanda just doesn't take to Judy, she thought.

For whatever reason, Amanda had told her almost nothing about herself. She was in her forties, but she never said anything about her past. Judy still didn't know what Amanda did for a living, or if she did anything at all. She didn't know whether Amanda had ever been married—although the absence of a wedding band indicated that she wasn't married now.

Judy was dismayed by how things were going. And time really was running out. Amanda could get up and leave at any moment. And here Judy was, still trying to decide whether to poison her or not.

Part of her indecision was simple prudence. Things had changed a lot during the last few days. Her last two killings were now in the papers. It seemed that some smart medical examiner had detected thallium in the corpses. It was a worrisome development.

She had a teabag ready with an altered recipe that used a little more arsenic and a little less thallium. But detection was still a danger. She had no idea whether the deaths of Margaret Jewell and Cody Woods had been traced back to their rehab stays or to their caregivers. This method of killing was becoming riskier.

But the real problem was that the whole thing just didn't feel right.

She had no rapport with Amanda Somers.

She didn't feel like she even knew her.

Offering to "toast" Amanda's departure with a cup of tea would feel forced, even vulgar.

Anyway, the woman was still here, exercising her hands, showing no inclination to go away just yet.

"Don't you want to go home?" Judy asked.

The woman sighed.

"Well, you know, I've got other physical problems. There's my back, for instance. It's getting worse as I get older. My doctor says I need an operation for it. But I don't know. I keep thinking that maybe therapy is all I need to get better. And you're such a good therapist."

"Thank you," Judy said. "But you know, I don't work here full time. I'm a freelancer, and today's my last day here for the time being. If you stay here any longer, it won't be under my care."

Judy was startled by Amanda's wistful gaze. Amanda had seldom made eye contact like this with her before.

"You don't know what it's like," Amanda said.

"What what's like?" Judy asked.

Amanda shrugged a little, still looking into Judy's eyes.

"Being surrounded by people you can't fully trust. People who seem to care about you, and maybe they do, but then again, maybe they don't. Maybe they just want something from you. Users. Takers. A lot of people in my life are like that. I don't have any family, and I don't know who my friends are. I don't know who I can trust and who I can't."

With a slight smile, Amanda added, "Do you understand what I'm saying?"

Judy wasn't sure. Amanda was still speaking in riddles.

Does she have a crush on me? Judy wondered.

It wasn't impossible. Judy was aware that people often thought she was gay. That always amused her, because she'd never really given any thought to whether Judy was gay or not.

But maybe it wasn't that.

Maybe Amanda was simply lonely, and she'd come to like and trust Judy without her even realizing it.

One thing seemed certain. Amanda was emotionally very insecure, probably neurotic, certainly depressive. She must be taking quite an array of prescription medicines. If Judy could get a look at them, she might be able to come up with a cocktail especially for Amanda. She'd done that before, and it had its advantages, especially at a time like now. It would be good to skip the thallium recipe this once.

"Where do you live?" Judy asked.

An odd look crossed Amanda's face, as if she were trying to decide what to tell Judy.

"On a houseboat," Amanda said.

"A houseboat? Really?"

Amanda nodded. Judy's interest was piqued. But why did she have the feeling that Amanda wasn't telling her the truth—or at least not the whole truth?

"Funny," Judy said. "I've lived in Seattle off and on for years, and there are so many houseboats in the waterways in these parts, but I've never actually been on one. One of the few adventures I haven't had."

Amanda's smile brightened and she didn't say anything. That inscrutable smile was starting to make Judy nervous. Was Amanda going to invite her to visit her on her houseboat? Did she even really *have* a houseboat?

"Do you do at-home visits for your clients?" Amanda asked.

"I do sometimes, but ..."

"But what?"

"Well, I'm not supposed to in situations like this. This rehab center would consider it poaching. I signed an agreement not to."

Amanda's smile turned a little bit mischievous.

"Well, what would be wrong with your paying me a simple *social* visit? Just stop by. See my place. We could chat. Spend some time together. See where things go. And then, if I decided to hire you ... well, that would be different, wouldn't it? Not poaching at all."

Judy smiled. She was starting to appreciate Amanda's

cleverness. What she was suggesting would still be bending the rules, if not breaking them outright. But who would ever know? And it certainly suited Judy's purposes. She'd have all the time she needed.

And the truth was, Amanda was starting to fascinate her.

It would be exciting to get to know her before she killed her.

"That sounds marvelous," Judy said.

"Good," Amanda chirped, not sounding the least bit sad anymore.

She reached into her purse, took out a pencil and notepad, jotted down her address and phone number.

Judy took the note and asked, "Do you want to make an appointment?"

"Oh, let's not get all regimented about it. Sometime soon would be fine. During the next day or two. But don't stop by unexpected. Call me first. That's important."

Judy wondered why that was so important.

She's certainly got a secret or two, Judy thought.

Amanda got up and put on her coat.

"I'll check myself out now. But remember. *Call* me."

"I'll do that," Judy said.

Amanda walked out of the room into the hall, singing some more of the lullaby, her voice sounding happier and surer now.

No need to weep,
Dream long and deep.
Give yourself to slumber's sweep.

As Amanda's voice vanished down the hall, Amanda sang the rest of it quietly to herself.

No more sighs,
Just close your eyes
And you will go home in your sleep.

Things were going Judy's way after all.

And this killing was going to be special.

CHAPTER TEN

Riley tried to ignore the tensions inside the FBI vehicle as she and Bill headed out to interview the wife of a poison victim. She thought that Barb Bradley could be a viable suspect. The fact that she delivered linens struck her as possibly significant. If the woman made medical deliveries, maybe she'd also had access to Cody Woods, who had admitted himself to a hospital and died there.

It was obvious that nobody in Seattle law enforcement was happy with the presence of two agents from Quantico. But then, none of those working on this case seemed happy with each other either.

Maybe the local animosity is catching, Riley thought. She had already found herself annoyed with both of the agents that Sanderson assigned to work with them. She told herself it was an irrational feeling, but her dislike persisted.

In spite of all that, it was good that she and Bill were going to interview Barb Bradley right away.

Are we going to really get lucky and solve this thing today? she wondered.

She knew better than to get her hopes up. Breaks like that were few and far between. It was more likely that progress was going to be slow and tough, especially due to all the infighting and power plays in the air.

The rain had ended and the air was starting to clear.

At least, Riley thought, *that could help make the trip more pleasant.*

Agent Jay Wingert was driving, and Riley and Bill were sitting in the back seat.

Wingert had the physique and good looks of a male fashion model—and the same complete lack of personality. Riley couldn't imagine that there was a single thought in that well-formed head with its perfectly groomed hair.

Agent Lloyd Havens was sitting in the passenger seat. Lean and wiry, he sported a pretentious pseudo-military posture and spoke in short, abrupt sentences. A chronic sneer didn't add to his charm as far as Riley was concerned.

Havens turned toward Bill and Riley.

"I thought you guys were here in an advisory capacity," he said. "To help develop a profile. Not to actually investigate the case. Agent Wingert and I are the team on this."

Riley heard Bill grumble and hurried to get in a reply first.

"Interviewing a suspect can help us develop a profile," she said. "We need as much information as we can pull together."

"Seems like overkill, the four of us interviewing Bradley," he said. "Might spook the suspect."

Riley was surprised to hear him say so. After all, Sanderson had insisted upon sending all four of them. But she couldn't disagree. Four was definitely going to be a crowd.

"Agent Paige, Agent Jeffreys," Havens added in that clipped, official-sounding manner of his. "No need to trouble yourselves. Agent Wingert and I will do the interview. You can wait in the car."

Riley exchanged shocked glances with Bill. Neither one of them knew what to say.

Is this brat really giving us orders? Riley thought.

Then it occurred to her that this was Sanderson's idea, and Havens was acting on his instructions. Maybe it was Sanderson's way of making his guests from Quantico feel thoroughly unwelcome.

Havens continued in his brazenly self-assured tone.

"Unusual case for a serial. Poisoning's not at all typical. A lesser-used method. Strangulation is much more common. After that, attack-type weapons—knives, guns, blunt objects, and the like. Up close and personal, that's the usual serial killer for you. This doesn't fit the usual parameters."

He was directing his comments to Riley, as if giving her a lecture on criminology.

A mansplainer if ever there was one, she thought with rising distaste.

And of course, he wasn't saying anything that she and Bill didn't know already.

"Oh, but there are always outliers," Riley said, fully aware of her own condescending tone. "Agent Jeffreys and I have seen all sorts. Our last serial killer shot people completely at random, purely for the love of killing."

Bill added, "My guess is that this killer isn't that type. Poisoning's personal. This one picks victims for a reason."

Riley nodded in agreement.

"Still, this one is definitely an outlier," she said. "Consider the gap between the poisonings and the actual deaths. Most serials want to witness the whole thing. They yearn for the satisfaction of watching their victims die by their own hands. This killer doesn't feel that way."

48

Riley took care to address her words directly to Havens, sounding as authoritative as she could.

"And that just might make the killer elusive, hard to catch. A whole segment of the usual clues is missing. There's no issue of transporting or not transporting the body—no disposal of it or trying to conceal it. You're right, this case definitely doesn't fit the usual parameters. Perhaps you've got your own theory, Agent Havens."

Agent Havens was looking distinctly uncomfortable now.

Still holding his gaze, Riley continued, "Agent Jeffreys and I know all about the usual parameters. Serial murder often provides some type of sexual gratification—or perhaps you already know that. We hunted down an impotent psychopath who posed female victims as dolls and another who had it in for prostitutes. But then, other perps go after a particular sex for different reasons. One of our cases went after women who were unusually thin, another targeted helpful women wearing uniforms. And still others are driven by something entirely different. That could be especially true if the killer is in fact a woman."

Bill chimed in, "And that's just part of what we have to sort out when we're working out a profile for you."

Riley added, "I wonder if these killings have a sexual component. Or not. What do you think, Agent Havens?"

Agent Havens looked truly cowed.

"Agent Jeffreys and I will take charge of the interview, if you don't mind," Riley said.

Havens nodded, then looked away from her. Riley couldn't help but smile. It felt good to put this arrogant little jerk in his place. Now she could focus where they needed to be—on the upcoming interview.

Again, she wondered if maybe they were about to get lucky. She deeply hoped so. It would be great if they could wind up this case and get out of this uneasy scene.

CHAPTER ELEVEN

Riley saw that the Seattle mist was lifting as Agent Wingert drove them south along the broad interstate that cut straight through the city. She hoped the case was about to clear up as well.

To their right, the handsome city stretched out toward Elliott Bay, while on their left lay a lovely park with trees, shelters, and picnic tables. Agent Wingert turned off the interstate onto a street that wound up the side of a hill into a working-class neighborhood. At the top of the hill, Wingert parked in front a modest little house with a spectacular view of the Seattle skyline.

Not far away, the bay sparkled through the waning mist. Riley could well imagine what the view would be like from here on a clear day. One could probably see Mount Rainier and beyond to the Olympic Mountains.

But she wasn't here to enjoy the scenery. The four agents got out of the car. A van was parked nearby with "Broomswick Linen Services" painted on its side. An old and beat-up Harley-Davidson chopper was pulled up close to the house.

The agents walked up onto the front porch and Riley knocked on the door.

"Who is it?" came a sharp reply.

"FBI," Riley called back. "We'd like to speak with Barb Bradley. We called ahead. You said you'd talk to us."

"Oh, yeah."

A moment later the door opened. Barb Bradley was a brawny woman with close-cropped hair. She was wearing long sleeves, but Riley saw that the backs of her hands and wrists were heavily tattooed. So was her neck down to the cleavage that showed above her shirt buttons. Riley guessed that she was pretty much covered with tattoos.

A gun rack on the wall was stocked with semiautomatic rifles. Riley's instincts told her that Barb Bradley was enough of a gun nut to also have pistols tucked away in ready reach—probably in the drawers of that nearby cabinet.

She remembered something that Chief McCade had said about her.

"Folks say she has a hair-trigger temper."

McCade hadn't mentioned that she was also armed to the teeth.

We need to watch our step with this one, she thought. *Things could get messy.*

Otherwise, the little house was pleasantly decorated. The presence of soft, pastel colors told Riley that Barb hadn't had much say in the decor. Like the gun rack, she looked thoroughly out of place here. Her late wife had surely made the interior design choices.

"We're very sorry for your loss of your wife, Ms. Bradley," Riley said.

Bradley looked away and said, "Yeah, well. I hope you didn't come all the way over here just to say that. Seems like kind of a wasted trip."

The woman didn't appear at all grief-stricken. Of course, a month and a half had passed since Margaret Jewell had died. But Riley had the feeling that Barb had never been devastated by her loss.

They were in a small room that doubled as a living area and a dining room. As Riley had feared, the four of them plus this burly woman made for something of a crowd.

"Hope you don't mind if I don't ask you to sit down," Barb Bradley said with a sneer. She crossed her arms in a defiant posture.

"So what do you want to know?" she said. "Seems to me the local cops asked me everything anybody could want to know."

"There have been some new developments," Bill said.

"It now looks like your wife's death wasn't an isolated incident," Riley said.

Bradley looked only mildly interested.

"No kidding," she said. "Well, as far as I'm concerned, it was still her own damn fault."

Riley was surprised.

"Why do you say that?" she asked.

"It happened after she'd been to a rehab center," she said. "I don't trust those kinds of places—hospitals neither. Maggie was always checking herself into hospitals. I make deliveries, and I see what's going on. Things go wrong, doctors fuck up, people get infections and die. I'm sure you know that. Who doesn't? But she didn't listen. She was in too much pain, she said. She went to that place for a couple of nights, and sure enough she died in her sleep the night she got home."

Riley looked at Bill. She could tell that he was puzzling over the same questions as she was.

"Ms. Bradley, I'm not sure you understand," Bill said. "Traces of thallium were found in your wife's system. Thallium didn't get there by accident. Margaret was murdered."

Bradley shrugged.

"Like I said," she replied. "She shouldn't have gone to that place."

Riley struggled to make sense of Barb Bradley's callousness. She'd come here thinking the woman would be a likely suspect. But now Riley simply didn't know what to think.

"What rehab center did Maggie go to?" Riley asked.

Before Bradley could answer, Wingert spoke up.

"She went to Natrona Physical Rehabilitation."

Riley was annoyed. Of course she wasn't surprised that the local FBI already knew about the rehab center. But she wanted to hear everything she could from Barb Bradley's own lips. Wingert had barely said a word during the drive here.

He picked a hell of a time to get talkative, she thought.

She gave him a stern look that she hoped would shut him up.

Then she said, "Ms. Bradley, what was the nature of Maggie's condition when she went to the center?"

Bradley scoffed loudly.

"'Condition'? Shit, she didn't have a condition. It was all in her head. She was always getting treatments of one kind or another. Cost us all kinds of money, put us in a world of debt. Doctors had a fancy name for what was supposed to be wrong with her."

"Fibromyalgia," Riley said.

"Yeah, and I looked it up," Bradley said. "Sure sounds to me like it's all psychological. And that was Maggie all over. Always complaining about numbness, aching, tingling, and being tired all the time. A regular psychological mess. Doctors just love to get their hands on suckers like her."

Riley thought for a moment.

Then she said, "Ms. Bradley, you're in the linen delivery business. Do you ever make deliveries to South Hill Hospital?"

"No. That's not in my zone. Why?"

"That's where the other victim died."

Bradley shrugged again.

"What'd I tell you?" she said. "Fucking hospitals."

"Do you happen to know a man named Cody Woods?" Riley asked.

"Name doesn't ring a bell," Bradley said. "Why?"

Riley studied the woman's face closely. But she couldn't tell if she was lying.

Meanwhile, Riley had been eyeing a colorful woman's scarf that was draped over a kitchen chair. She doubted that it had been

52

there during the whole month and a half since Margaret Jewell died. And it didn't look like something that Barb would wear.

Riley walked over to it and fingered it.

"Nice scarf," she said. "Maggie's?"

"No," Bradley said.

She obviously didn't want to elaborate. Riley waited for her to say something more.

"It belongs to a neighbor. Lulu. She spends some time over here."

Riley could see that Barb was getting visibly impatient now.

"I've moved on, OK? I've been through a couple of relationships since Maggie died. Sue me. Life goes on."

Then Havens spoke up.

"Were you and your wife having marital problems, Ms. Bradley?"

Riley stifled a groan. This pompous guy really was a bull in a china shop. For one thing, it was a stupid question. The cops had already figured out that the couple had been having problems. Pressing Barb Bradley about it was only going to aggravate her.

Sure enough, Bradley's eyes darkened with fury.

"Is that any of your business? Goddamn Feds."

"Just answer the question, please," Havens said.

"Why? I'm an American with rights. I don't have to answer any questions from government stooges like you."

Riley could see a change in Havens' expression. She sensed exactly what he was thinking. He was sure that Barb Bradley was guilty and it was time to take her in.

Not only pompous, she thought. *A moron as well.*

Sure enough, Havens reached for the cuffs on the back of his belt. Riley could see that Barb had detected the movement. The woman moved closer to the cabinet that Riley had noticed. Her hand reached toward a drawer.

Riley knew the situation was about to get deadly.

CHAPTER TWELVE

Split seconds were passing. But from Riley's point of view, everything seemed to slow down. It was her ingrained reaction to life-threatening situations—especially when they involved a firearm.

Brandishing his cuffs, Havens said, "Barbara Bradley, you're under arrest for the murder of Margaret Jewell."

But before Havens could finish his sentence, Bradley had the drawer open. In an instant, the gun was in her hand. She swung around and aimed it straight at Havens.

From Havens' deer-in-the-headlights expression, it was obvious that he had no idea what to do.

It's up to me, Riley realized. As her mind snapped into action, time seemed to slow down even more.

After years of training and experience, the four steps of disarmament had become reflexive to Riley.

The first step was to *clear.*

Riley stepped right in front of Bradley. But the weapon was pointed at her only for a fleeting instant. She simultaneously snapped her body sideways and gripped Bradley by her hand, pushing the muzzle clear of any human target.

Time was crawling along in microseconds now.

The next step was to *control.*

Barb was about to try to point the gun toward her again. She reinforced her grip to keep that from happening.

The next step was to *disarm.*

Still holding Barb by one hand, she grabbed the muzzle by the other, twisting it loose from her grip.

The final step was to *disable.*

And this step happened almost on its own. Suddenly, Riley was facing the would-be shooter, pointing her own weapon at her. Bradley raised her arms in surrender.

Riley held Barb's gaze for a moment. She looked thoroughly cowed now. She wasn't going to be any further danger.

Without a word, Riley put the gun back into the open drawer and shut it.

"We're through here," Riley said.

Havens started to protest.

"Agent Paige—"

"I said we're through here," Riley said, locking eyes with

Havens now.

Havens glared at her like she'd lost her mind. Wingert was standing there with his mouth hanging open.

Riley turned toward Barb Bradley again.

"Thank you for your time, Ms. Bradley," Riley said. "Like I said, we're sorry for your loss."

Bradley smirked broadly at Riley—an admiring smirk, she was sure.

Followed by Bill, Riley herded Havens and Wingert out the front door. She heard the door slam behind them as they walked toward the car. Before they got into the car, Havens turned to Riley.

"What did you think you were doing back there?"

He gave her a sharp shove in the chest.

Riley felt her mouth twist into a smirk.

Oh, how I hoped you'd do that! she thought.

She grabbed Havens' arm and twisted it behind him, shoving him face first against the car.

"Hey!" Wingert cried out.

Holding Havens fast, Riley spoke in his ear with mock-sweetness.

"Agent Havens, please correct me if I'm wrong. Did you just make a threatening move against a superior?"

"No," Havens said.

"Are you sure? Agent Jeffreys, what's your opinion?"

Bill couldn't contain a chuckle.

"Sure looked to me like a threatening move," Bill said.

"Now that's not nice," Riley told Havens, speaking as if he were a naughty child. "I'm sure that Chief Sanderson would disapprove. And he doesn't even like me."

Havens grunted helplessly. Riley let go of his arm and looked at Wingert.

"Agent Wingert, get in the car and drive," she said. "We've got more work to do today."

The four agents got in the car, and Wingert started to drive.

After a few moments of tense silence, Havens spoke to Riley through clenched teeth.

"I still don't know what you thought you were doing."

"Beating the odds," Riley said. "Agent Jeffreys, how often do disarming attempts end in the firing of a weapon?"

Bill chuckled a little.

"About ninety percent of the time," he said.

"Really?" Riley said, feigning surprise. "Wow, those are some pretty steep odds. I'd say we got really lucky."

Havens was trembling all over with fury and frustration.

"You made a mistake back there," Havens said.

"Oh, really?" Riley said. "Tell me, Agent Havens, have you ever been in a gunfight? Because that's what was about to happen. And that woman was probably an excellent shot. Agent Jeffreys, maybe you can talk him through it."

There was a note of pleasure in Bill's voice as he described what he'd observed.

"You went for your cuffs, she went for her gun. She'd have shot you dead before any of us got our weapons out. Then it would have been up to the rest of us to bring her down."

Riley nodded in agreement.

"There'd be at least one officer down," she said. "And probably one innocent civilian as well."

"Innocent?" Havens barked in disbelief. "She drew a weapon! The woman was ready to kill us!"

"She was," Riley said. "Your information was right about that. She has a terrible temper."

Havens was sputtering with outraged confusion.

"She hated her wife. She acted happy that Maggie had died."

Riley summoned up her patience so she could explain.

"No, Barb didn't *act* happy to see Maggie die," Riley said. "She didn't *act* anything. She *was* happy to see her wife die. Sincerely and truly. She considers it a lucky break, and she doesn't care if we know it."

"So what?" Havens asked. "She wanted her wife dead, she killed her, and now she's happy."

Riley groaned aloud. But she knew that she wasn't being persuasive. She had a much more precise reason for knowing that Barb Bradley didn't kill her wife. But how could she put it in words that this dolt could understand?

She knew that Bill was thinking along the same lines. And fortunately, Bill knew exactly how to say it.

"The woman's an asshole," Bill said. "We can't arrest her for being an asshole. Life is unfair that way. There ought to be a law against assholes, but there isn't."

If there were, there'd be one fewer people in this car, Riley thought.

Bill continued, "Serial killers are seldom assholes. They're vicious, sadistic, pathological, unable to feel empathy, sometimes crazy, often charming, always manipulative. But your basic garden-variety assholes? Practically never. That woman might get mad enough to kill, but she's not a serial. My guess is she's never killed anybody in her life. That might have changed today. She might have made her first kill."

Riley smiled. Her partner had nailed what had been on her mind.

But Havens didn't seem to be the least bit swayed.

"We should have hauled her in for resisting arrest," Havens said.

Riley had had enough of Havens' stupidity. It was time to shut him up.

"Wingert, stop the car," she said.

Wingert said, "Huh?"

"Just pull over and stop."

Wingert obediently pulled over to the curb and stopped.

Riley said to Havens, "If you want to arrest her, be my guest. It's a pretty short walk from here. You can book her and go to her trial and even visit her in jail. But don't waste the rest of our time. We've got a serial poisoner to catch."

Havens stared at her in silent disbelief.

"OK, Wingert, let's go," Riley said.

Wingert started driving again.

Riley doubted that this was the end of her difficulties with this pair. She was pretty sure that Havens would complain to Chief Sanderson. And Sanderson would almost certainly take his side.

It's going to be a pain in the ass, she thought.

Any hopes she had of solving this case quickly were dashed. And the local help was going to be worse than useless.

A clever killer was still out there somewhere, as shifty as the Seattle fog.

It was going to be up to her to figure out who it was.

CHAPTER THIRTEEN

At the next morning's meeting, Riley found Division Chief Sean Rigby to be a daunting and weirdly demoralizing presence. She thought that Rigby, who outranked even Team Chief Sanderson, looked like an undertaker presiding over a funeral.

Or maybe more like a vulture, Riley thought.

Yes, that was more like it. He looked like a vulture hunched and looming high in a tree, looking down and waiting for someone to die so that he could dine on dead flesh.

For one thing, the black-clad, rail-thin, cadaverous man refused to sit down. He managed to dominate the room by leaning against a wall while everybody else sat around the FBI conference table. Riley was next to Bill. On the other side of the big table sat Maynard Sanderson along with Wingert and Havens, all looking unhappy.

As far as Riley was concerned, this case was going to be tough enough without rivalries and infighting. But the room reeked with unspoken hostilities.

For his part, Sanderson looked sullen, brooding, and palpably resentful—hardly the blustering blowhard he'd been yesterday. He barely made eye contact with anybody, least of all Rigby.

The only person who didn't look intimidated by Rigby was Van Roff, an overweight, socially inept technical analyst. He was at the end of the table, busy on his laptop computer, and he seemed oblivious to all that was going on around him.

After the meeting got underway, Rigby spoke to Sanderson.

"I understand that your team interviewed Barbara Bradley yesterday."

"They did, sir," Sanderson replied. "I'll let Agent Havens report on that."

Despite his own nervousness, Havens managed to maintain that clipped, pseudo-military delivery of his.

"Our team concluded that Margaret Jewell and Barbara Bradley, a married lesbian couple, were having marital troubles before Margaret was killed," he said. "During the interview Barb Bradley was aggressive and belligerent and not cooperative. Nevertheless, we came to the conclusion that she doesn't fit the profile of a murderer, especially not a serial."

"Oh?" asked Rigby in a low, ominous purr. "How did you come to that conclusion?"

Havens exchanged looks with Sanderson. Riley was sure that Havens had already told Sanderson about her actions at Jewell's house.

Sanderson nodded, obviously cuing Havens to continue.

Riley braced herself for trouble.

"Sir, I came to a different conclusion during the interview," Havens said. "I was placing Bradley under arrest. She resisted. She drew a weapon. A semiautomatic pistol."

Havens paused, apparently trying to decide how to best spin what came next.

"Agent Paige successfully disarmed Bradley. Then we left."

Rigby's heavy black eyebrows jerked upward.

"Oh?" he said. "You didn't apprehend Bradley?"

"No, sir. That was my intention, but Agent Paige was the ranking agent. She overruled my wishes."

"Your *wishes*," Rigby said, with just a trace of mockery in his voice. "Tell me, Agent Havens. Did Bradley have any other guns in her possession?"

Havens gulped.

"Yes, sir," he said.

"How many, do you think?"

"I have no idea, sir."

"And was your team prepared to confiscate *all* of those weapons?"

Havens' face twitched.

"Probably not, sir."

"Do you have any reason to assume that she didn't have a permit for her guns?"

"Not really, sir."

Rigby's mouth shaped into a smirk.

"Not really, eh?"

A chilly silence fell over the room.

Rigby said, "Agent Havens, I take it that Agents Paige and Jeffreys were the ones who decided that Barbara Bradley didn't fit the profile."

"They were, sir."

"And they decided not to clutter up our investigation by bringing the woman in?"

"They did sir."

"And are you in agreement?"

Haven winced all over.

"I am, sir."

59

"Well, then."

Rigby then turned his silent, withering gaze on Riley.

I may not be out of the woods yet, she thought.

Riley knew that it had been Rigby's idea for her and Bill to come in from Quantico. He clearly didn't have much confidence in Maynard Sanderson and his team. But how much confidence did he have in Riley and Bill at this point? Although she was independent of his authority, she didn't want to get on his bad side.

And she still didn't understand what kind of politics were at work here.

It's like we got dropped into a jungle without a map, she thought.

She figured she'd better start finding out what was going on. But who could she ask? She doubted that anybody here was likely to be forthcoming.

"So we can eliminate Margaret Jewell's spouse," Rigby finally said. "What did we find out about the other victim—Cody Woods?"

Rigby nodded toward Bill, who hadn't spoken yet.

Bill said, "After we interviewed Bradley, we talked to everyone we could find who knew Woods. His grown-up son and daughter are both married with kids. They've been pretty much estranged from Woods for years. Nothing rancorous, it's just that Cody Woods got to be pretty solitary over the years. His first wife died, his second wife was unfaithful, and he had a heart attack, and he sort of pulled back from any and all relationships. People who worked with him said he was something of a loner—likeable but sad, a harmless loser."

"So," Sean Rigby added, "you didn't find anybody with reason to want him dead."

"We did not," Bill agreed.

Rigby scanned everybody's faces ominously.

"Sounds more and more like we're dealing with a serial who is quite ordinary in one sense," he said. "This is someone who is killing for the sake of killing. The question is, has he killed anybody else? For all we know, he's been committing murders for years, and these are just the first ones we've noticed."

Riley spoke up. "Barb Bradley said that Margaret had been in a rehab facility. Although she died at home, she was most likely poisoned earlier, possibly at that facility. Are we seeing any indication that we're looking for a healthcare worker?"

Havens said, "Cody Woods had been in a hospital and then he returned to the same hospital and died there. He must have been poisoned in between his hospital stays. That could have happened at home or anywhere else that he went."

"Have you checked out Natrona Physical Rehabilitation?"

"Of course we have! We found nothing unusual about Jewell's treatment there."

Rigby turned toward the technical analyst, who was gripping a candy bar in one hand and typing with the other.

Rigby said, "Mr. Roff, I wonder if you could run a search—"

"Already on it," Roff interrupted. He apparently hadn't been as oblivious as he'd seemed. "And I think maybe I've got something. About a year and a half ago, a woman named Arlis Gannon complained that her husband, Keith, was trying to poison her. He was working as a hospital orderly at the time. The cops couldn't find any evidence and decided that Arlis was just paranoid. The couple separated and divorced. Keith got booted from his hospital job because of his temper, and he recently did time for assault. Now he's working in a convenience store."

Rigby stroked his chin thoughtfully.

"Interesting," he said. "And he worked at a hospital. Can you find anything to suggest he may have had access to either Cody Woods or Margaret Jewell?"

Van Roff rattled away at his keyboard for a few moments.

"Not that I can see," he finally said. "He worked at Nazareth Hospital. Cody Woods got surgery at South Hills Hospital, died there too. It doesn't look like Keith Gannon ever worked there. Margaret Jewell got treatment at Natrona, and it doesn't look like Gannon worked there either."

"Any overlap of personnel between South Hospital and Natrona Rehab?" Rigby asked.

"Already looking," Roff said, typing. "No, I don't see any."

Rigby thought for a moment.

"Check him out anyway," he said.

Riley spoke up again. "I think it's more likely that the killer is a woman."

Rigby gave her a sharp look. "But almost all serial killers are male. Right?"

"Yes, but I'm getting a different sense of this one. And poison is more of a woman's weapon."

"You've developed a profile?"

"I can't say that yet," Riley replied. She wasn't ready to explain her gut feelings to this group.

Maynard Sanderson complained, "We brought you here to

61

develop a profile. Instead, you're just confusing the issue."

Rigby shot the team leader a look that shut him up. Then he turned to Bill.

"And you?" Rigby demanded.

"No solid profile yet," Bill said. "But I've learned to trust my partner's instincts."

Riley heard Havens snort with derision. Sanderson was obviously struggling to keep quiet.

Rigby snapped, "Interview Gannon. Get on it right away. That will be all."

Riley had seldom heard orders more terse and blunt. Everybody was shifting in their chairs, getting ready to carry out Rigby's command. But Sanderson seemed to have summoned up the courage to complain directly to his boss.

"Before we leave, I want to say for the record that Agents Jeffreys and Paige have insinuated themselves into this case much more than I'd expected—or wanted. When you said you were bringing in BAU people to help, I expected them to advise, not investigate. I'm not at all pleased—especially with Paige's behavior yesterday."

Rigby nodded.

"Agent Sanderson, your displeasure is noted. And disregarded."

Sanderson looked punctured like a balloon. Riley almost felt sorry for him.

Rigby added, "If you and your team had come up with anything resembling a profile, I wouldn't have had to ask the BAU for help. You have yourself and your subordinates to blame. Agents Jeffreys and Paige have carte blanche here in Seattle as far as I'm concerned. I expect you to follow their lead."

As Rigby turned to leave, he stopped and locked gazes with Riley.

His look conveyed an unmistakable message.

I'd better watch my step from now on, Riley thought.

Without another word, Rigby strode out of the room. Wingert and Havens were hanging their heads like scolded puppies.

Riley exchanged looks with Bill. She could see that he was as dumbfounded as she was.

Sanderson was struggling to regain his dignity and some semblance of command.

"You've heard your orders," he said to all present. "Find out where Keith Gannon is and interview him right away."

Riley didn't much look forward to charging into someone else's house with Wingert and Havens. Besides, she felt a hunch coming on.

"Agent Sanderson, I'd like to take some time to pursue a theory of my own," she said.

Sanderson growled, "Hell, go right ahead. You heard what Rigby said. Carte blanche. You're like royalty here. Go ahead and waste your own time. My people will solve the case."

Sanderson shoved his notes into his briefcase and strode out of the room. Wingert and Havens conferred with Roff, who was searching for Keith Gannon's address and contact information.

Bill leaned over to Riley.

"Coming up with an idea?" he asked quietly.

"Nothing solid yet," she said.

"Want my help?"

Riley was about to say yes, but after a glance at Wingert and Havens decided otherwise.

"I think you'd better stick with Tweedledum and Tweedledee and make sure they don't screw things up," she said. "Keith Gannon might be a viable suspect or he might have some sort of connection to the killer, but I don't trust them to find out on their own."

Bill nodded and joined the group talking to Roff.

Riley stepped out of the FBI meeting room and into the hallway. She took out her cell phone and called the Seattle medical examiner's office. The receptionist quickly connected her with Prisha Shankar. The chief medical examiner's calm, professional voice came as a relief after the tense meeting.

"Hello, Agent Paige," Shankar said. "How is the case going?"

"Well, that's what I wanted to talk to you about."

"Are you navigating the political waters successfully?" Shankar asked.

Riley smiled a little. She hadn't planned to discuss the local power plays, but she was glad Shankar had brought the matter up.

"It's pretty tricky going," Riley said. "I just came out of a meeting with Sean Rigby and Maynard Sanderson."

Riley thought she detected a hint of a chuckle.

"Oh, dear," Shankar said. "Those two are like oil and water."

"What's the problem between them?"

"They've been rivals for years, ever since they were rookies. Rigby recently got promoted to division chief, the top of one food chain. He's determined to lord it over Sanderson. He wants to make sure that Sanderson never gets to be more than a team leader. He'd just love to find an excuse to bust him down to a lowly field agent. Just try to stay out of their crossfire. You'll be OK."

Riley sighed.

"Easier said than done. Rigby wants us here, Sanderson doesn't. We're right in the middle. I'm afraid they think of Agent Jeffreys and me as pieces in their little chess game."

"I see. Well, just remember, you're a pair of BAU hotshots and they're just a couple of local flunkies."

Riley laughed a little. Seattle was a major city and the FBI agents were hardly powerless. Even so, Shankar's dryly irreverent tone was somehow reassuring. Riley wished that a thoroughgoing professional like Shankar was in charge of the investigation.

"I don't assume you called me to talk about all that," Shankar said.

"No," Riley said. "I just wanted to pick your brain a little."

"I'd love to help."

Riley paused to think for a moment.

"I've never worked a case just like this before," Riley said. "Do you think it's possible that our serial killer is a healthcare professional?"

"Could be," Shankar said. "I'm not the best person to ask, though. The person you want to talk to is Solange Landis. She's the director of the Tate School of Nursing here in town. I'll put you in touch with her."

"She's familiar with this question?"

"She's studied it long and hard," Shankar assured her. "Landis has presented papers at academic conferences and even served as an FBI consultant."

"Well then, thanks for the contact," Riley said.

Shankar added, "Ask her to tell you all about the Angel of Death."

CHAPTER FOURTEEN

The cafe where Solange Landis had agreed to meet Riley was a pleasant change after the turbulent atmosphere at the FBI building. Riley gazed around at the large images of water and sky painted on the walls. Live flowers in a vase on their table added to the feeling that they were sitting outdoors on a sunny day. She sipped her coffee and waited patiently for the information she was seeking.

"So you want to know about the Angel of Death," Landis said. She seemed to savor the phrase.

The nursing school director was a sharp-dressed woman, wearing a business suit rather than a uniform. Her dark hair was carefully styled and showed no sign of gray. It was clear to Riley that this woman had gone to some trouble to create an efficient and ageless appearance.

"Dr. Shankar said you had some knowledge of the subject," Riley said.

"Indeed I have. I've given it quite a lot of study."

"The 'Angel of Death' refers to a certain *type* of killer," she said. "A killer who poses as a medical caregiver—or if you prefer, a caregiver who abuses his or her trusted role in order to kill. And I take it you think that this killer you're looking for might fit that profile."

"It's only a theory," Riley said. "Hardly even that yet. Little more than a hunch. And it's out of my area of expertise. The FBI doesn't get called in on such cases often. I've been told that's because medical co-workers go into denial while the killings are going on. They don't want to believe that such a thing is happening right under their noses."

Solange Landis nodded in agreement.

"Yes, and by the time they have to admit what's going on, the identity of the killer is pretty obvious. There's not much investigating left to do. Such cases are very rare, of course. My guess is that your hunch is a real long shot."

"Could you tell me about some specific cases?" Riley asked.

Landis shrugged. "Well, the most notorious case is surely Dr. Josef Mengele, the Nazi concentration camp physician who performed hideous experiments on prisoners. He was said to whistle happy tunes while committing his crimes, and charmed his child victims with smiles and candy, getting them to call him 'Uncle Mengele' before he tortured and killed them."

Riley shuddered at the thought.

"You look shocked," Landis said with a note of curiosity. "I wonder why."

"That kind of evil is hard to fathom."

Landis smiled.

"Even for a seasoned FBI agent?" she asked. "Tell me, how was Dr. Mengele any different from other monsters that you've known?"

Riley was startled. She had to admit it was a valid question. Just during the last year, she'd hunted killers who had whipped and starved victims, tormented others with chains, or humiliated women even in death by grotesquely posing their naked corpses.

"Of course, Mengele tortured and killed thousands," Landis said. "The criminals you bring to justice aren't nearly so prolific. But I think it's wise not to try to *quantify* evil—to say that one monster is more evil than another just because of the numbers of people they kill. The thing that most strikes me about evil is its sameness. It seems to me that monsters are pretty much alike. But you've had much more hands-on experience with monsters than I. What do you think?"

Riley didn't know what to say. The conversation had taken a turn that she hadn't expected—a strange turn that somehow bothered her.

"I suppose I scare you a little bit," Landis said with a rather dark grin. "I tend to have that effect on people. After all, I run a school that teaches the healing arts. You're probably wondering why I should be fascinated by so-called healers who abuse their trust to torture and kill. Why do I go to so much trouble to learn about them?"

"That question did cross my mind," Riley said.

Landis squinted in thought for a moment.

"I'm sure you know the motto of my profession," she said. "'First, do no harm.' I take that motto very much to heart. I teach my students to do so as well. But I think that the saying 'Know thyself' is just as important. Evil creeps up on us unawares, and before we know it, we become complicit in it."

"I'm not sure I understand," Riley said.

Landis took another slow sip of her coffee, then said, "Consider the case of Genene Jones, the pediatric nurse who killed babies in Texas hospitals. At one of those hospitals, the staff noticed that an unusual number of babies were dying. But the staff fell prey to that denial we just talked about. They just couldn't bring the truth out in the open. So instead of tracking down the killer, they got rid of all their children's intensive care nurses and restaffed the unit. Genene just moved on to another hospital, where she killed six more babies before she was caught. Was that negligent staff any less guilty of those murders than Genene Jones herself?"

Landis leaned toward Riley and spoke with quiet passion.

"I truly believe that denial is our most dangerous enemy. And that motto—'First, do no harm'—doesn't it suggest that even the kindest and gentlest of us has a capacity to do harm? And how can we heal others when we also harbor the desire to hurt? Because we do, you know. Cruel demons reside in all of us."

Landis paused, holding Riley's gaze.

"You must know quite a lot about demons," she said. "I imagine you have a few demons of your own."

Riley shivered as a memory came flooding back.

She had caught up with Peterson.
He was monster who had kept both Riley and April in cages.
He had tormented them in the dark with a propane torch.
Riley's lust for revenge was overwhelming—as cold and cruel as the shallow river where they both stood knee-deep in water.
She lifted a sharp, heavy rock and smashed him in the head with it.
He fell down, and she struck him again and again.
She crushed his face as the river turned red with blood.

She snapped herself out of her memory. Solange Landis was still gazing at her intently.

"The most terrible thing about evil is that it's *easy*," Landis said.

Riley was deeply unsettled now. She sensed that Landis also harbored some memory of inflicting harm, of deliberate cruelty.

What might it be? Riley wondered.

Suddenly, Landis smiled that disarming, impish smile of hers.

"Of course, some Angels of Death pose as Angels of Mercy. You've probably heard of Richard Angelo, who poisoned patients in West Islip, New York, during the 1980s. His goal was to save their lives and convince the world that he was a hero. But more of his patients died than were saved. Do you think your killer might be of that type?"

Riley shook her head.

"I don't think so. Ours administers his poisons and then leaves the patients to die. He's got no interest in saving them. The lag between poisonings and death is part of why he's proving so elusive."

"I see," Landis said. "But you haven't told me what substances he uses."

"Thallium seems to be his poison of choice."

Landis looked surprised.

"Thallium? Oh, then I wonder if you're looking for a medical caregiver at all. Thallium has almost no medical uses to speak of. Angels of Death tend to use medications that they have at hand— muscle relaxants, painkillers, and the like. I'm afraid you might be wasting your time even talking to me."

"It doesn't seem to be pure thallium," Riley said. "It's some kind of a cocktail. Dr. Shankar said that it contained traces of Prussian blue—an antidote to thallium. Are Angels of Death ever inclined toward experimenting on their victims?"

"Very rarely, but ..."

Landis fell silent for a moment.

"Someone comes to mind ... but I'm reluctant to say anything."

Landis fell silent, staring into space.

"I really need to know," Riley urged her.

"Well ..." the nursing director said, then stopped again. After a moment she looked directly at Riley and continued, "There's a former student of mine, Maxine Crowe. She graduated several years ago. I was fond of her, and she was very bright. But lately, she's been in some trouble. She got fired from a hospital job. I gather it was because she experimented with medications. She's still working—doing home care work, I believe. I hate to think that she might be your killer, and I don't want to get her into further trouble. But she always had an odd streak, and there have been rumors. I can help you find her. I'll call my secretary."

Landis took out her cell phone and dialed a number. She asked her secretary for Maxine Crowe's contact information, then waited.

Riley felt skeptical.

"I don't know about this, Landis," Riley said. "An 'odd streak' isn't much of a reason to suspect someone of murder."

Landis's smile faded away.

"Is that true, Agent Paige? How do you know? My guess is that most murders go completely undetected. Who knows who might commit them?"

CHAPTER FIFTEEN

Bill watched closely as Agents Wingert and Havens fired questions at the suspect. The man sitting on a box in the corner glared up at them, an adolescent sneer on his face. Bill guessed him to be about thirty, but he had the manner of a snotty high school kid who'd just been hauled into the principal's office.

They were in the stockroom of a convenience store interviewing Keith Gannon, whose ex-wife had once accused him of trying to poison her. Bill stood back and gave Wingert and Havens room to work. At least they weren't making a mess of things this time and he wanted to observe how the suspect responded.

"We hear that you've got a short temper," Havens told Gannon.

"Yeah, we hear that it's what got you fired from your job as a hospital orderly," Wingert added.

"That's right," Gannon replied. "I punched out another orderly."

"Why did you do that?"

"I didn't like him. Why does anybody punch out anybody? Hey, are you going to haul me down to the station or someplace for questioning? Because I sure hate this job, and I'd love to have an excuse to clock out early."

Havens took a step toward him.

"Did you poison your wife?" he asked.

Gannon shrugged.

"You asked me that question three times already," he said.

"And you still haven't answered," Wingert said.

Gannon let out a rude snort of laughter.

"Look, I keep saying. First, she's not my wife anymore. We're divorced. Second, she's alive, isn't she? What more do you need to know about it?"

Bill crossed his arms and listened as Gannon kept playing games with Wingert and Havens. So far, Bill wasn't sure whether the guy was actually a viable suspect. And of course, Riley seemed to be sure the killer wasn't a guy at all.

Bill decided to just let Wingert and Havens keep doing what they were doing. But the whole case was troubling him ... the discussion of poisoning triggered terrible memories that he'd been keeping at bay for days now.

Bill and his brother were standing at the base of the stairs. Dad was helping Mom come down the stairs. Her whole weight was on him, and she couldn't support herself, she was so weak from an hour of vomiting and nausea. She was pale and sweating and crying from the pain.

There was panic in Dad's eyes.

"We're going to the hospital," he said.

Bill shoved the memory from his mind. He tried to focus on the man being questioned. The one who had worked in a hospital.

But he heard himself say aloud, "She was crying from the pain."

"What?" Wingert asked. Both he and Havens jerked around to face Bill.

Bill shook his head to try to clear it. An idea was forming and he couldn't push it aside. He stepped forward and grabbed Gannon by the front of his shirt, pulling him to his feet.

"Then who did poison Arlis?" he demanded.

"Hold it," Wingert cried.

But Bill was lost in a maze of ancient memories and current fury.

"Who were you working with?" he shouted in Gannon's face. "When you got tired of your wife, who did you get involved with? Did you find someone who could help you get rid of Arlis?"

He shoved Gannon back against the wall and saw that he had triggered the man's temper. It gave him a sense of deep satisfaction.

Bill easily dodged the punch that Gannon threw and slugged the man in the solar plexus. He watched Gannon stagger backward and begin to collapse. He liked that sight.

Then Havens stepped in front of Bill, yelling, "Snap out of it, man."

The fog in Bill's mind cleared and he stepped back.

Gannon was gasping for breath and Wingert was helping him sit back down on the box in the corner.

"Sorry," Bill said. "I guess this jerk really got to me."

He couldn't help but note that Havens and Wingert were both looking at him with new respect in their eyes.

Somehow that brought home the enormity of the mistake he had made.

*

Solange Landis had given Riley an address where she should be able to find Maxine Crowe. The LPN was now working as a palliative caregiver. That fact alone stirred Riley's suspicions. What couldn't a poisoner get away with while caring for patients who were thought to be already dying?

It was an unsettling question.

When Riley arrived at the house, she was struck with a gut feeling that something was strange about the place. She couldn't quite put her finger on why she felt that, but the house itself struck her as very odd. It was a large old bungalow in a staid-looking middle-class neighborhood. The house appeared well cared for, but it somehow had an abandoned look about it.

The yard had been mowed, but there was neither shrubbery nor a flowerbed to offer a touch of color. When she stepped up on the porch, she saw that there were no chairs, no tables, no sign that anyone had ever spent time there.

Riley peeked through the big front windows. There didn't appear to be any drapes or blinds hung at all. The late afternoon sunlight sloped through the panes and shone inside across a bare hardwood floor.

Stranger still, the interior seemed to have been gutted. The space was vast and empty, as if a single room took up the whole bottom floor. And like the porch, there wasn't a piece of furniture in sight inside.

She looked again at the note that Landis had handed her. This was definitely the address where Maxine Crowe was supposed to be working with a patient in her last weeks of life.

Nothing is what it seems here, she thought.

She had no idea what to expect—or to prepare for.

Riley knocked sharply on the door and waited.

No one answered.

She knocked again and waited some more. Still no one answered.

What was going on in there? Was someone hovering over another victim? Or was the murderer alone inside, using this seemingly empty house as a hideout?

Finally she turned the doorknob. The door was unlocked, and she pushed it open.

She called out, "This is the FBI. I'm looking for Maxine Crowe."

A ghostly woman's voice replied, echoing as if disembodied.

"What do you want?"

"Are you Maxine Crowe?"

"Yes."

"I only want to talk to you."

Silence fell for a moment.

"Go away," the woman said.

Riley kept her hand close to her gun and she walked on inside. In the sloping, dusty rays of sunlight, now she could see the room more clearly. It really was a huge room that had probably started off as two or three rooms.

One long wall was completely covered with mirrors. Stretching at waist height along the mirrors was a dance barre.

This room had been a dance studio—whether long ago or recently, Riley couldn't tell.

"Where are you?" Riley called out.

"I said go away."

Then Riley heard the murmuring of another voice. A conversation seemed to be going on. Riley followed the voices across the studio to an open door on the other side. She peered into a much smaller room.

In the middle of the smaller room was a hospital bed with an IV stand next to it. In the bed lay a tiny, emaciated, white-haired woman. Standing next to her was a youngish, white-clad woman with a long, birdlike face and enormous, probing eyes.

Riley found Maxine Crowe's expression inscrutable, but that wide-eyed stare made her think of some predatory creature.

Maxine raised her fingers to her lips, cautioning Riley to be silent.

The old woman in the bed kept talking in a weak, croaking voice.

"But I keep forgetting—is Millicent bringing her little girl tomorrow?"

"No, the day after tomorrow," the caregiver said.

The old woman let out a hoarse, rasping chuckle.

"I'm so excited about seeing her! If you'd told me when I was your age that I'd live to be a great-great-grandmother, I'd never have believed it. Someday it will be your turn. Or do you want to have children, Maxine?"

"I haven't decided."

"Well, you've got time. It must be wonderful, knowing your whole life is ahead of you."

The old woman was holding a small plastic object with a button on it. Her hand was trembling so much that she could barely hold onto it. She kept trying to push the button with her thumb.

"Oh, I can't do it anymore," she said with a sigh. "And the pain is so terrible. Could you do it for me?"

Now Riley understood that the button controlled the IV drip.

Probably morphine, she thought.

Or might it be something more sinister?

Maxine gently took the button out of the woman's hand. She held the button in front of the woman's eyes and squeezed it. A smile of relief crossed the woman's face. Her whole body relaxed.

"Oh, that's better. Please do it again."

Maxine squeezed again.

"A little more, please," the woman said.

Maxine squeezed yet again.

Then again.

And again.

The woman's eyes closed and she seemed to fall fast asleep.

Riley felt a kind of helplessness that she'd seldom felt before. Was she witnessing a medical treatment or a murder in progress?

"What's in that bottle?" Riley demanded.

Maxine turned and looked at Riley with a mysterious smile.

"What do you *think* is in this bottle? You don't know, do you? And I'm quite sure you'll never guess."

CHAPTER SIXTEEN

Riley's doubts vanished in a shudder of horror. This woman had to be the killer she was looking for. And she had to stop her this very minute.

Riley reached for her handcuffs.

"Maxine Crowe, I'm placing you under arrest. For attempted murder."

Maxine's eyes opened wide.

"For *what*?" she said.

"You heard me. Murder. You will also be held responsible for the death of three victims that we know about. And I am witness to this attempt."

Maxine's smile broadened.

"Let me show you something," she said.

She rolled up her left sleeve. Riley was surprised to see that she had an injection port in her own arm. Then she disconnected the IV tube from the sleeping woman's port and inserted it in her own.

She repeatedly pushed the button. Riley could hardly believe her eyes. The liquid in the bottle was now going into Maxine's own vein just as it had gone into the vein of the patient.

Maxine's eyes sparkled with mischief.

"There," Maxine said, pushing the button again and again. "Do you still think I'm a murderer?"

"What's in the bottle?" Riley asked again.

"What do you *think* is in the bottle?"

Riley was beginning to understand.

"Apparently nothing," she said slowly. "Not morphine, anyway. Saline solution, maybe."

Maxine nodded and softly laughed.

"I'm sure you've heard of placebos," she said. "Now you've seen how they work."

Riley pointed to the port in Maxine's arm.

"But why—?"

"Just an experiment. You see, placebos can work even when you *know* they're placebos. I've been testing this placebo's effect on me. And to tell the truth, I'm feeling a little bit high right now."

She disconnected the tube from the injection port.

She asked, "But what's all this talk about murder?"

"The FBI is investigating some recent poisonings here in Seattle," Riley said. "Possibly a serial killer."

"And I seemed like a possible suspect? Why?"

"We strongly suspect that the killer may be a healthcare worker."

"Ah," Maxine said with a sigh. "And you came looking for me because I've gotten in trouble for some unorthodox treatments? Well, yes, I've done some unauthorized experimenting. All of it has to do with placebos. People understand so little about the body's untapped healing powers. Legitimate research has been too slow for my taste. So I took matters into my own hands."

Maxine looked away rather sadly.

"Perhaps I really did go too far," she murmured.

The whole thing seemed unreal to Riley, almost like a dream. She wondered if Maxine Crowe was really in her right mind. At the very least, she was dangerously irresponsible.

But one thing she didn't seem to be was a deliberate killer.

"How long has she got to live?" Riley asked, indicating the patient.

"A day or two at most," Maxine said. "Organ failure is already underway. Don't worry, I've always got real morphine on hand in case the placebo doesn't work. That sometimes happens. I'd never allow anybody to suffer—not for the sake of an experiment or anything else. Anyway, I'm really doing this for her sake. I think it's better for her."

Riley remembered the snippet of conversation she'd heard when she first came in.

"Who is she?" Riley asked.

"Her name is Nadia Polasky," Maxine said. "She's ninety-nine years old. She was a dancer and a choreographer and teacher for longer than either of us has been alive. Probably both of us put together. She kept right on working until just five or six years ago."

Riley felt a touch of awe. The woman must have been a true force of nature.

What would it be like to live so long? Riley wondered.

What might Riley herself live to see? Would she still be working so late in life? Would she *want* to spend all those years facing demons—not just in criminals but herself?

Riley asked, "Do you think she'll live long enough to see her great-great-granddaughter?"

Maxine shrugged.

"What great-great-granddaughter? She never had any children at all, never even got married. From what I've been told, her work in dance was her whole life."

"I don't understand," Riley said. "She was just talking about being a great-great-grandmother."

"I'm not sure I do either. The best I can figure is that she spent her whole life fantasizing about what it would be like to have a family. She's an extremely creative and imaginative woman, so those fantasies must have been very vivid. Now that she's falling into dementia, she's forgotten that they *were* fantasies. She believes that all of it was true. Well, I'm not going to tell her otherwise. Her illusions are the most powerful placebos of all. They keep her at peace."

Riley's mind reeled. She remembered that feeling she'd had when she got here—a feeling that nothing in this house was what it seemed.

I had no idea how right I was, she thought.

"I still don't understand why anybody thought I might be capable of murder," Maxine said. "Certainly some people have disapproved of my methods, but nobody ever accused me of poisoning anyone."

Riley felt rather puzzled by this as well.

"I talked with your old teacher—Solange Landis. She said—"

Maxine interrupted.

"Professor Landis? I should have known."

"Why?" Riley asked.

"We weren't exactly on good terms when I graduated from her school."

Riley was taken a little aback.

"But she spoke well of you," Riley said. "She said you were bright and that she was fond of you."

"We liked each other at first, but then …"

Maxine paused, stroking her patient's hair.

"Have you ever been to her house?" Maxine said.

"No."

"It's very strange. She's very strange. She's got images of death everywhere—antique photos of funerals and coffins, a Civil War embalming table, real human skulls, morbid engravings and paintings. A few times she invited me and some other students over to her house to drink and talk. The talk went on late into the morning hours—and it sometimes turned toward interesting ways to kill people. Not serious talk, of course. Just letting off steam, joking and having fun, scaring each other a little."

Maxine thought for a moment.

"Still, it was too weird for me, and I told her so. I stopped going. Things were never the same between us after that."

Riley thanked Maxine for her time. As she crossed the empty dance studio, she found odd images churning around in her mind—two women discussing methods of murder in a setting of human skulls and grisly mementoes. She began to mull over how she might arrange to visit the home of Solange Landis.

As she stepped down from the empty porch into the unadorned yard, she realized that it was late in the day now. She wondered how Bill had done with his interview of a possible suspect. She would check in with him and they would plan what to follow up on tomorrow.

Like the Seattle mist, troubling thoughts permeated everything about this strange, disturbing case.

Nothing is what it seems, Riley thought.

CHAPTER SEVENTEEN

Amanda Somers was pleased when she saw Judy Brubaker walking along her private dock toward her home on the water. Through her window, she could see that Judy was glancing up and down the dock, looking rather confused. She was undoubtedly expecting something more modest.

Poor thing, Amanda thought. *Maybe I should have warned her.*

When Judy got to the front door, Amanda pressed the buzzer to let her in.

"I hadn't realized that this would be a gated houseboat community," Judy said. "I'm glad you told you the gatekeeper to let me in."

"And I'm glad you called before you came over," Amanda said. "As I told you, it was important to do that. Otherwise he would have made a fuss and demanded identification and phoned me for clearance, and it would have been a bother for everybody. Of course, maybe I should have told you *why* it was important. It didn't occur to me."

"Oh, it's all right," Judy said.

Then Judy just stood staring around at the spacious interior with its clean modern lines and sleek, comfortable furniture. Amanda kept forgetting that her home on the water might not be exactly what visitors had assumed they would see. She'd long since grown comfortable here. She loved her bedroom upstairs with huge windows looking out over the water, and her rooftop deck that made her feel like she owned the sky.

Of course, it sometimes seemed like more space than Amanda needed.

Still, it was little more than a cottage in comparison to her place up in Moritz Hill. Amanda liked the comparative snugness. What she liked most about the houseboat was the privacy. The homes here were close together, but everyone in this community respected each other's space. If anyone here knew how famous she was, they never mentioned it.

As far as her neighbors here on the wharf were concerned, she was just an ordinary person who lived here part of the time. They were all used to her coming and going, being away for weeks at a time. They never intruded to ask why she left or where she went.

As Judy looked around, her curiosity gave Amanda a moment to study her a little.

She was dressed just like she had been back at the rehab center—in a plain jogging suit. Her auburn hair was arranged simply with bangs, and she wore no makeup. The reading glasses hanging around her neck were the only thing about her that looked especially stylish.

Amanda liked Judy's plain demeanor, and she always enjoyed the marvelous stories the therapist liked to tell. She hoped that she had found a friend she could trust. She wasn't sure, but she hoped so. Her life could be awfully lonely.

Now Judy was wandering about the place rather freely, peeking into the kitchen and dining room. Right away, she seemed to Amanda like someone who could make herself at home just about anywhere.

But was that a good thing or a bad thing?

Still looking around, Judy said, "When you said a houseboat, I guess I was picturing …"

She let the sentence trail off.

"Something more like a mobile home?" Amanda asked.

"I suppose so," Judy said. "It's not what I expected."

"Well, my real estate agent insisted that it's not a houseboat but a 'floating home.' But that sounds so pretentious. I just feel awkward saying it."

Judy was looking out the window now.

"Then it doesn't actually go anywhere?" she asked. "I mean, it's not really a boat?"

Amanda chuckled a little.

"No, you won't find any engines, gas tanks, or steering wheels. Instead, I've got all the standard necessities—running water, connections to the city sewer pipes, and electricity. You could say that I've traded mobility for comfort. But I love the feeling of living on the water. Sometimes the whole place actually rocks gently. I hope you don't get seasick!"

Judy's smile broadened.

"Seasick, me? Not a chance!"

Judy's roving about was starting to make Amanda a little nervous—an irrational feeling, she told herself.

"Would you like to sit down?" Amanda said.

"I'd love to. Thanks."

Judy fairly sank into one of the deep white chairs. Amanda sat on a nearby sofa.

"How are you feeling?" Judy asked. "Your wrist, I mean? Oh, I know this is just supposed to be a social visit, but …"

"My wrist is better, thanks," Amanda said.

She started doing that little exercise with her palms and fingers—the "spider doing pushups on a mirror."

"The exercises you taught me work wonders," Amanda said.

"I'm glad to hear that," Judy said.

The two women sat in silence while Amanda kept doing that exercise, pushing her fingers together, then apart, then together.

She doesn't know what to say, Amanda thought. *I don't either. We don't have anything to talk about after all.*

Finally Amanda offered, "Would you like something to drink? I've got coffee ready. Or we could have a little brandy, if you don't think it's too early in the day."

An odd look crossed Judy's face.

"A glass of water would be nice," Judy said.

Amanda managed not to frown. She didn't like that answer. And she didn't like the way Judy said it. She wasn't sure why. But it was the first thing Judy had said that seemed somehow calculated and deliberate.

Amanda walked into the kitchen and filled a glass of water from the faucet.

Then she stood alone in the kitchen for a moment.

She was really starting to feel uncomfortable now. She told herself that it didn't make sense, that she had no reason to feel uneasy around Judy.

But Judy had been so chatty when they were in the rehab center. So friendly. Why was she behaving oddly today?

It's people, Amanda told herself. *Why can't I ever just trust people?*

She knew the answer, of course. There were too many people in her life—so many that she had to come here to get away from them. And she couldn't trust any of them. She'd learned that from long, hard experience.

She knew that people often thought she was neurotic and even paranoid, even if they seldom said so.

But she knew better. It wasn't really her problem.

It was like she'd told Judy back at the rehab center:

Users. Takers.

Everybody wanted a piece of her. Why should she expect Judy to be any different? But she reminded herself not to rush to judgment. Maybe Judy *would* be different. That would be wonderful.

She walked back into the living room and handed the water to

Judy.

"Thanks," Judy said.

Another awkward silence fell.

"You haven't told me very much about yourself," Judy said.

Amanda shrugged.

"Oh, there's so little to tell. Everything about me is so boring."

Judy tilted her head in a curious way.

"I've got a feeling that's not true," she said. "For example, how did you come to live in a place like this?"

Amanda's unease was growing.

What did she mean by "a place like this"?

Probably a place so big and expensive.

She wants to know how rich I am, Amanda thought.

"I like living on the water, that's all," she said, trying not to sound defensive.

It was a lame thing to say, and she knew it.

Judy just kept looking at her with an inquisitive expression.

"You're an odd duck, aren't you?" Judy said.

Amanda didn't reply. Judy's smile was starting to look rather chilly to her.

Then Judy asked, "May I use your bathroom?"

"Of course," Amanda said, pointing. "It's right over there."

Judy set the glass of water on the end table and headed toward the bathroom.

Amanda couldn't control her sense of suspicion anymore. As soon as Judy shut the door behind her, Amanda crept over to the door and put her ear against it.

Sure enough, she heard the medicine cabinet door open.

Of course it was full of all kinds of prescription medicines—fluoxetine and bupropion and sertraline for depression, trazodone and hydroxyzine and alprazolam for sleep and anxiety, and several others to manage chronic pain in her wrist and back and elsewhere.

Obviously, Judy was in there taking a quick tour of Amanda's medical history. She probably could have read that history at the rehab center, so why was she so interested in checking up on it now?

Amanda wasn't shocked. Other people had done this in her home. But her disappointment was crushing.

She hurried back to the sofa and sat down again. When Judy came out of the bathroom, Amanda didn't look like she'd moved from her spot.

Judy sat down and took a sip of water.

What do I do now? Amanda wondered.

Confronting Judy about what she had just done would be both messy and futile. She'd probably deny it altogether. Still, it was time for at least a little honesty.

"Judy," she said, leaning toward her, "I'm afraid this has been a mistake."

"What's been a mistake?"

"Your coming over."

Judy looked startled but not really shocked.

Amanda said, "It was my mistake, I invited you, but … well, you don't know me very well, but I'm a solitary person, and I really do like to keep to myself. This must seem very peculiar. I hope you understand."

Judy's kindly smile startled Amanda a little.

"Of course I understand," she said. "You have every right to your privacy. I didn't mean to intrude."

"Not at all," Amanda said. "Like I said, I *did* invite you."

Judy glanced around a bit, as if getting ready to leave.

"There's no need to hurry off," Amanda said.

"Oh, I appreciate that," Judy said. "In fact, I was just thinking … I believe I told you that I have a special tea recipe that I carry around with me everywhere. Everybody says that it's absolutely delicious. For some reason, we never had a chance back at the center to try it."

Amanda smiled. This wasn't going to be nearly as awkward as she'd feared. Judy wasn't really a bad sort. She was just too nosy. And Amanda had zero tolerance for nosiness. But there was no need to end things abruptly or rudely.

"I'd love a cup," she said.

Amanda just sat and relaxed while Judy rustled around in her kitchen, making tea. When Judy served her, Amanda took a long sip.

She thought it tasted a little bitter, but she didn't want to hurt Judy's feelings, so she kept sipping away at it until the cup was empty.

CHAPTER EIGHTEEN

Riley was at her hotel window looking out over Seattle by night when her phone rang. Her heart sank when she saw that the call was from home. She thought that it was likely to be some kind of problem.

When she'd left, Jilly had been pretty shaky in her transition to being part of the family. Riley had been braced for the possibility of bad news ever since she'd been in Seattle. It bothered her that she felt that way. She wondered if the day would come again when she could look forward to calls from home.

And sure enough, as soon as Riley answered, Jilly's voice said, "You've got to get me out of that school."

Riley almost groaned aloud, but she didn't say anything for a moment. On the phone, there was only the sound of a TV in the background.

Finally Riley said, "I can't get you out of that school."

"Why not?"

Riley stopped herself from trying to explain all the reasons why not. If she started yielding to Jilly's every demand to explain things, she'd be on her way down a slippery slope with her. Besides, Jilly was going to have start dealing with the realities of her new life.

"What's wrong with the school?" Riley asked.

"I can't catch up with the classes. Kids ignore me. I can't make new friends. Nobody's going to like me. I want to go to school with April."

"Jilly, we talked about this. You're in middle school, April's in high school. Going to the same school with her is just not possible. I know it's hard to fit in at a new school. But this is only your second day. Give yourself some time."

She heard Jilly pop her gum. It was a very unsettling sound.

"What if I went and got myself a job?" Jilly said.

Riley shivered a little. The last time Jilly had decided to get a job, she'd tried to become a prostitute.

"You're only thirteen," Riley said. "You can't work yet."

"When are you coming home?"

Riley couldn't help but feel a pang of guilt. Here it was again—the impossibility of balancing her job with raising kids.

Why did I ever try to take this on? she wondered.

Riley said, "I'll come right home when this is over. Jilly, you know what my job is like. I'm not the kind of mom who can be there all the time."

Jilly was sounding more and more upset. Riley was afraid she was going to cry.

"I just feel so out of place. I've always felt this way. But I thought I'd feel different here."

Riley didn't know what to say.

Then Jilly said, "Ryan wants to talk to you."

Riley was both relieved and surprised. She hadn't expected her ex-husband to be there.

Ryan said, "Hi, Riley. How are things going for you?"

"We're finding a lot of dead ends," she said.

"Tell me about it," Ryan replied. "I'm going to move out onto the back deck where I can hear you better."

Riley realized that Ryan wanted to talk more confidentially. She said, "I'll wait."

She heard a door opening and closing, and then Ryan's voice came back on the line.

"I just heard what Jilly was saying," he said. "Not that I was eavesdropping. We all just finished dinner and are sitting in the living room watching TV. I figured maybe you and I should talk."

"How has she been with you?" Riley asked.

"She's been pretty low. She's got a lot of self-image problems. No self-confidence. She expects everything to turn out bad. I guess that's not surprising, considering the life she's had."

Riley felt deeply grateful to Ryan for being there. It was a strange feeling, after years of having to distrust him.

"What am I going to do with her, Ryan?" she asked.

"Well, you're not alone in this. I stayed over last night, and I'll stay tonight too. I'll make sure she's OK. And April and Gabriela are spending a lot of time with her. April's helping her with her schoolwork. She says that Jilly is smarter than she thinks she is. She'll get caught up."

Riley was starting to relax a little. It was comforting to know that her family was pitching in to help.

"What class is she having the most trouble with?" Riley asked.

"Social studies."

"Maybe you could help her with that. She'd probably like the attention."

There was a pause.

"I guess I could," Ryan said. "I never spent time doing homework with April. Guess I can make up for some of that now."

There was gentleness in Ryan's voice that Riley had seldom

heard over the years.

"Ryan, I'm so glad you're there. This whole thing would fall apart without you."

"It feels good to help. Sorry it's taken me so long to … well, you know."

Riley smiled.

"I know. Thanks. Get back inside. I'm sure it's cold out there."

They both said goodbye and hung up.

Riley stood looking out the window again. The mist was clearing up, and she could see the lights of the Space Needle with its flying-saucer-shaped restaurant hovering 500 feet about the city. Off to one side, she caught a glimpse of Seattle's enormous Ferris wheel on the nearby waterfront. Seattle was a beautiful city, even in the fog.

Of course, she wasn't here to enjoy the scenery. Still, she was just getting ready to meet Bill for dinner in the hotel bar. Maybe that wouldn't be all business.

*

A little while later, she was sitting with Bill in a cozy booth as they waited for their hamburgers. The hotel bar and cafe was dimly lit and comfortable. Riley's bourbon on the rocks was helping her relax. But she reminded herself to take it easy. Drinking too much had gotten her into trouble in the past, especially with Bill.

She remembered with a shudder a drunken late-night phone call to Bill when she had told him that she thought they should have an affair. That had been six months ago, when his own marriage hadn't broken up yet, and Riley's divorce from Ryan hadn't been final. That had been a low point for her. And it had nearly destroyed both her friendship and her working relationship with Bill. She wasn't going to let anything like that happen again.

She and Bill were filling each other in on their activities that day. Riley had told him about her visits to Solange Landis and Maxine Crowe.

Bill had just finished telling her about interviewing Keith Gannon with Havens and Wingert at the convenience store.

"I really blew it," Bill said. "This case is getting to me more than I realized."

"I know exactly how that goes," Riley said. You've seen me do that more than once." Then she asked. "Do you still think Gannon is a suspect?"

"No, I actually think that I completely misread that one," Bill said. "Havens and Wingert have still got their suspicions. That's OK, it should keep them occupied while you and I solve the case. But Solange Landis sounds like a strange customer."

Riley took a sip of her drink.

"Strange is right. I just went to her for information, and had no idea I'd wind up thinking she might be a suspect. I called Roff, told him to try to find out if she had any connections with the victims. So far he hasn't turned up anything. Still, I'd like to get a look at that house of hers. I'm definitely going to set that up as soon as I can."

"I guess we've done all we can do for today," Bill said.

"I guess so," Riley said.

It didn't feel like a very satisfactory day's work, though. It had left them with more questions than answers.

The waiter brought their hamburgers, which looked delicious. Riley was just starting to take a big bite of hers when her phone buzzed. She saw that it was a text message from Blaine.

The message read …

Hope all is going well. When do you think you'll be getting back? I'll make dinner.

Riley was a little surprised. She'd barely thought about Blaine since she'd come to Seattle. She wasn't especially pleased. She was still feeling disappointed and even angry that he'd moved away.

Now he's acting like nothing has changed, she thought.

And he wanted to know when she'd be getting back.

Riley didn't feel like giving him an answer. She put the phone back in her bag.

"Who was it?" Bill asked.

"Nobody," Riley said.

Bill just stared at her with slight smile on his face. He'd obviously detected that the text had made her uneasy.

"I said it was nobody," Riley said.

Bill just kept looking at her.

"It's my ex-neighbor, OK?" Riley said.

"Blaine?"

"Yeah."

She'd already told Bill about Blaine, including the fact that Blaine had moved.

"Aren't you going to answer him?" Bill asked.

"No."

"Why not?"

Riley leaned toward Bill.

"I don't know," she said. "Why are you asking me all these questions?"

Bill shrugged.

"I've been worried about you," he said. "You're dealing with a whole lot of stuff, especially with a new teenager in the house. I can tell it's got you stressed."

"It's nothing to worry about," Riley said. "I've got plenty of help at home. April's there, and Gabriela. Ryan's pitching in too."

"Ryan?" Bill asked with a note of surprise.

Riley sighed. She wished she hadn't said Ryan's name.

"Don't tell me you're thinking about getting back together with that jerk," Bill said.

"What if I am?"

Bill's eyes widened. He looked like he couldn't believe what he was hearing.

"Look, we've been working together since practically forever," he said. "We've gotten each other through worlds of crap. Do I need to remind you of everything that guy did to hurt you? Because I can remember every detail."

"Things are different now. He's different."

Bill shook his head with a growl of disapproval.

"It's your choice," he said. "But from what you've told me, Blaine's a good guy, someone you can count on."

"That turned out not to be true," Riley said.

"Why, because he moved across town? That's nothing, Riley. And here you are, not even answering his messages."

Riley glowered at Bill.

"Leave it alone, OK?" she said.

"OK."

They said little else as they finished eating their hamburgers.

*

Riley was walking through a wet, dense fog.
She was holding two girls by the hand.
One was April, the other was Jilly.
But they weren't teenagers. They were both little girls.
They asked Riley in unison ...
"Where are we going?"

"Somewhere safe," Riley said.

But it wasn't true.

The truth was, Riley had no idea where they were, or where they were going. She couldn't see anything around her. There were shadowy figures moving through the fog everywhere—predatory shadows, all of them dangerous and deadly.

How could Riley find safety for April and Jilly in this impenetrable mist?

One of the figures walked toward them. Riley couldn't tell if it was a man or a woman.

"Who are you?" Riley asked.

A laugh rumbled through the fog.

"Who do you think?"

The voice sounded barely human.

Riley knew right away—it was the poisoner, the killer she'd been hunting for.

The figure started to move away into the swirling whiteness.

Riley reached for her gun, but it wasn't there.

She let go of the girls' hands and hurried after the vanishing figure.

"Mom, where are you going?" April called out.

"Don't leave us here!" Jilly said.

The voices broke Riley's heart. She didn't want to leave them. But she had a job to do. She had no choice.

"I'll come back for you," Riley said.

But how was she ever going to find them again in this fog?

Riley was awakened by the sound of her phone ringing. She was shaking all over from the dream. She wasn't sure which had terrified her most, the figure in the fog or her abandonment of the girls.

She tried to clear her head as she answered the phone and heard a familiar voice.

"Agent Paige, this is Chief Rigby. I need you and Agent Jeffreys right away. We've got another body."

"Do you know who it is?" Riley asked.

"We sure do," Rigby said. "And the press is going to eat this one up. The victim is Amanda Somers."

Riley jumped out of bed.

"Amanda Somers?" she said.

"I thought maybe you'd heard of her. We're meeting at Parnassus Heights Hospital. Wingert and Havens will pick you up

ASAP."

Rigby ended the call.

"Amanda Somers!" she whispered aloud.

The case had taken a turn that she couldn't have imagined.

CHAPTER NINETEEN

The morning fog was still thick when Riley and Bill stepped out of the hotel. Agent Lloyd Havens was waiting for them outside. He hastily ushered them into the FBI car. Agent Jay Wingert was driving again.

"Tell me what we know," Riley said to Havens.

"It's a writer this time," Havens said. "Somebody famous. Amanda something."

Riley bristled.

"Amanda *Somers*," she said. "Please don't tell me you've never heard of her."

"I remember her name from somewhere," Havens said.

"She wrote some kind of bestseller, right?" Wingert said.

Riley was aghast at their ignorance.

"She was more than a writer," she said. "She was a legend. And her book was a lot more than just a bestseller. Haven't you ever read *The Long Sprint*?"

"Not me," Havens said.

"Me neither," Wingert said.

Riley glanced at Bill, who looked as annoyed as she felt.

What are they teaching kids in school these days? Riley wondered.

Bill told them, "Amanda Somers wrote a really great novel quite a few years ago. Then she became a total recluse. She never did interviews, and she never appeared in public. There have always been rumors that she was working on another book, or maybe several. Thousands upon thousands of readers have been waiting anxiously all this time. This news is going to crush their hearts."

Havens and Wingert looked like they couldn't care less.

Riley felt an ache in her throat. The sadness of what had happened was just hitting her.

She'd read *The Long Sprint* when she was still in college—not for a class, but because everybody was reading it and loving it. *The Long Sprint* was one of those rare novels that touched and changed lives. It was an epic saga about an adventurous and rebellious young woman named Emerson Drew. Like thousands of other young women, Riley adored Emerson Drew and wanted to be just like her.

And like so many other readers, Riley had long hoped that Amanda Somers would write another book—maybe even a sequel about Emerson Drew. Riley had often wondered what had become of the beloved character. How much like her own life had Emerson's life been?

Now maybe we'll never know, Riley thought.

"How did it happen?" Bill asked.

Havens said, "A neighbor spotted her body floating in water late last night. The neighbor called nine-one-one, then dived in and fished her out and tried to revive her. The paramedics arrived promptly, but it was too late. She was pronounced dead on the spot."

Riley tried to make sense of what she was hearing.

"In the water?" she asked. "Do you mean a swimming pool?"

"No, in Lake Union," Havens said. "One of the fancy houseboat communities there. She lived in one of those multimillion-dollar floating homes. Kind of a super houseboat."

Riley couldn't quite picture what he meant. She'd seen houseboats in the bodies of water that threaded through and around Seattle, but she'd never gotten very close to them.

Bill asked, "Are we positive that she was poisoned, like the other victims?"

"Yes, we are," Havens said. "Because of who she was, Chief Medical Examiner Prisha Shankar got called in to do the autopsy personally. She found traces of thallium right away. That's when we got the call."

Riley's head was buzzing with questions. How had the murderer gotten access to her? Was the murderer now pursuing high-profile targets? Rigby had been right when he said that the press would soon be all over this. A lot of publicity was the last thing the team needed right now. How much worse were things about to get?

"Take us to this houseboat," Riley told Wingert and Havens. "I want to see it."

"Later," Havens said. "First we've got a big meeting at Parnassus Heights Hospital."

Wingert drove skillfully through the morning traffic, but Riley was impatient to get on with the investigation.

Why, she wondered, *do we have to detour for yet another meeting?*

The case had taken on new urgency, and she was more eager than ever to track this awful killer. But, she realized, she wasn't in a position to give orders right now. With a sigh of resignation, she settled back into the car seat.

When Wingert pulled up to the hospital, Local Division Chief Sean Rigby was waiting outside. His usual icy demeanor was now one of palpable alarm.

"Get ready," he said, ushering the agents inside. "We're in for a rocky time of it."

Riley couldn't imagine what he meant by that. But when she, Bill, and the others stepped into the large meeting room, she was buffeted by bodies and deafened by chatter. News of Amanda Somers' death had spread like wildfire, and reporters were already swarming.

The crush of people reminded her of the shadowy figures from her dream.

Here they were, crowding her from all sides.

And the fog is here too, Riley thought with despair.

It was the impenetrable fog of chaos and confusion.

CHAPTER TWENTY

The suffocating heat of the overcrowded room hit Riley hard after the damp, chilly air outside. Local Division Chief Rigby ushered her along with Bill and Agents Wingert and Havens to seats at a large conference table.

Reporters were jammed against each other all around the table, taking pictures and videos and scribbling notes. Seated at the table were some people Riley knew and some she hadn't seen before.

Rigby took a seat nearby, looking anxious and uncertain. Team Chief Maynard Sanderson was seated beside him, struggling to maintain his starched, official composure. Police Chief Perry McCade was sweating profusely, and his walrus-style mustache was twitching nervously.

Seated at the head of the table was a man who seemed to be in charge. He had the mannequin-like stiffness and the frozen smile of a politician.

Riley now fully understood that this was a press conference, not an investigative meeting. She didn't know whose idea it had been, but it was a lousy one. A PR stunt like this was going to make the case much harder.

The only person Riley was glad to see was Chief Medical Examiner Prisha Shankar. Perhaps she'd bring an element of sanity to whatever was about to unfold.

The man at the head of the table stood up.

"For those of you who don't know me," he said, "I'm Briggs Wanamaker, Director of Parnassus Heights Hospital. The local FBI Field office and I want to confirm some tragic news. The famous writer Amanda Somers was pronounced dead last night from undetermined causes."

Reporters tried to yell Wanamaker down with a barrage of questions, but he managed to silence them with his own booming voice.

"Ms. Somers was hospitalized here a couple of weeks ago for a completely unrelated condition. She also spent a short time at the Stark Rehab Center. We at Parnassus Heights want to express our condolences to Amanda Somers' legion of readers, and to her son and daughter, Logan Somers and Isabel Watson, who are here with us today."

Wanamaker gestured toward a man and a woman. They seemed to be making an effort to appear appropriately grief-stricken. It looked more like veiled gloating to Riley.

A male reporter shouted out.

"Can you confirm that Amanda Somers received surgery here for carpal tunnel syndrome?"

"No comment," Wanamaker said.

But the reporter wasn't going to back down.

"Does that kind of surgery often involve a risk to the patient's life?"

Wanamaker snapped back, "The surgery had nothing to do with it."

Riley stifled a gasp. It was a blunder, and she could tell by Wanamaker's fallen expression that he immediately knew it. Now the questions came piling on.

"Does the hospital accept any responsibility for possible misdiagnosis?" asked one reporter.

"Was medical malpractice involved?" yelled another.

Wanamaker raised his arms and tried to subdue the group.

"Please, we have additional statements for you, and then we will be open to questions. The division chief of the Seattle FBI field office, Sean Rigby, would like to make a statement."

Rigby stood up and for a moment he looked like he might head for the exit. Riley sensed that he now understood the disaster he had helped create by setting up this meeting. He read from a piece of paper that he managed to keep steady in his hand.

"Last night at approximately twelve thirty, Amanda Somers' neighbor Dale Tinker spotted a body floating in the water next to Somers' floating home. Ms. Tinker is with us today."

He gestured toward a frightened-looking woman. As far as Riley was concerned, it made no sense that she was even here. Riley wondered which had been the greater shock for her—discovering the body or getting dragged into this PR insanity.

Riley could see that she was in no condition to make a statement of her own.

Even so, Rigby obviously expected her to say something.

Cowering in her chair, Dale Tinker spoke in a barely audible voice.

"I saw her in the water. It's not far between our houses, so I jumped in. I pulled her back up onto her deck. I tried to do CPR, but …"

Her voice froze for a moment and she looked dazed.

"I didn't know who she was," she said, almost weeping now. "I've known her for years, and she was always just Amanda. I didn't know she was *that* Amanda. The neighbors only knew her as Amanda. I even read her book, and I didn't know."

The woman couldn't say anything more.

A reporter said to Rigby, "You haven't said anything about the cause of death."

Rigby said, "We can't give any details yet. It appears that she fell from the upper deck of her floating home into the water."

"So you think she drowned?" the reporter asked.

Rigby hesitated.

Then he said, "No comment."

Riley was cringing now. Those two words were like red meat to a pack of wolves. The reporters all started asking questions at once.

Could he possibly be handling this any worse? Riley wondered.

One reporter managed to make herself heard over the rest.

"I see that the chief medical examiner is here. Do the authorities have any reason to suspect foul play?"

Another chimed in, "We understand that the FBI is investigating two poisonings. Is this death related to that investigation?"

Yet another pointed to Riley.

"Isn't that BAU Agent Riley Paige, the well-known profiler? Why has she been brought in?"

Dr. Prisha Shankar looked thoroughly exasperated. Riley sensed that she, too, thought this meeting was worse than useless.

"No comment," Rigby said again. "I'd like to give Amanda Somers' son and daughter a chance to speak."

Logan Somers stood up.

"Isabel and I just want to say that this is a terrible shock. Our mother had been depressed lately, but we hadn't realized how desperate she was. If we'd only known, if we'd only seen the warning signs ..."

He acted as though he was too overwhelmed with emotion to say more. Riley didn't find him the least bit convincing.

Logan sat down, and his sister, Isabel Watson, spoke in a calculatedly regretful tone.

"My brother and I wish we'd have known," she said. "If we'd known, maybe we could have done something."

Riley was completely dumbfounded. She could see that everybody else at the table felt the same way.

The room was in a greater uproar than ever. The flock of reporters was demanding to know whether Amanda Somers had committed suicide. Things were completely out of control.

Rigby called out, "This meeting is over."

Despite noisy protests, hospital security officers deftly herded the reporters out of the room.

Logan Somers and Isabel Watson both rose. With solemn expressions, they each thanked everyone rather ceremoniously. Then, looking rather smug and self-satisfied, they left.

By the time the throng was gone, hospital director Briggs Wanamaker had lost what little remained of his carefully cultivated political poise.

He barked at Rigby, "I told you to keep the FBI out of this meeting. You should have just let me handle it."

"You'd have botched it even more," Rigby shot back. "You should thank me and my people for saving you from yourself. If the press got wind of what was really going on, you'd be in a lot more trouble than you already are."

Riley couldn't contain her frustration a moment longer.

"Whose idea was this damned meeting, anyway?" she said, almost shouting.

Rigby and Wanamaker turned toward her, startled. Then they stared at each other, looking somehow both accusing and ashamed. Riley could see that they had cooked this whole mess up together. Why either one had thought it would be a good idea, she couldn't possibly imagine.

Riley said, "Mr. Wanamaker, I'd like you to leave. I need to confer with my law enforcement colleagues."

Looking thoroughly cowed, Wanamaker took what was left of his dignity and left the room.

Riley glared at Rigby and Sanderson.

"I've got some questions of my own," Riley snapped. "And I'd better get some answers right now."

CHAPTER TWENTY ONE

All eyes snapped toward Riley, and everybody fell silent. Her ears were still ringing from the racket that had filled the room just a few minutes before. But the place wasn't so suffocating now, and she could breathe more easily.

At least she now had the full attention of everybody in the room.

"That whole scene was a farce," she said, managing to keep her anger under control. "Right now, those reporters know as much about Amanda Somers' death as Agent Jeffreys and I do. For all I know, they're as well informed as anybody here. And that's a disaster. It's about time we all got a few things straight."

She noticed that two people were smiling slightly—Bill and Dr. Shankar. They'd been sharing her frustration all along.

Then Riley said, "First of all, what were her son and daughter talking about? Agent Havens said that traces of thallium were found in the victim's body. So what was all this about suicide? *Did* Amanda Somers commit suicide? Did she take pills, jump off that platform and drown, or both? If she did, what are all of us doing here?"

Riley was relieved that Prisha Shankar was the first to speak.

"She didn't drown. That was the first conclusion we were able to come to. And she most certainly did not commit suicide. What you were told is correct. We found traces of thallium in her system. Even if we didn't already have a pattern of thallium poisoning, it's not a substance anyone would be likely to use for suicide."

Bill was jotting down notes.

"So what were her kids talking about?" he asked.

Everybody was silent for a moment.

"I've got a hunch about that," Shankar finally said. "Everybody knows that Amanda Somers was notoriously reclusive. I'd be willing to bet that she and her children had been estranged for years. So all their talk about how depressed she was and how worried they were about her was just brazen hypocrisy. Right now they're looking to inherit her fortune."

Riley was starting to understand what Shankar was getting at.

She said, "And there's nothing to boost an author's posthumous sales like suicide."

Shankar nodded.

"Right. Better than murder, and much, much better than an

accident or natural causes. Especially for a writer like Amanda Somers. It would add to her already considerable mystique. She'd be tortured and unhappy as well as reclusive. It all adds up to the stuff that literary legends are made of."

It made sense to Riley. Too much sense. "And besides," she added, "there wouldn't be all those inconvenient questions about who would kill her and why."

Shankar nodded and continued, "And you can bet that new books by Amanda Somers will be published in the near future. Posthumous works, one right after another. Very likely cribbed together from notes and drafts, the kind of stuff that Somers would never have allowed to get into print when she was still alive."

The possibility saddened Riley. She'd spent years looking forward to a new Amanda Somers novel, especially one about Emerson Drew. But this was not what she'd been hoping for at all. And Somers' children were definitely muddying the waters for the investigation with this talk of suicide.

Police Chief Perry McCade was stroking his mustache, listening with interest.

"So should we be looking at the kids as suspects?" he asked.

Team Chief Sanderson had been glancing at Division Chief Rigby. Riley sensed that he was becoming emboldened by his superior's lapse in self-confidence.

"Nothing's off the table," Sanderson said.

"But we'd have to connect them to the other poisonings," Rigby added, apparently trying to reassert his authority. "That is, if Amanda Somers was poisoned by the same killer."

"What do you think, Dr. Shankar?" Rigby asked.

Prisha Shankar didn't have to stop to think.

"I'm all but sure of it, since thallium was involved," she said. "My team has been examining the cocktails used on the other two victims. They're really quite sophisticated, and the killer varied the recipe both times. Margaret Jewell's concoction included heparin, a blood thinner. Cody Woods' mix included the hormone epinephrine. The killer was trying for slightly different effects and symptoms. Or perhaps delaying one death while bringing another along more quickly."

Riley asked, "Any preliminary information on the cocktail used on Amanda Somers?"

Shankar drummed her fingers on the table.

"It's too soon to say much about it," she said. "But it did contain traces of suxamethonium chloride."

"And what effect would that have?" Bill asked.

"It's a muscle relaxant. It can cause short-term paralysis."

Riley asked Shankar to spell out the name of the substance. She wrote it down. Then she turned to Police Chief McCade.

"Chief McCade, I assume that you've already sent cops to the houseboat. What have they found out so far?"

McCade looked over some notes.

"Amanda Somers' floating home is in a gated community," he said. "My people talked to the gatekeeper who was on duty yesterday afternoon. He buzzed in only one guest. Amanda had told him she was expecting a visitor. She just said a friend would ask for her and to let her in. She didn't give the gatekeeper a name. We asked the nearest neighbors who might visit, but they had no idea. But we've still got other people to interview."

"Did the gatekeeper give a description?" Riley asked.

"He said she was pretty nondescript—middle-aged, reddish-brown hair. She was wearing a jogging outfit."

Riley tapped her eraser against the table, considering what to ask next.

"Did you get any images from surveillance cameras?" she asked McCade.

"The cameras on Somers' houseboat were turned off. The cameras on the dock got grainy images. Just a woman wearing a cap, you can't see her face. The gatekeeper's description is more useful."

Riley mulled this over. She'd been starting to consider Solange Landis a suspect but this didn't sound like the nursing school head that she had talked to yesterday morning. At least, not unless she was wearing a disguise. Could Solange have gone from their morning chat over coffee to a murderous visit to a famous writer? It was a question she couldn't answer.

Riley turned to Prisha Shankar, who looked alert and attentive as usual.

"Dr. Shankar, how does the visitor fit in with a time frame for a poisoning scenario?"

Dr. Shankar squinted in thought.

"I'm not sure," she said. "Thallium doesn't normally work that fast. But the cocktail might have been designed to speed things up. Suxamethonium chloride might have accelerated the effects. It *could* have been the visitor, but it's just as likely that the victim had already been poisoned by then."

Riley wasn't sure whether to address her next question to

99

Sanderson or Rigby. The political tensions between them were as palpable as ever. Rigby was determined to stay at the top of the local FBI food chain, at Sanderson's cost if possible. Sanderson was anxious not to get eaten. No matter which of them Riley addressed, the other was going to be offended.

What a pain in the ass, she thought.

She glanced back and forth between them, hoping to show no preference.

"Give us an overview of the case so far," she said.

Rigby jumped in before Sanderson got a chance to speak.

"We've got three murders that we know of—all poisonings. The first was Margaret Jewell, who died at home in November. She'd recently been treated for fibromyalgia at Natrona Physical Rehabilitation. Cody Woods died a week ago. He'd gotten knee replacement surgery at South Hills Hospital awhile back. He checked himself back in because he felt unwell. He died there soon afterward."

"And both appeared to have died from heart attacks," Riley said.

"That's right," Sanderson said.

Rigby jumped back in. "And now Amanda Somers. She was also hospitalized for a procedure that is not usually life threatening. And she was also poisoned."

Riley asked, "Has our technical analyst found any overlapping personnel between the hospital where Cody died and the rehab clinic where Jewell was treated?"

"No," Sanderson said.

"Have him check again," Riley said. "Include the hospital and the rehab facility that treated Amanda Somers. Tell him to go over the records with a fine-toothed comb. We're not necessarily looking for physicians, nurses, and caregivers. Check out cleaning personnel, delivery people, social workers, visitors—anybody who might have come and gone without drawing a lot of attention. Tell him to keep an eye out especially for a woman who meets the description of Amanda Somers' visiting friend."

Sanderson jotted down the instruction.

Riley turned to Chief McCabe.

"Give me the address for Amanda Somers' houseboat," she said. "Agent Jeffreys and I will go over there right away."

McCabe nodded and wrote down the address.

Riley scanned all the faces at the table.

"I don't need to tell you that we've got a mess on our hands," she said. "Amanda Somers' death makes this case personal for millions of people. Things are going to keep right on getting tougher. We've got three victims now, and those are only the ones we know about. There may have been others. There are going to be more unless we put a stop to it."

Riley made eye contact with Rigby and then with Sanderson.

"We'll have no more press conferences if we can possibly avoid them," she said. "That means no more rookie mistakes. Understood?"

The two FBI chiefs nodded. Neither of them looked at all pleased. Again, Riley detected a slight grin on Prisha Shankar's face.

"This meeting's over," Riley said.

As everyone left the conference, Bill leaned over to Riley.

"Well done," he said quietly.

But Riley wasn't in the mood for congratulations. Now that the meeting was over, she realized yet again that Amanda Somers was gone, and that she'd never read another book by her. Even if new books supposedly by her came out, they'd probably be just patched together by ghostwriters and editors. The thought made her terribly sad.

Snap out of it, she told herself.

She had to keep her head in the game.

Next, she would get a look at that houseboat where Somers had died. She hoped to find something there that others had missed.

CHAPTER TWENTY TWO

Mount Rainier was never out of sight as Bill drove them to Amanda Somers' home. Riley gazed out the car window at the snow-covered peak, so beautiful in the sunshine. It seemed a picture of majestic tranquility—not what it actually was, an active volcano that might erupt at any moment.

It struck Riley as a fitting image.

Just like this case, Riley thought. *Ready to explode.*

Of course, if Mount Rainier were to erupt, it could easily destroy a large part of the city. A series of murders seemed paltry by comparison, but murders were the one thing that she could put a stop to.

Riley was glad that she and Bill had commandeered an FBI vehicle of their own today, instead of riding along with Wingert and Havens. She was sure that the two local agents were just as glad to be rid of them.

As Bill wended their way past several waterfront communities, she saw houseboats of various types and sizes clustered closely together along shared docks. They were colorful and lively looking, with people bustling about obviously engrossed in everyday matters. Farther out in the water, small sailboats took to the breeze.

Soon they arrived at the gate for the community where Amanda Somers lived. Bill braked to a stop, and the gatekeeper stepped out of his comfortable-looking shack. As he walked over to the car, Bill opened the window.

"You must be from the FBI," the man said.

Bill and Riley introduced themselves and showed their badges. He was a tall, lanky man with a good-natured face. Riley guessed that he was about her own age.

"Come right on through," the gatekeeper said. "You can park just inside."

The man opened the gate, and Bill drove past it and parked in the private lot. The man was standing nearby when they got out of the car and he shook hands with each of them.

"I'm Evan Highland," he said. "I was working here yesterday afternoon, and—"

He stopped short and slouched awkwardly. Riley could tell that he was having trouble processing what had happened.

She'd recognized his name right away. The local police had interviewed him shortly after the discovery of Amanda Somers' body. He hadn't been on duty when the body was found, but he had been here when the visitor had arrived.

Before leaving the hospital, Riley had read a transcript of his description of the woman. He was an observant man, and his description was very nicely detailed.

Even so, Riley wanted to ask him just a few more questions.

"I wonder if you could tell anything more about the visitor you buzzed in yesterday," she said.

A pained look crossed Highland's face.

"Do you think she might have been the killer?"

Riley was sorry to have to bring it up. She didn't want to tell him that he might have let a murderer into Amanda Somers' home. Besides, Prisha Shankar had expressed her doubts. According to her, it was likely that Amanda Somers had been poisoned before the visitor arrived.

"We really don't have any idea yet, Mr. Highland," Riley said. "Has anything occurred to you about her since you talked to the police?"

Highland shook his head.

"I can't think of anything else," he said. "She had the most ordinary face you could imagine. Ordinary lips, chin, eyes, nose. I remember thinking that at the time—'this is the most ordinary-looking person I've ever seen in my life.'"

He chuckled sadly.

"Kind of a contradiction in terms, huh? How can you look more *ordinary* than everybody else?"

Riley jotted his words down.

"Was she wearing makeup?" she asked.

"No."

"Do you think she was wearing a wig?"

Highland paused for a moment.

"Maybe. Her hair was reddish-brown, like I told the cops yesterday. It was hanging straight and she had bangs. Yeah, maybe it could have been a wig. A good one if it was."

Riley was picturing Solange Landis in her mind. With a simple disguise, she could probably fit the description. But it was still a rather dim possibility.

Bill asked, "Are you sure she didn't have any other visitors that day? Earlier than the visitor you described?"

Highland shook his head.

"No," he said. "I didn't buzz in anybody else to see her."

"How about visitors to see other people?"

103

"It was a quiet day. Just a couple of people, but nobody that I didn't know."

Riley knew that FBI agents had already thoroughly checked everyone who had come through that gate on the day of the murder. And they had questioned all the neighbors without turning up any suspects.

Now another possibility occurred to her. If the killer wasn't a neighbor or a visitor, it appeared that only one other person would have had access to Amanda Somers.

That person was the gatekeeper himself.

Riley eyed him carefully, looking for any sign of anxiety. If he was the killer, she could surely detect some telltale sign of guilt.

In fact, he seemed to be quite unsettled. But Riley sensed that wasn't guilt. This man was bothered by something more than the possibility of having failed in his professional duties.

"Can you think of anything else?" she asked.

Highland squinted thoughtfully.

"She was kind of plain, but she had a nice smile. She seemed— generous, I guess. Amanda—that's what I called her—didn't have guests very often. I was glad that someone nice had come to see her."

Highland had a faraway look in his eye.

He said, "You know, I was one of the only people around here who knew who she really was. She was just 'Amanda' to her neighbors. I still don't quite believe it. Whenever she came and went, she'd always stop and talk to me."

Highland's eyes filled up with tears.

Riley and Bill exchanged glances. She knew that they had both realized the same thing.

Bill said, "You read her book, didn't you?"

Highland nodded.

"Years ago," he said. "Long before I ever met her."

"So did both of us—Agent Jeffreys and I," Riley said.

Highland had trouble speaking for a moment.

"That book changed my life, made me see myself and the world in a whole new way. I should have told her, I guess, but ... she wanted so much to be left alone, because this was the place where she didn't have to *be* Amanda Somers. I thought it wouldn't be right. So I never even mentioned it."

He fell silent. Riley could see regret in his eyes—regret at never asking a world of questions, regret at never having thanked her for her wonderful book.

This man was definitely no killer.

"You did the right thing," Riley said.

"Thanks," he said. He didn't sound very convinced.

Highland gave directions to Amanda Somers' home, and Bill and Riley started walking toward the docks.

"He's not our man," Bill said.

"No," Riley said. "He's grieving, just like all the rest of her readers. And he's struggling with guilt on top of that."

Riley observed the neighborhood as they walked. She had heard the houses here described as floating homes rather than houseboats. Now she could see why. The houses were quite enormous, and some of them were architecturally elegant.

Off to the side, she could see much smaller homes—true houseboats, with pointed bows. They reminded Riley of RVs, except that they were on the water. Those obviously could move about on the water. She'd been told that the larger ones were permanently moored.

The floating homes were lined up along several interconnecting docks. Even in this expensive neighborhood, the decor ranged from kitschy to elegant. As they walked along, Riley saw potted trees, sculptures, and garden gnomes on the decks.

They found Amanda Somers' home at the end of a dock. It was larger than most of the other houses, a big modern box shape. Riley and Bill stepped under the police tape and walked toward the front door.

Just then Bill's phone rang. Bill checked to see who was calling.

"It's Rigby," he said. "I guess I'd better take this. You go on inside."

Riley opened the door and stepped into the house. She had to catch her breath. The place looked even bigger inside than it had from outside.

A strange feeling came over her—a chill that went down to her bones.

She had been sad about the author's death until now, but this was different.

She was filled with a peculiar and unsettling kind of awe.

I'm alone in the house where Amanda Somers died, she thought.

But somehow, the place didn't seem completely unoccupied.

CHAPTER TWENTY THREE

A shudder ran through Riley's body as she gazed into the large, sparkling living room with its big windows overlooking the water. Waves of emotion swept through her. She knew they were not her own emotions, but powerful sensations that seemed to fill the space all around her.

The most powerful emotion of all was loneliness.

The sheer size of the place added to that feeling. That Amanda Somers chose to live alone here seemed strange, and somehow terribly sad.

And yet she hadn't been entirely alone during her last day alive. Riley still felt the visitor's presence. Had Amanda's last, rare houseguest been her killer?

That was what Riley hoped to find out.

Riley's first impression of the place was that everything looked so startlingly pristine. The white sofa and chairs could only belong to a person without children or pets. It was also obvious that Amanda never expected to come in wet from water sports. Nor did she have guests who might do so. It was likely that she never went into the water for the fun of it.

It seemed ironic—to live in a floating home but have no interest in the water. Riley wondered what had attracted Amanda here in the first place.

Something else seemed odd to Riley. She'd been in writers' homes before. She'd never been in one that was this neat. In her experience, creative people were at least somewhat disorderly. But this house was immaculate.

It made Riley wonder whether Amanda Somers had stopped writing altogether. Despite all the rumors about more books in the works, maybe she'd simply given up after writing *The Long Sprint.*

But maybe there was another reason for how the place looked.

This is where she came to escape, she reminded herself.

Perhaps Amanda Somers' mansion up on Moritz Hill looked very different. If she did her writing up there, at least parts of it would be cluttered with evidence of creative outpouring.

Riley didn't know, and it was pointless to wonder. After all, it was here that Amanda Somers had been murdered.

Keep your mind on the case, she reminded herself yet again.

Her eyes rested on an unfinished drink on the coffee table.

She picked the glass up and sniffed the stale drink.

A bourbon drinker, like me, she thought.

But the bourbon was diluted. Amanda Somers apparently preferred her whiskey with more water and ice than Riley did.

She remembered something that Prisha Sanders had said about how Saddam Hussein had assassinated dissidents.

"When some of them were released from prison, they were offered congratulatory drinks to toast their freedom."

Was the drink poisoned?

The theory didn't click for her. There was only one glass for only one person. Amanda had made the drink alone, and she'd sat down to drink it alone.

Riley put the glass down exactly where she'd found it. Then she walked into the very modern kitchen. Two clean teacups and saucers had been washed and left in the drying rack.

Riley felt a tingling sensation.

She'd had a hot drink with her visitor, Riley thought. And Prisha Shankar had said thallium might be delivered in a drink.

Riley wondered if they'd shared tea or coffee.

In either case, Amanda Somers had cleaned up after the visitor had left. She had still been alive and able to function then.

The carafe in the coffeemaker was empty. But of course, Amanda Somers might have washed it when she washed the cups and saucers.

Riley opened the garbage pail. A few papers and other scraps were still inside, but she saw neither coffee grounds nor teabags. That seemed odd. What had they used the teacups for?

Finding nothing more of interest in the kitchen, Riley stepped back into the living room. A chronology of events was starting to form in her mind.

Bill stepped back inside.

"Rigby wants us to go to the South Hills Hospital when we're finished here," he said.

"The hospital where Cody Woods died?" Riley asked.

"Right. The director there might be able to help us."

Noticing the glass on the coffee table, Bill asked, "Do you think her drink might have been poisoned?"

"No, she'd barely started drinking it," Riley said. "I don't think she even knew she'd been poisoned when she fixed it. My guess is that her visitor had been gone for hours. It was probably late at night."

She stood still and thought for a moment.

"She started feeling sick as soon as she sat down to drink it," she said. "She decided to go upstairs for a nap."

Riley walked toward the stairs that led to the second floor. Bill followed behind her. At the base of the stairs was a small table with some scattered books on it. She could tell by two bookends that the books were normally neatly placed. The woman who kept her home this tidy wouldn't tolerate even this slight disorder.

"She was dizzy and nauseous by the time she got here," she said. "She stumbled and knocked these books over."

As Riley and Bill continued up the stairs, Riley saw that some pictures on the walls on each side were hanging askew.

"She kept staggering as she went up the stairs, bumping into the walls," Riley said.

In the hallway at the top of the stairs, a carpet was bunched up in places.

"She was stumbling badly by the time she got here," Riley said.

They walked into a spacious bedroom. The bed was made, but slightly disheveled. The pillow had a head-shaped dent in it, which was slightly stained. Riley bent over and sniffed the pillow.

"She was sweating when she finally lay down," she said. "She must have started to realize that something was very wrong. Or perhaps she was too dizzy and disoriented to think much of anything at all."

Riley was beginning to empathize with the victim's agony. She felt a bit sick to her stomach.

This wasn't what she wanted.

Usually at a murder scene, Riley could step into the mind of the killer.

She wasn't used to identifying with the victim.

But she had to make the most of it.

"She was miserable lying down," Riley said. "She couldn't sleep. Her head may have been spinning and hurting. She decided she needed a breath of fresh air. She sat up. Maybe she got a bit of a second wind, was able to walk more steadily."

Riley retraced her steps in the hallway, then continued onto the outside deck.

"Why didn't she call nine-one-one?" Bill asked, following her.

"She was delirious. She no longer had a clear idea of what she was doing."

"The police said that she fell from the roof," Bill said.

With Bill behind her, Riley walked up the stairs that led to the roof from the deck.

"She must have had some vague idea she'd be more

comfortable up here," Riley said.

Indeed, the air on the roof patio was remarkably crisp and clean. The area had square patches of artificial grass and real potted plants. An elegant furniture set with a sofa, a chair, and a coffee table looked like it would fit well in an expensive living room, although Riley was sure that the upholstery was thoroughly weatherproofed. One of the sofa cushions was turned awkwardly.

"She collapsed here for a while," Riley said. "Maybe she even passed out. When she came to, she got up and made her way over here."

Riley followed the woman's steps to the railing overlooking the water, with Seattle on the opposite shore. The air was clear now, and Riley could see far across the water. But the view would have been different then. She imagined it by night, with scattered lights shining through the mist over the water. It must have been lovely. Perhaps Amanda was even able to enjoy the view for a moment or two before ...

Before what?

Then she remembered something that Prisha Shankar had said this morning. The poisonous cocktail had contained a certain substance—Riley couldn't remember the multisyllabic name off the top of her head, although she had it written down in her notebook.

For the moment, the name didn't matter.

Riley recalled Dr. Shankar's exact words about the substance.

"It's a muscle relaxant. It can cause short-term paralysis."

Riley could feel what Amanda must have felt—a tidal wave of weakness and despair as her body ceased to obey her.

But the question remained—had Amanda's final houseguest poisoned her?

If not, who could possibly have done so?

Riley closed her eyes and tried to capture Amanda's final thoughts before she tumbled over the rail.

She'd felt betrayed ...

All I wanted was a friend to talk to, to pass the time with.

So I allowed someone into my lonely home

And my guest did this to me.

And now I'm going to die just as I've lived—alone.

Riley felt a growing certainty.

Now she remembered something that Highland had said about the visitor.

"She seemed—generous, I guess."

He'd also said ...

"I was glad that someone nice had come to see her."

Riley's certainty grew stronger by the second.

Yes, it had been that final houseguest.

The visitor had been charming—too charming. She was capable of kindness, perhaps even believed herself to be a kind person.

And yet she was a true outlier. The killers Riley had hunted before had watched their victims die. That was part of their compulsion—to exult in the painful final moments of those they killed.

But this one was capable of a magnitude of cruelty Riley had seldom encountered.

She thought nothing of leaving her victims to die alone.

She had left even this loneliest of women to die alone.

There was a strange emptiness inside her, an abyss that even she knew nothing of.

She doesn't even know what kind of monster she is, Riley thought.

Riley's eyes snapped open. She looked at Bill. He clearly saw that she had come to a realization.

"What is it?" he asked.

"It was the visitor," Riley said.

Then with a gasp Riley added, "And she's truly insane."

CHAPTER TWENTY FOUR

Riley's jaw tightened as she and Bill walked into South Hills Hospital. She was still jangled by the disaster at Parnassus Heights Hospital earlier that morning. She wasn't sure what to expect at South Hills, but she had no reason to think anything might be much better here.

This was where Cody Woods had died. Of course, the local cops and FBI agents had already interviewed the hospital director and much of the staff. Now she and Bill were going to start in on them all over again. In Riley's experience, interviews like this seldom went well. People who were tired of being questioned often got nervous and defensive.

When they met Director Margery Cummings in her office, Riley breathed a sigh of relief. She was a pleasant woman with a ruddy complexion, and she greeted them with handshakes and a hearty smile.

"I heard about the meeting at Parnassus Heights," Cummings said. "Sounds like it was quite a scene."

Riley and Bill glanced at each other. What could they discreetly say to her about this morning's debacle?

Cummings laughed a little. She seemed to sense their awkwardness.

"Gossip gets around fast in the medical community," she said. "I'm pretty new to Seattle. But I've heard lots of stories about Briggs Wanamaker. He's got a taste for grandstanding. I try not to follow his example."

Riley smiled a little uneasily. Although she found Cummings' cheerfulness refreshing, it also struck as just a little bit odd. The idea that a patient in her hospital had been poisoned didn't seem to weigh on her mind very much.

Cummings got up from her desk.

"Come with me," she said. "I've got my people waiting for you."

She led Riley and Bill up an elevator and through a hallway to the hospital's staff lounge. Some twenty people were there—orderlies, nurses, physicians, and even maintenance workers. All of them had worked on the floor where Cody Woods had been a patient during the times in question.

Riley was relieved that this meeting was nothing like the catastrophe at Parnassus Heights. Everybody was cooperative and patient as she and Bill asked them questions they had surely been asked before.

Still, the whole effort didn't seem very productive to Riley. Most of these people had excellent memories. The floor team chief had kept careful records of work shifts and general comings and goings.

Might a supposed visitor to another patient have gotten into Cody Woods' room either time when he was here?

The staff didn't think so, and Riley herself soon realized that it was highly unlikely. Director Cummings ran a tight ship, and her staff was vigilant. A stranger straying among the rooms would surely have caught somebody's attention.

Probably just a wasted trip, Riley thought.

Not that a wasted trip was completely unexpected. Dead ends like this were part of an investigator's routine. What mattered was leaving no stone unturned.

Riley and Bill were about to end the meeting when a nurse's hand shot up.

"Excuse me," she said, "but does anybody else remember that patient awhile back—the guy who kept saying he was being poisoned?"

There was a general murmuring among the staff. Yes, some of the people remembered.

"We checked him out," a young physician said. "There was nothing to it."

"I thought so at the time," the nurse who had spoken said. "But now that this has happened, it makes me wonder."

Cummings looked surprised.

"Who are you talking about?" she asked.

"It happened about a month before you took over," the nurse said. "What was his name, anyway?"

Another nurse was bringing up information on a tablet.

"George Serbin," she said. "He was here for about a week with a case of pneumonia. We seriously looked into his complaints, but didn't find anything to back them up. We followed up after he was released. The last we heard, he was alive and well."

"Do you have any contact information for him?" Riley asked.

"I've got it right here," the nurse with the tablet said.

Bill wrote the information down. Riley and Bill thanked everybody and called the meeting to a close.

As they rode back down the elevator, Bill commented, "Maybe at last we have a live witness."

"I really hope so," she replied. "Our interviews have led us exactly nowhere so far."

As soon as they got outside, Riley dialed George Serbin's number on her cell phone. She got a monosyllabic answer.

"Yeah?"

"Am I speaking to George Serbin?"

"Yeah."

The man's voice was very odd—slightly high-pitched and nervous sounding.

"I'm Special Agent Riley Paige of the FBI. My partner and I would like to ask you a few questions in person."

A silence fell.

"What about?" Serbin asked.

"We just talked to some of the personnel at South Hills Hospital," Riley said. "They said that you thought you'd been poisoned. We're checking into it."

Serbin's voice cracked with alarm.

"I'm OK," said.

Riley glanced at Bill.

He doesn't sound OK, she thought.

"Are you sure?" Riley asked.

"Yeah," he said, "I made a mistake. I was wrong."

"We'd like to make sure," Riley said. "We want to hear your story. Are you home right now?"

An even longer silence fell.

"Yeah," he said.

Then he ended the call.

"What do you think?" Bill asked.

"He's scared of something," Riley said. "We'd better check him out."

She and Bill headed straight for their car.

George Serbin had sounded so strange on the phone that she had to wonder whether he was a prospective victim or a suspect.

*

The apartment building was a short drive from the hospital. It was a simple structure, no different from a dozen others lined up along several city blocks. Once they confirmed the location, Riley and Bill walked up to the second floor and knocked on his door.

"Who is it?" the occupant called out.

"Agents Paige and Jeffreys, FBI," Riley said. "I called you a short while ago."

"Oh."

Riley heard the clatter of chains and deadbolts.

The door opened into a tiny, rather untidy efficiency apartment. George Serbin was a swarthy little man with a frightened expression on his face.

"May we come in?" Riley said.

"Sure," Serbin said, stepping out of the way.

Serbin didn't offer them a place to sit. He paced about uneasily, avoiding eye contact. He struck Riley as extraordinarily awkward— as if he didn't trust his own skin and wanted to get out of it.

Riley glanced around the single room. She noticed that the windows were covered inside with clear insulation sheets. That seemed peculiar to her. The weather here in Seattle hadn't seemed especially cold so far.

Bill said, "Mr. Serbin, you were hospitalized fairly recently for pneumonia. The staff said that you complained that you were being poisoned. What was that all about?"

Serbin waved his arms as he talked in that odd, high-pitched voice. He sounded to Riley almost like a cartoon character.

"Yeah, well. Like I said, it was a misunderstanding. I wasn't accusing anybody of anything."

"Could you tell us what happened?" Bill said.

"It was nothing. Really, nothing."

Serbin continued to pace.

Riley's eyes fell on a laptop computer sitting on the Formica-topped kitchen table. She was surprised to see herself, Bill, and Serbin on the screen.

She asked, "Mr. Serbin, are you recording us on video?"

"Kind of," he said warily.

After a pause, he added, "Actually, we're live on Facebook."

Riley didn't know what to say or do. She had no idea how many of Serbin's friends might be watching—maybe a handful, or maybe hundreds.

Fortunately, Bill seemed to know how to handle the situation. He walked over to the computer and spoke directly to the screen.

"Hi, folks," he said. "I appreciate how you're all watching out for Mr. Serbin here. Your loyalty and vigilance is admirable. But I promise, my partner and I don't mean him any harm."

He took out his badge and displayed it for the camera.

"I'm Special Agent Bill Jeffreys, FBI," he said.

He nodded at Riley. She peered into the camera, flashing her own badge.

"I'm Special Agent Riley Paige."

"We're here to conduct a perfectly routine interview," Bill said, looking into the camera again. "The thing is, we really can't do this with lots of people watching. So Mr. Serbin is going to log off now. I guarantee that he'll be back online in fifteen minutes. If not—well, you know who we are and who we work for. You can hold us to account."

He turned toward Serbin with a friendly smile. Looking somewhat relieved, Serbin logged off.

"You can't be too careful these days," Serbin said.

"I agree," Bill said. "But why did you think you were being poisoned at the hospital?"

Serbin shook his head almost frantically.

"I wasn't being poisoned *at the hospital*," he said. "I was being poisoned *everywhere.* Surely you know all about it. That must be why you're here."

Riley and Bill looked at each other.

Riley said, "Mr. Serbin, I assure you, neither my partner nor I have any idea what you're talking about."

"You're going to have to spell it out for us," Bill added.

Serbin sat down at last. He seemed to relax a little.

"You guys really don't know about it, do you? I guess you don't have clearance at that level. Oh, man. You don't even know the truth about who you work for. We're all getting poisoned—or at least everybody's exposed to it. But only a few of us are actually targeted."

Serbin shrugged, as if he thought he was making all the sense in the world. Then he gestured toward a window.

"Come over here," he said. "I'll show you."

Riley and Bill looked with him out the window. The sky was still mostly clear, with just a few clouds.

"I'm talking about that right there," he said, pointing.

Riley saw a long, narrow white cloud.

"It's a vapor trail from a jet," she said.

"Yeah, and that's how they're doing it. My people call them 'chemtrails.' They keep changing the formula to target people with specific genes. They've got all of our DNA on file, so it's easy to do. When I got sick, I knew they were after me. But then I got better, and I realized I'd been taken off the list. They changed the formula."

Riley's heart sank.

So that's what the insulation sheets are for, she thought.

He was taking precautions in case "they" changed their minds.

She'd heard the chemtrails conspiracy theory before, but she'd never met anyone who took it seriously. It was right out there with other silly memes, such as the notion that Seattle's Space Needle was actually a flying saucer parked there by aliens.

George Serbin was nothing but an exceptionally batty conspiracy theorist.

"You understand what I'm saying, don't you?" Serbin asked.

"Yes, we do," Riley said, trying to sound more patient than she felt. "You've told us all we need to know."

"Thank you for your time," Bill added.

Serbin started with alarm as Riley and Bill went to the door.

"But you can't go back," he said. "Not knowing what you know now. You won't be safe. My people can take care of you. We'll protect you. We'll help you disappear. Just say the word, we'll get right on it."

Riley managed to suppress a smirk.

"We'll just have to take our chances," she said. "Our job, you know."

Serbin looked crestfallen. He obviously sensed that he wasn't being taken seriously. Before he could say more, Riley nudged Bill through the door and followed him out.

They walked in silence down the hall. Then, at the top of the stairs, Bill slouched and sat down.

He shook his head. "We're not getting anywhere, Riley," he said. "We couldn't even prevent a new victim from being poisoned. Amanda Somers shouldn't have had to die. And we're not stopping this killer from taking whoever comes next."

Riley understood what he meant. She squeezed his hand.

"Come on," she said. "Let's go somewhere where we can talk."

CHAPTER TWENTY FIVE

Although Riley and Bill had both ordered sandwiches in a sparkling little deli, they weren't actually eating them. Riley had taken a few bites, and Bill hadn't touched his at all. Now they both just sat staring at their food.

I guess neither one of us feels much like eating, Riley thought.

She gazed at her partner with deep concern.

"You've got to talk about it, Bill," she said. "You've got to tell me what's getting to you."

He didn't speak right away. Riley could see that he was struggling with himself.

"It happens every time I have to deal with a situation that involves the word 'poison,'" he said.

It happens? Riley wondered for a moment. Then she realized what he meant.

"You mean flashbacks?"

Bill nodded.

"Mom was in so much pain," he said. "She was crying so much from the pain. It was ..."

He stopped for a moment.

"And here we are, getting nowhere fast," Bill said. "We've only been here three days, and we've lost another victim. That's three victims that we're aware of, but you and I both know there have probably been others—earlier victims who were never spotted. We have no idea how many. And I'm too close to it to do my job. I'm not thinking straight."

Riley understood perfectly. She felt a similar kind of stress, although for different reasons. For her it was a question of priorities—stopping an evil murderer here in Seattle, or taking care of dire problems at home. Knowing that she couldn't have it both ways was nagging at her all the time.

"Maybe you should work this one without me," Bill said. "Meredith can send Lucy Vargas to replace me. She'd do a great job. Right now I'm just dead weight."

Riley was alarmed. A change like that could be disruptive. She was sure that it wouldn't do any good. And she didn't want Bill to quit on this case. She knew he would regret it later if he left.

She leaned across the table toward him and spoke in a gentle but firm voice.

"You're not dead weight," she said. "You're never dead

weight."

Bill didn't reply.

"Tell me the truth, Bill. Do you really *want* off this case?"

Bill shook his head no.

"So what do you really want?"

Bill's face tightened with resolve.

"I want to solve this case so bad I can taste it," he said.

Riley smiled and patted his hand.

"Well, then," she said. "Let's consider that question settled."

Bill smiled a little and his whole body seemed to relax.

"OK," he said. "Let's get back to work. Do we have any leads at all?"

Riley fell silent. She remembered something that Solange Landis had said to her.

"The thing that most strikes me about evil is its sameness. It seems to me that monsters are pretty much alike."

The more Riley thought about that statement, the more it struck her as very odd.

For one thing, she didn't think it was true. She'd seen evil in all manners and forms over the years. And these recent murders seemed unique among all the cases she could remember.

Had Solange Landis even meant what she said?

Riley wondered about the nursing school director.

Landis had managed to cast suspicion upon Maxine Crowe, which proved to be a dead end. Had she just been getting back at an adversary, or was it something more sinister?

Was Landis deliberately misleading her?

Riley had a gut feeling that the woman wasn't to be trusted. It was the kind of really strong feeling she'd long since learned not to ignore.

She told Bill, "I can't help suspecting Solange Landis."

"The head of that nursing school?"

"Right. Something is really off about that woman."

"It makes sense. It seems unlikely that anyone outside the healthcare profession had access to all three victims. We should follow up on her. What kind of information have you got so far?"

Riley thought for a moment.

"I asked Van Roff, the tech analyst, to find out whatever he could about her. He gave me a file of stuff. I read through it and didn't see anything odd. He didn't find any connections between Landis and the three victims."

"Sounds to me like you'd better take another look," Bill said.

Riley opened her laptop. She clicked open the file and skimmed through it.

"It's mostly routine stuff," she said. "Date of birth, Social Security number, home address, phone number. She'd been married and divorced and has always used her maiden name."

Riley scrolled through more records.

"She got her nursing degree from Rosin Medical College in Dover, Delaware—a really prestigious school. After that she worked as a nurse for years and got glowing reports and recommendations. About ten years ago, she was hired to be the director of a small nursing school in Cincinnati. She did great work there, building up the nursing program and developing a sterling reputation."

Then Riley came to some news stories about how Landis had gotten her current job.

"When the Tate School of Nursing here in Seattle started looking for a new director, they were delighted to find her. They hired her in a heartbeat. And her reputation just keeps getting better and better."

Riley squinted at the records uncertainly.

"Maybe my hunch is wrong," she said. "She's got a perfect record."

Bill looked over the information thoughtfully.

"Maybe too perfect," he said.

Riley felt a tingle of understanding.

"That's it," she said. "That's what's been bothering me. It's all too perfect. She's just a bit too good to be true."

"So we look for what's wrong," Bill said.

"Where should we start?"

Bill shrugged.

"At the beginning," he said.

Riley immediately understood his meaning. She got online and found a phone number for Rosin Medical College. She dialed the number on her cell phone and put the call on speakerphone so both she and Bill could listen and talk.

When the female receptionist answered, Riley said, "This is Special Agent Riley Paige, FBI. My partner, Bill Jeffreys, is also on the line. We need for you to look through your records for information about a past student. Her name is Solange Landis."

Riley told the receptionist the year when Landis graduated.

"That was more than twenty years ago," the receptionist said. "We don't have electronic records going back that far. It's all on paper. But I can check on it and get back to you tomorrow."

Riley held back a groan of frustration.

"We really need it today," she said. "This for a murder investigation."

"I'm afraid that's impossible," the receptionist said, sounding quite irritated.

Bill leaned toward the phone.

"Then make it possible," he said. "Find the records right now, or we'll send a team there. We'll put your whole office on lockdown and turn everything upside down until we can go through everything."

Riley almost laughed. Bill was acting like his old self again.

"Okay," the receptionist said. "I'll call you back shortly."

"Make that *very* shortly," Bill said.

The call ended. Bill and Riley smiled at each other. It felt good to be getting something done. Now they both started in on their sandwiches with much more appetite than before.

Only a few minutes passed before the receptionist called. She sounded flustered and anxious.

"Don't shoot the messenger, OK? But I can't find any record at all of a student by that name. No evidence that she enrolled, much less graduated. Are you sure you've called the right school?"

For a moment, Riley wondered if she had made a mistake. She looked again through the documents in the file that Van Roff had given her. Sure enough, it included a diploma, a nursing certification, and a sterling academic transcript—all from Rosin Medical College.

Riley looked closely at the document in front of her.

"Her middle name is Alexandra," Riley said. "Might her records have been filed with that as a first name?"

"No," the woman said. "We've had some students named Landis, but not a Solange or an Alexandra. Sorry."

"Thank you for your time," Riley said. "You've been a great help."

Riley and Bill stared at each other in stunned silence.

"Forged," Riley said. "Her whole academic record was forged. It's really rather brilliant. She went to incredible lengths."

"Everybody who hired her just assumed the records were real," Bill said. "Nobody inquired directly with the school."

"They sure look authentic," Riley said. "It's hardly any wonder that she hasn't been found out."

"Until now," Bill added.

They sat looking at each other for a moment.

Is this the break we've been hoping for? she wondered.

"I think we should give Solange Landis a call," Riley commented.

"I agree," Bill said.

Riley dialed the number for Landis's office and put the phone on speakerphone again. Landis's secretary quickly connected them to the director herself.

"Agent Paige," Landis said pleasantly. "I was wondering if I was going to hear from you again."

"My partner, Agent Bill Jeffreys, is also on the line."

"Hello, Agent Jeffreys. I'm pleased to make your acquaintance. But how is the case going? Did you check out Maxine Crowe?"

Riley paused before replying.

"I interviewed her," she said. "I believe we can eliminate her as a suspect."

"Oh."

A brief silence fell.

Then Landis said, "Well, I know that's not good for you. But I must admit I feel a little relieved. I'd hate to think that one of my own students had become a coldblooded killer."

Again, neither Riley nor Bill said anything. They wanted Solange Landis to feel uncomfortable. Perhaps she'd say something to give herself away.

"Well," Landis said at last, "how can I help you?"

"We've got a few more questions we'd like to ask," Riley said.

"Of course. I'm in my office right now. Why don't you drop on by?"

Riley remembered Maxine Crowe's description of Landis's home.

"She's got images of death everywhere ..."

Riley said, "We'd like to talk with you at home."

Now Landis sounded distinctly uneasy.

"May I ask why?"

"We'll explain when we see you."

Riley and Bill waited for a few seconds.

"I'm working into this evening," Landis finally said. "Could you come by at around eight o'clock?"

"That would be fine," Riley said.

Solange Landis gave them an address, and the call ended.

Bill and Riley looked at each other.

"I think we just got really lucky," Bill said.

I hope so, Riley thought.

And yet it was hard to believe. True, Solange Landis had based her whole career on forged records. But it had been a fine career even so, and she'd taught many people in the healing arts. She'd done a lot of good in the world.

Was she really a murderer?

Riley remembered something else that Landis had said.

"Cruel demons reside in all of us."

CHAPTER TWENTY SIX

Nightfall couldn't come early enough for Riley. Solange Landis had said they could come to her house about eight o'clock. She and Bill spent the rest of the afternoon preparing themselves for their visit.

Riley thought that maybe they were about to make an arrest in this awful case. Of course, they didn't know for sure yet, but if this really was their lucky break, she didn't want to leave any loose ends. She double-checked with Van Roff, going over details of Landis's forged documents. Bill researched the legal penalties for using forged records.

As eight o'clock finally approached, Riley and Bill drove into a cheerful, well-lighted neighborhood in northern Seattle. Even after dark there was a fair amount of activity. Some people were jogging, others were walking their dogs.

The area was lush with trees and plants, and older traditional houses were mixed with occasional townhouse complexes. Since Riley had been in Seattle, she had noticed that some of the local townhouses were very modern in design. But this row of narrow homes with pitched roofs was more traditional looking, rather like her own home back in Virginia.

They parked in front of Landis's townhouse, went to the front door, and rang the doorbell. Solange Landis greeted them, wearing a business suit and high-heeled shoes.

Landis seemed cheerful and relaxed, betraying none of the uneasiness Riley thought she'd detected on the phone earlier. She invited Riley and Bill inside.

Riley was immediately taken aback by how ordinary everything looked. The living room was similar to Riley's, except that this one had newer, more stylish furniture.

Where was all the macabre decor that Maxine Crowe had hinted at—the images of death, the human skulls?

Had Maxine Crowe been lying?

Had Riley written her off as a suspect prematurely?

On the wall were some photographs of a girl at different stages of her life, from a toddler discovering a swing set to a teenager graduating from high school. Solange Landis appeared in most of those photos, beaming happily over the girl. The pictures seemed affectionate. Nothing about this room was at all disturbing.

Landis noticed Riley's interest.

"That's my daughter, Chloe," she said with a trace of melancholy. "She's away, in her first year of college. The place feels so empty without her. Her father, my husband, left years ago. I live alone now."

An absent father, Riley thought.

Of course it reminded her of how Ryan had been over the years until recently. But Riley couldn't help but wonder whether the disappearance of Landis's husband might have a more sinister cause.

Landis said, "But you said on the phone that you had some more questions for me. What can I help you with?"

Bill said, "First of all, we'd like to know if you ever had any contact with Margaret Jewell, Cody Woods, or Amanda Somers."

Landis glanced back and forth between Bill and Riley.

"Those names don't sound familiar—except of course Amanda Somers. I've read her book but I never saw her professionally. Didn't she die very recently?"

Then her eyes widened.

"Wait a minute. Those are the names of the poisoning victims, aren't they?"

She added with a wry smile, "Oh, dear. Am I a suspect?"

"We just want to ask you a few questions," Bill said.

Landis emitted a short chuckle and clapped her hands.

"I *am* a suspect, aren't I? And I thought you were here because of my expertise. But then, in a way you are, aren't you? Well, this is a new experience for me. I must say, I feel oddly flattered. Come on downstairs where we can talk more comfortably."

Riley and Bill followed her downstairs to a room with dark wallpaper. Heavy curtains hung on the windows and the room was lit by thickly shaded lamps. It wasn't a large room, but it was well-furnished so that a small group of people—perhaps six or eight—could sit together and talk.

This was obviously the place that Maxine Crowe had spoken of—a lair where dark stories and thoughts were shared. Maxine had claimed that she stopped coming to see Solange Landis because the setting and the conversations held there too weird for her.

They are pretty weird, Riley thought, as she looked over the macabre touches and decor. There were a few real human skulls here and there. The walls were hung with engravings of monsters, ghouls, and chimeras. Amongst them were many antique photographs. Some of those showed corpses resting in coffins. Others looked like really old family portraits, although there was something strangely morbid about them.

Landis seemed to notice Riley's curiosity.

She explained, "Those are death portraits. In the old days, when photography was new, families posed for photographs with their departed loved ones. They often went to a great deal of trouble to make those corpses look as if they were alive."

She pointed to different pictures and explained.

"Here you see two children posing with their dead little sister. In this one, a dead man is sitting with his favorite dogs on his lap. This one shows a dead little girl cuddling her beloved dolls. Here are two little girls holding hands—I'm not sure which one is dead. You'll notice that the deceased's eyes are always open."

Landis fell silent, letting the chilling effect of the pictures sink in.

"I suppose it seems morbid to most people," she said with a sigh. "But I think it was a touching tradition. Perhaps we've lost something essentially human as we've distanced ourselves from the realities of death."

Then turning to her visitors, she said, "But I'm being very rude. I haven't offered you anything to drink. I'd offer you a beer or some wine, but of course you're on duty. Would you like some tea or coffee?"

Riley resisted the impulse to look at Bill. She was sure he was thinking the same thing—that Landis was deliberately toying with them. Would she really be so brazen as to poison two FBI agents in her own home? Riley doubted it, but she couldn't be sure, and of course Bill must have felt the same way. Landis seemed to be getting some twisted amusement from their uncertainty.

"No, thank you," Riley said.

"We're fine," Bill added.

"Please sit down, make yourself comfortable."

Riley and Bill sat together on a settee with dark, plush upholstery. In front of them, an odd-looking piece of furniture was in service as a coffee table. It looked very old, with slender legs and a cane latticework top. Riley wondered what its original use might be.

As she sat, Landis again observed her visitors' curiosity.

"This is a true antique," she said. "It dates back to the nineteenth century. It's been restored, of course, and the wicker weaving is new. Have you ever heard of a 'cooling board'?"

"I can't say I have," Riley said.

"Me either," Bill said.

Landis patted the thin wicker top.

"Well, today we take refrigeration for granted. But back in those days, storing dead bodies in preparation for a funeral was very difficult, especially in warm weather. Bodies were kept on cooling boards like this one. Ice underneath the latticework kept them cool. The lattice allowed blood and fluids to drain."

A nostalgic look crossed Landis's face.

"Cooling boards have long since been replaced by refrigerated storage units and metal embalming tables—not nearly so elegant, I think. Call me old-fashioned, but it seems to me that progress comes at the price of grace and style."

Landis looked and Bill and Riley with an inquisitive expression.

"You said that you'd eliminated Maxine as a suspect. Why?"

Riley studied the woman's expression. Riley and Bill needed to handle this carefully. The goal right now was to get Landis to tip her hand, to say or do something that revealed her guilt.

Riley said, "When we met, you told me that Maxine Crowe had gotten into trouble for experimenting on patients."

Landis nodded.

Then Riley added, "But you didn't tell me that she was experimenting with placebos, not anything actually poisonous."

Landis tilted her head curiously.

"Placebos? I didn't know."

Riley peered at Landis ever more closely. Was she lying? Riley usually found it fairly easy to detect a lie during an interview. But something in Landis's perpetually sardonic expression made her difficult for Riley to read.

Riley said, "You never mentioned that you and Maxine weren't on very good terms when she left your school."

Landis gazed back at Riley intently.

"Was I supposed to? When we met before, I didn't know I was a suspect."

Riley didn't reply.

"Oh, I see. Maxine told you some rather sinister stories about my little gatherings right here in this room. And you seem to have jumped to some rather disagreeable conclusions."

Riley still said nothing. Both she and Bill knew that the best tactic was to say and ask as little as possible. They must let Landis do most of the talking—hopefully until she tripped herself up.

Landis wrinkled her brow.

"Agent Paige, are you suggesting I deliberately steered you

toward Maxine Crowe as a distraction?"

Riley held her gaze quietly.

"I had hopes for Maxine Crowe," Landis said. "But I think I made my educational goals pretty clear to you earlier. *Denial* is the healer's worst enemy. That's what my meetings here are all about. They separate the students who can face hard realities from those who can't."

Still silent, Riley kept her eyes locked on those of the other woman. Neither of them blinked.

Landis continued, "I expect my students to be able to look death in the eye, to see it for what it is. Maxine had—how would I put it?—a weak stomach for the sort of work she was training for. She graduated and got her credentials, but I've never given her my wholehearted recommendation. She's obviously still sour about that, but it can't be helped. There are some things you just can't teach."

Landis broke their eye contact, glancing back and forth between Riley and Bill. Was it out of nervousness? Riley still couldn't tell.

Then a slight smirk crossed Landis's face.

"You've got no proof. You can't very well arrest me just because a disgruntled ex-student thinks I'm morbid."

Again, Landis was toying with them.

But did that prove she was a murderer?

She's right, Riley thought. *We've got no proof—not yet, anyway.*

Riley and Bill had reached a stalemate. They were left with only one option. Riley glanced at Bill and saw that he was thinking the same thing.

Bill got from the settee, walked over to Solange, and urged her to her feet.

He said, "Solange Landis, you are under arrest for a class C felony."

Landis's mouth dropped open with disbelief as he began to cuff her.

"What?"

Riley got up from the settee.

"It is illegal to use or hold a fraudulent postsecondary degree," Riley said. "The penalty in the state of Washington can be five years in prison and a ten-thousand-dollar fine."

"I don't know what you're talking about," Landis said.

And for the first time, Riley knew that she was definitely lying.

127

"I think you do," Riley said.

As Riley and Bill led Landis out of her house, she stammered in shocked confusion.

"But if I did … I'm not saying I did, but … surely the FBI has better things to do than … Don't you have a murderer to catch? … Please, I have a daughter, I try to do what's right."

Riley said nothing as Bill pushed their captive into the car.

It was a good arrest, but not as good as Riley had hoped.

They still hadn't proved that Solange Landis was a murderer.

And if she's guilty, Riley thought, *she's still got lots of tricks up her sleeve.*

CHAPTER TWENTY SEVEN

Early the next morning, Riley felt a tingle of excitement as she and Bill drove within view of Amanda Somers' mansion on Moritz Hill.

She really lived here, Riley thought.

An author who had profoundly touched Riley's life had lived right here.

The thought was truly awe-inspiring.

Still, the place was certainly not what Riley had expected. It looked more like the dwelling of some medieval lord than the home of a great American author. The facade was half-timbered, its dark wood framework standing out against pale plaster. Impressive as it was, it seemed antiquated and out of place in a modern city.

Bill parked the car in the private lot next to the house.

"I hope this isn't a waste of time," Bill said as they walked toward a pair of tall ornamental gates at the front of the property.

Riley hoped so too. It hadn't been her idea or Bill's to come here this morning. Chief Sanderson had called them very early and appealed to them to stop by the mansion right away. He said that Amanda Somers' son and daughter wanted to talk to them.

Riley understood Sanderson's reasons. Now that the public's attention was focused on a famous author's death, mollifying Somers' children in every possible way was a huge PR concern.

But Solange Landis was in custody. Riley knew that they needed to focus their energy on Landis—on determining her guilt or eliminating her as a suspect. Sanderson had said that Landis was still denying anything to do with the murders. The Seattle police and the local FBI had searched her home and office and found nothing suspicious—certainly not any poisons.

This was a side trip, and not at all to Riley's liking. She and Bill were due at a meeting at the field office as soon as they finished here. They needed to get their visit done quickly.

As they walked through the gate, an extremely well-dressed man stepped out of the house to greet them in a formal manner.

"I'm Cromer, the late Ms. Somers' butler," he said in an upper-class English accent. "And you are Agents Paige and Jeffreys, I believe. Come right this way. You are expected in the library."

Cromer led them through two large doors into a tiled foyer. Through an open door, Riley glimpsed a spacious living room with lots of dark wood paneling.

She felt as though she'd stepped into the distant past—and like the outside of the house, none of this looked anything like what she'd expected. In her mind's eye, she compared this very traditional mansion to the very modern houseboat. How had the same woman lived in both places? Riley had sensed that Amanda Somers had been comfortable on the houseboat. How could she possibly have enjoyed living in a place like this?

Everything looked perfectly neat and clean, just as things had at Somers' floating home. It didn't look like the dwelling of a vibrantly creative person. It didn't even look real. The house looked more like an elaborate stage set than a home.

Riley kept flashing back to Somers' unforgettable book, *The Long Sprint,* and its vital protagonist, Emerson Drew. Amanda Somers had created a world full of characters that had seemed realer than real, livelier than life. It just didn't make sense that she'd called this darkly burnished museum of a place her home.

Cromer led them into the library. He introduced them to Amanda Somers' son and daughter and departed. Logan Somers and Isabel Watson were sitting at a large antique mahogany table poring over reams of manuscript pages.

Riley breathed a little easier as she looked around. The library was chaotic and messy—much more the sort of creative environment that Riley had expected. The walls were covered with bookshelves filled with hundreds of haphazardly arranged volumes, many left open, others piled carelessly atop of one another. Books and papers were even lying on the floor and on all the furniture. It didn't appear that anyone had dusted the place in a very long time.

She probably didn't allow it, Riley guessed.

An old-fashioned mechanical typewriter sat on a plain wooden desk, still holding a page of unfinished manuscript. There wasn't a computer in sight. It appeared that Amanda Somers hadn't entered the electronic age even after all her years of writing.

Riley wasn't the least bit surprised. Somers had belonged to a literary tradition that was fading away. Such authors had no desire to keep up with the latest technology.

Logan Somers peeked up at Riley and Bill over a pair of reading glasses.

"We're glad you're here," he said.

Isabel Watson didn't even look at them.

"Have a seat," she snapped.

Riley and Bill had to move piles of books off of two straight-backed chairs in order to sit down. For a few moments neither of their hosts said anything more, so Riley kept surveying her surroundings. An open door led to a bathroom. Riley noticed a small daybed in one corner. Riley sensed that Amanda Somers slept there much of the time. In fact, Riley guessed that she seldom left this room whenever she was in this house.

She hated this house, Riley realized. *This library was her sole refuge here.*

Riley then took a moment to study the faces of Somers' children. In her notorious reclusiveness, the author had never allowed her picture to appear on copies of her own book. Riley hadn't seen a photograph of her until just yesterday. Then she had been struck by the humanity and depth of character of that face—exactly the demeanor Riley would have expected in the author of *The Long Sprint.*

And now did Riley see any resemblance between these two adults and their mother? Their faces had much the same shape, and their chins and noses were similar. But their features seemed small somehow, and devoid of any real feeling.

Riley found no trace of the penetrating soulfulness she'd seen in Amanda Somers' photograph.

Maybe it skipped generations, Riley thought.

Unlike their mother, Logan Somers and Isabel Watson were palpably shallow people. Riley also sensed that they had been estranged from their mother for a very long time.

Finally, Logan Somers pushed some papers aside and looked up at Riley and Bill with an insincere smile.

"Great house, isn't it?" he said.

"We encouraged Mom to buy it when it came on the market," Isabel Watson added, barely looking up from what she was reading. "We thought it was perfect—really suitable to a person of her literary stature."

Riley noticed a distinct hollowness in how Isabel said those words, "literary stature," as if she didn't fully understand what they even meant.

Logan Somers shook his head and added in a bitter tone, "Mom didn't spend nearly enough time here. She kept going off on her own, staying on that damned boat."

"That stupid boat," Isabel said. "We tried to talk her out of buying it. What a waste of money."

Her tone was chilly and uncaring.

Money, Riley thought. *That's all they care about. Mom's money.*

And now they were hovering over stacks of Somers' unfinished manuscripts like vultures.

Bill said, "Chief Sanderson said you wanted us to come talk with you. What about?"

Logan smiled again.

"We just wanted to make sure that we're on the same page," he said.

Riley exchanged glances with Bill.

"What 'page' is that?" Bill asked.

Neither Logan nor Isabel replied for a moment. Isabel finally put her papers aside and looked at Bill and Riley.

"We understand that you've taken a suspect into custody," Isabel finally said. "A woman."

"We have," Riley said.

Logan and Isabel looked at each other, then back at Riley and Bill.

"Well, you just have to do your job, I guess," Logan said with a shrug.

Riley felt somewhat puzzled.

"What do you mean?" she asked.

"You have to eliminate all other possibilities," Logan said.

"Other possibilities?" Bill asked.

Logan emitted a slight chuckle.

"Other than suicide, I mean. That's what Mom's death was, of course. I think we all know that."

Riley felt a flash of anger.

"We don't know any such thing," she said.

Bill added, "Your mother was killed by an elaborate cocktail of rather unusual poisons—hardly what most people would use for suicide."

Isabel smiled a haughty smile.

"Our mother was hardly 'most people,'" she said. "She was a creative genius, after all. But you're investigating a serial case, aren't you? Well, it simply doesn't make sense that our mother's death had anything to do with that. The other two victims were too … well, ordinary. They had nothing in common with our mother."

Riley remembered what Dr. Prisha Shankar had said to her about how suicide would add to the market value of Amanda Somers' work.

"She'd be tortured and unhappy as well as reclusive. It all adds up to the stuff that literary legends are made of."

That's what this was all about—complete control of an author's posthumous reputation. Riley sensed that Bill felt as annoyed as she did. But as usual, he maintained a tactful tone.

He said, "I assure you that we'll do everything we can to uncover the exact circumstances of your mother's death."

With a slight smirk, Isabel said, "Agent Jeffreys, we *know* the exact circumstances. And her agent has hired a PR firm to handle the story of her last days. I'd hate for the police and the FBI to contradict that story."

Riley's mind boggled at the woman's brazenness.

She said, "And I'd hate for you and your brother to be charged with obstruction of justice. You'd better not let that 'story' of yours go public before we finish our investigation."

Isabel's expression darkened, and the room suddenly seemed a few degrees colder. She gestured toward the enormous piles of manuscripts.

"Agents Paige and Jeffreys, you're looking at a literary treasure trove," she said. "There are at least five unpublished novels here. It's a dream come true for our mother's legion of readers. Why spoil their enjoyment with a sordid scandal?"

The woman's hypocrisy astounded Riley. Neither of these people wanted to avoid a scandal. They just wanted it to be a scandal of their own choosing—suicide rather than a murder, especially if it was just one among other murders. And with all the money they were about to inherit, they could afford to hire an expensive team of lawyers and successfully buck an obstruction charge. They could make this investigation much more difficult than it already was.

Or was something more sinister at work?

Amanda Somers' death must be their dream come true, Riley thought.

They'd lived in the shadow of their mother's fame for their whole lives, and they'd never been able to exploit it.

Had one or both of them decided to cut their mother's life short?

Their eager plunge into their mother's manuscripts and anticipated rewards certainly suggested a motive.

Riley struggled to make sense of the possibility. Did either Logan or Isabel have the backbone to carry out a murder—or a series of murders to cover up for this one? Maybe not, but they could have hired someone else for the job.

Bill's voice interrupted Riley's thoughts.

"I think we're through here," he said in a tense, angry voice.

133

"Thank you for your time."

Isabel rang for the butler, who escorted Riley and Bill out of the house.

As they walked toward the car, Bill said, "Do you get the feeling that we were just talking to a couple of viable suspects?"

"I don't know, Bill," Riley said. "It did occur to me, but I just don't know."

*

When Bill and Riley drove up to the FBI field office a few minutes later, they saw a crowd of people standing around the front entrance.

"What the hell's going on?" Bill asked.

Many of the people were armed with cameras and microphones. Riley had been hoping for a productive discussion of an ongoing investigation. Instead, she and Bill were about to walk into another media ambush.

She could feel her anger rising.

She also felt Bill clutch her arm and heard him mutter, "Try not to scare the nice reporters."

CHAPTER TWENTY EIGHT

When the crowd of reporters spotted Riley and Bill, they rushed forward and surrounded them, mikes held high and cameras flashing. Riley was furious—though not with the reporters, most of whom she recognized from the disastrous hospital meeting yesterday. She knew that they were only doing their job. But somebody had released news about the case prematurely. And Riley was livid at whoever that "somebody" was.

The reporters called out as they crushed around Riley and Bill.

"Agent Paige!" shouted one.

"Agent Jeffreys!" yelled another.

"Is it true that you've made an arrest in the poisonings case?"

"How does it feel to have solved the case so quickly?"

Riley and Bill pushed reporters away, trying to make a path to the front door.

"You know we can't discuss a case under investigation," Bill yelled.

"But the investigation is over, isn't it?" shouted a woman with a camera.

"How did you determine that Solange Landis was the killer?" yelled a man with a microphone.

"What was her motive?" called out another reporter.

Riley and Bill managed to get to the front door without answering any questions. A pair of security officers was standing just outside.

"Don't let them into the building," Riley told the officers.

The officers nodded and moved toward the crowd. Riley and Bill hurried deeper into the building and out of sight of the mob outside. Riley took a moment to catch her breath.

"Damn it," she gasped. "I thought we were coming to a meeting to discuss how the case was progressing."

Bill shook his head.

"Well, from what we were just told, the case has been closed. Too bad we had to hear about it from reporters instead of our team."

"Yeah, I wonder whose fault that was," Riley said.

They hurried up a flight of stairs to the FBI conference room. When they stormed inside, Riley was shocked to see almost everyone looking quite pleased with themselves.

Maynard Sanderson sat on one side of the big conference table with Agents Lloyd Havens and Jay Wingert flanking him. They all had wide smiles plastered on their faces.

As usual, Division Chief Sean Rigby was expressing his dominance by standing while the others were seated.

By contrast, Van Roff appeared to be oblivious as usual. Again he sat at the far end of the table, busy on his laptop.

Chief Rigby displayed a crooked, self-satisfied smile.

"You're running a little late, Agents Paige and Jeffreys," he said.

"Yeah," Riley said, resisting the impulse to pace about angrily. "We got slowed down a bit in front of the building.

Rigby made a guttural sound that seemed to be the closest he could get to a chuckle.

"Oh, the reporters, you mean. You can't blame them for wanting to congratulate you on a job well done. In fact, we all want to congratulate you. Have a seat, both of you."

Bill was shifting his weight from one foot to the other.

"I'd rather stand, thanks," Bill said.

"Me too," Riley said.

Rigby's smile faded a little. He didn't sit down either. Riley sensed that he was determined to vie for dominance and would stay on his feet as long as she and Bill did.

"Why is the media so sure that we've got our killer?" Riley asked.

Rigby said, "All I told them was the truth—that we've made an arrest. And I told them the name of the suspect."

Maynard Sanderson added in a blustery voice, "Great job, you two. I have to admit, I wasn't crazy about bringing you in from Quantico. But Chief Rigby made the right call. You've done a great job."

"We're not through yet," Riley said. "Agent Jeffreys and I want to interview the suspect."

Rigby shook his head.

"That won't be necessary," he said.

"What do you mean, it won't be necessary?" Bill said.

Sanderson said, "You two have already done all the heavy lifting. Our people can handle the rest. We can get a confession out of her. She's already starting to crack. You two can go back to Quantico now."

Riley was almost shaking with anger. She didn't know what to say. She was relieved that Bill spoke instead.

"Agent Paige and I understand that you've not found any evidence at Solange Landis's house—no poisons of any kind."

Rigby shrugged.

"Well, that's to be expected," he said. "She's smart, and she knows how to cover her tracks. But it's only a matter of connecting a few more dots. We all know she's our killer."

"All we know is that she's guilty of fraud," Bill said. "That's not the same as multiple murders."

Rigby stared hard at Riley and Bill.

"The circumstantial evidence is overwhelming," he said. "You know that as well as anybody. Because of her position at her school, she could have gotten access to any kind of medical facility. That means she could have gotten access to any of our victims."

"'Could have,'" Bill grumbled. "That's a long way from proof."

Riley looked at Van Roff, who seemed to have been paying no attention to what anybody was saying. He was still poring over his computer.

"What are you doing, Mr. Roff?" Riley said.

"Still looking," Roff said in a distant voice. "I'm tracking down people who might have had access—physical therapists, mostly."

Riley almost sighed with relief.

At least someone here is still on the job, she thought. *If only I could get through to the others.*

"Listen to me," she said. "This case isn't nearly as open-and-shut as it seems. If Solange Landis is guilty, believe me, she's still got some tricks up her sleeve. She won't be easy to pin down. If she's not guilty, we've still got a killer out there."

Rigby took a few steps toward Riley and Bill.

"I appreciate your diligence," he said, sounding more impatient now. "But it really is over."

Rigby crossed his arms and glowered for a moment.

"I'm sure you've both got more urgent work waiting for you at Quantico," he said. "Would you like me to arrange your flight back?"

"No, thanks," Bill muttered. "We'll take care of it."

"Do it soon," Rigby said. "You may go now. The rest of us can take things from here. And thanks again."

At long last, Rigby sat down at the head of the table and faced the others, who turned their attention to him. Riley and Bill were now shut out of whatever was going to be discussed next. They left the room.

As they stepped out of the building, they were relieved to see that the pack of reporters had apparently moved on to some other story.

"Guess they got bored waiting," Bill said.

"God only knows what kind of story they're going to spread now," Riley said.

They walked in silence toward their car for a moment.

"What do you think we should do now?" Riley asked.

"I don't know about you," Bill said. "But I could use a drink."

"Good idea," Riley said.

*

A little while later, Riley and Bill were settling into a booth at the hotel bar. The bar was busy with lunchtime business, but the booth was very private. Bill waved away the waiter, saying, "We'll order in a few minutes."

He made a call to Brent Meredith at Quantico and they delivered a brief report to him on speakerphone. Riley made her complaints clear about wrapping the case up so fast.

"I agree with you that there are still some loose ends," Meredith replied. "But Rigby is the guy who requested you in the first place. If he thinks your work is through there, that's his decision. Unless you have some overriding evidence to the contrary."

Riley sighed. "We've got nothing solid," she said. "But I don't like this, sir."

"You don't have to like it. That's just the way things are."

A short silence fell.

"I'll expect to see you in my office in the morning," Meredith said.

"Yes, sir," Bill agreed. He ended the call.

Bill and Riley just looked at each other for a moment.

"I've got to admit, I'm relieved," Bill said wearily. "I can't get out of here soon enough."

Riley was shocked.

"What are you saying? I'd think that you'd be especially anxious to close this case right."

Bill's brow furrowed.

"I am. I really am," he said. "But this whole thing is eating me alive. And it wouldn't do any good to stay here. The case *is* closed, according to everybody except—"

He stopped short of finishing his sentence. Riley bristled.

"Everybody except me?" Riley said. "Is that what you're

138

saying?"

Bill didn't reply.

"Bill, I want you to look me straight in the eye and tell me that you're satisfied that we've got Solange Landis dead to rights."

Bill locked gazes with her, but again he made no reply.

Finally he said, "I'm calling the pilot to get the plane ready to take us back to Quantico."

Riley could hardly believe her ears.

"You go right ahead and make that call," she snapped. "But you'll be getting on that plane alone. I'm staying here until I'm sure that the job gets done right."

Bill's eyes widened with alarm.

"Riley, are you crazy? You heard what Meredith just said. He's expecting both of us to report to him tomorrow morning."

Riley could feel her throat tightening with anger.

"Yeah, well, it wouldn't be the first time I ignored an order."

Bill looked truly worried about her now.

"No, it wouldn't," he said. "But it might be the last. Riley, you've been suspended and fired and reinstated time and time again. Sooner or later your luck is going to run out. When are you going to stop playing with fire?"

Riley almost had to bite her tongue. How could Bill, of all people, be ready to give up like this?

Finally she said, "You go ahead and make that phone call. I'm going to order a drink."

"Riley—" Bill began.

She slid out of the booth and strode across to the bar. She ordered a double bourbon on the rocks. While she was waiting, she found herself wondering …

Am I wrong?

Everybody else seemed to be so certain that the case was closed. She wasn't exactly sure why she didn't feel the same way. Now she regretted being so harsh about it with Bill.

The bartender served her drink and she paid for it.

I need to talk things over with Bill, she thought.

But when she turned toward the booth, she saw that he wasn't there.

He'd gone to his room, of course, to pack up for the flight home. He hadn't even stayed to order lunch.

Riley wondered if she ought to do the same.

It wasn't too late to change her mind.

She walked back to the booth, slid in, and took a sip of her drink.

She realized that some vague, unformed doubt had been nagging her ever since she and Bill had arrested Solange Landis.

What was it exactly?

Then Riley remembered that moment on the upper deck of Amanda Somers' floating home.

She'd caught a fleeting glimpse of the killer's mind. And she'd realized two things beyond a shadow of a doubt.

The murderer was a woman …

And she's completely insane.

Did Solange Landis fit that profile?

It wasn't impossible. She'd dealt with psychotics who managed to present a sane face to the world. And Landis was very much a mystery to her.

But Riley couldn't shake off her doubts.

Just then her phone buzzed. She saw that the call was from home. She answered and heard April's frantic voice.

"Mom, you've got to get home right now! Jilly's in real trouble!"

"What happened?" Riley asked, trying to stay calm.

"I don't know, Mom. I just got home, and Gabriela's scared to death. She just got a call from Jilly's school. Jilly cut out of her last couple of classes. And she didn't come home. We don't have any idea where she is."

Riley felt panic rising. April had gone missing in the past, and she had been in terrible danger.

It doesn't have to be the same kind of thing, she told herself.

"Daddy wants to talk to you," April said.

Riley felt a slight relief to hear that Ryan was there. Then she heard Ryan's voice.

"Riley, I'm sorry this happened. I've been doing my best. But April and Gabriela and I can't watch her every single minute. She was supposed to be at school."

"It's not your fault, Ryan."

"Should we call the police?"

Riley thought for a moment.

"No," Riley said. "It hasn't been long enough, and the police won't do anything. We'll call them later if—"

She couldn't finish the sentence.

She said, "I'm coming home, but I can't get there until tonight. Can you stay there with April and Gabriela?"

"Of course," Ryan said.

Riley breathed a sigh of gratitude.

"Thank you, Ryan," she said.

"I wish there was something I could do."

"You're doing all you can. I—I really appreciate it."

The call ended, and Riley sat staring at the phone for a moment.

Hurry, she told herself. Bill was getting his stuff together to fly back to Quantico. She had to go with him.

After all, the FBI was sure she'd caught the Seattle killer.

Why couldn't she convince herself that was true?

CHAPTER TWENTY NINE

The woman sat at her kitchen table scanning the front page of today's newspaper.

The headline blared ...

Nation Mourns Death of Beloved Author

The woman clicked her tongue with dismay.

For the second day, the front page was filled with news about Amanda Somers' death.

The woman's latest victim was getting far too much attention.

She was surprised to see that the story was still oddly contradictory about the cause of death. It seemed that Somers' children were calling it a suicide, while the local police and the FBI were investigating it as a murder.

"You'd think people could make up their minds about something so serious," she muttered aloud.

Anyway, she had to be more careful from now on. The police and the FBI were all too aware that there was a poisoner at large. They were already trying to track her down. How long would it take before this latest death was linked to a certain freelance healthcare provider?

She got up from her table and walked over to a shelf where she kept a dozen cell phones lined up on a rack. Each one was clearly labeled with a name—Susan Guthrie, Esther Thornton, Michelle Metcalf, Miranda Oglesby ...

She picked up the phone labeled Judy Brubaker.

She'd been Judy Brubaker when she had poisoned Amanda Somers.

Just yesterday a clinic had called this very phone asking if Judy Brubaker was available. She'd politely told them that no, Judy Brubaker had to leave town for a family emergency.

But now it appeared that Judy Brubaker needed to disappear for good.

It made her sad.

She'd liked Judy Brubaker.

Everybody had liked Judy Brubaker.

But like Hallie Stillians a few days ago, Judy Brubaker had to go. Just like others had disappeared over the years.

She took the phone over to the kitchen counter and pulled a

heavy wooden rolling pin out of a drawer. She rolled it back and forth over the phone, cracking and crushing the thing until she was sure that it was completely destroyed.

She tossed the phone into the trash.

Then she sat down at the table again and gazed around her kitchen. She sighed contentedly. She loved this house so much! It was amazing how happy she'd been living here. Even after a whole lifetime, she never tired of her cozy home. She'd taken great care to keep it exactly as it had been during her childhood—a shrine to her perfect life.

She sighed at the thought that not everybody's childhood had been as happy as hers. Not everybody's life was as rich and meaningful.

How sad!

This kitchen was her favorite room. It had ruffled curtains and pretty dishes lined up on painted shelves. She especially adored the old-fashioned canisters, which had belonged to her mother. They were decorated with colorful fruit and flowers, and were labeled for their intended ingredients—coffee, tea, sugar, flour, and the like.

During her childhood, her mother had worked magic with the ingredients in those big-lidded tins. She remembered with special fondness Mother's soft, brightly glazed orange cookies, which took a whole day to prepare and bake.

Of course, those canisters now held very different ingredients.

That was because life was very different.

She wasn't a little girl anymore.

She had responsibilities now—responsibilities she didn't always understand.

Often it seemed perfectly clear why she must end people's lives.

Sometimes it was because someone was in pain or unhappy or lonely.

Or sometimes it was because people were wicked and bad and had lived useless, harmful lives.

Oddly enough, Cody Woods had been both of those kinds of people. She hadn't known whether to pity him or hate him. All she knew was that she'd had to stop him.

She wasn't nearly so certain just why Amanda Somers had to die. But she'd felt that terrible necessity deep in her bones, and she'd known that it had to be done.

Somehow, she always knew what had to be done, even when she didn't understand why.

She closed her eyes and again imagined herself soaring above the world on great black wings.

But was it really just imagination?

As time passed, she was becoming more and more convinced that those wings were real. She could actually feel them sprouting out of her shoulders. No one in the world could see them, but they really were there.

She really was an angel.

And like all angels, she had an eternity of work to do.

It was lonely work—sometimes almost unbearably so.

No one would ever understand.

Now don't go feeling sorry for yourself!

She opened her eyes and shook off her reverie.

She had some serious decisions to make.

She'd been using thallium for a long time—much too long.

Now the authorities would be watching out for it, and besides, it acted too fast—she needed something much, much slower.

Fortunately, she'd already prepared to make the necessary change. But it wasn't going to be easy. And it would place her own life in terrible danger. She had to be brave—and extremely careful.

She got up and walked over to the kitchen counter and opened a lower cabinet. There was only one object inside—a little gray strongbox with a combination lock.

She'd never written down the combination—it seemed too dangerous.

But she'd practically engraved it on her memory.

To the right thirteen, left thirty-six, then right again twenty-four.

She wasn't going to open it now, of course. The very idea made her shudder. Inside was a little vial with a rubber stopper that was hermetically sealed with something waxy. Inside the vial was a clear liquid.

She'd stolen the vial about a year ago from a college chemistry lab, where it had been rather carelessly stored in a cabinet marked "REFERENCE TOXINS."

Whatever that means.

At the time, she hadn't known what a foolhardy risk she was taking just by handling the vial. Then she did some research that scared her half to death.

Once she'd grasped how dangerous the substance was, she'd bought the little strongbox, locked the vial inside, and stored it under the counter where the temperature was cool and steady. She vowed never to touch the vial or even open the strongbox until the time came when she'd need to change her methods.

And now, it seemed, that time had come.

But did she have everything she needed?

She knew she did, but decided to check anyway, just so she'd feel safer.

She opened another cabinet and looked through its contents. Yes, most things she would need had been stored for safekeeping— a pair of laminated gloves, another pair of long-cuffed heavy-duty gloves, a set of chemical splash goggles, a supplied air respiratory system with a full-face mask, and a white lab coat.

She giggled a little at the daunting array.

So much armor, such a little bottle!

The only thing missing was an eyedropper, and that would be easy to come by.

All in all, the gear had cost her nearly a thousand dollars. But she had no doubt that it had been an excellent investment. She had always known that she would need it some day.

Was she brave enough to use it now?

Just then a cell phone rang. She walked over to the rack full of phones and saw that the call was for Esther Thornton.

Oh, yes, Esther.

She hadn't been Esther for quite some time.

Esther was an outwardly stern New Englander with a dry sense of humor. People didn't always take to Esther right off the bat, but they always warmed up to her in just a few minutes. There was a world of warmth behind Esther's formidable facade.

She answered the phone.

"Esther? This is Molly Braxton at Ormond Rehab."

She replied in a rough-edged New England accent.

"Oh, yes, Molly. How are you? It's been ages."

Molly chuckled.

"Yes, it has, hasn't it? Well, we've got a new patient who's suffering from vertigo."

Her interest was piqued. She hadn't dealt with a vertigo patient in a very long time.

"Really? What's the cause?"

"Inner ear dysfunction. And of course, we need someone who can give the proper physical therapy."

"And you thought of me! I'm flattered. When do I start?"

"As soon as you can get here, I suppose."

"I'll be right there."

She jotted down the information that Molly gave her and ended the call in Esther's typically brusque manner. Then realized she ought to have asked a bit more about the patient. She didn't even know the patient's name or whether it was a man or a woman.

Well, I'll know soon enough.

She'd also know pretty soon whether this patient was marked for life or for death.

CHAPTER THIRTY

Riley felt helpless as she looked out the airplane window at the slowly creeping landscape below. It would be hours before she got home.

What might happen between now and then?

What was happening right now?

She got out her cell phone and typed a text message to Ryan.

Has Jilly come home?

A few seconds passed before Riley got a reply.

No. I'm sorry.

Riley typed a final line.

I'm on my way.

Ryan replied, *I'm glad.*

Riley put the phone back in her bag and stared out the window again.

"What are you thinking?" Bill asked.

Riley had almost forgotten that he was sitting beside her.

"I'm just feeling so—so over my head in everything," Riley said.

She was surprised to feel her throat catch. It was all she could do to keep from crying.

"I wish there was something I could do," Bill said.

Riley squeezed his hand for a moment, then let go. She was glad he was here, and he was doing plenty just by sitting there and saying very little. She could trust Bill not to say a lot of stupid hopeful things, like, "I'm sure everything will be all right," or, "She'll be home any minute now, just you wait and see."

Shallow people always said things like that, and Riley hated it. But Bill always knew what to say and what not to say—and when to say nothing at all. Sometimes she felt that she didn't appreciate him enough.

"I'm sorry I snapped at you earlier," Riley said.

Bill didn't reply.

Maybe he's still angry, Riley thought.

"I was wrong," Riley said.

Bill's furrowed his brow.

"Maybe not. I don't know. I'm not happy with how we left things back there. And …"

Bill's voice trailed off. Riley knew what he was leaving unsaid. He felt bad that he'd let his emotions run away with him. The childhood trauma of his mother's poisoning had undermined his objectivity, made it hard for him to do his job, and now he felt like he was running away from it.

But Riley couldn't blame him. Some cases triggered terrible memories. She knew that from hard personal experience.

"We had our orders," Riley said. "We're officially off the case."

"I don't know, Riley. Let's face it, neither one of us thinks we tied this case up with a nice little bow on top. Maybe we should have stayed, and to hell with orders. You know, sometimes I envy you your ..."

He seemed to be searching for the right word.

"Stubbornness?" Riley asked with a smile.

Bill smiled too.

"Let's just call it your healthy capacity for insubordination."

Riley let out a sad chuckle.

"Yeah, well—you and I both know it's going to get me fired for good one of these days."

Bill laughed softly.

"At least you'll have your integrity," he said.

"Integrity's overrated."

"No it's not."

Riley said nothing for a moment. She sat looking out the window again.

"I don't get it, Bill," she said at last. "All I'm trying to do is give Jilly a safe and comfortable home. Back in Phoenix, she had good reason to run away. Her father was abusive and cruel, and God only knows what else she had to deal with. But I've done everything I can to make things better. Why is she still running away?"

Bill thought for a few seconds.

"It must all be new to her," he finally said. "She never expected the kind of life you're giving her. And she doesn't ... know how to live it, I guess."

Riley remembered what Ryan had told her recently.

"She's got a lot of self-image problems. No self-confidence."

Bill and Ryan seemed to be on the same wavelength about Jilly. Riley appreciated both of their insights.

"Do you think she'll learn?" Riley asked.

Bill didn't reply, just looked at her sympathetically.

Riley sighed a little. No, it wasn't Bill's way to say stupid hopeful things—not when he didn't know any better than she did

148

whether things would get better. And that was just as well.

She put pushed her seat back and closed her eyes. The rumble of the engines was comforting. She breathed slowly and let herself slip off to sleep.

Riley was moving about through a thick, damp fog.

She was all alone and didn't know where to go.

Then she saw a dim figure moving toward her.

The mist lifted just a little, and Riley could see that it was her mother.

"Mommy!" she cried out. "You're all right!"

But then came a flash and a bang, and suddenly there was a bleeding hole in Mommy's chest.

Mommy still stood there, looking faintly surprised. She touched the wound, then looked at her hand, which was covered with blood.

Riley wanted to rush toward her, but found that her legs were rooted to the spot.

"Mommy, we've got to get you to a hospital," she said.

"No," Mommy said.

"We've got to! If we don't, you'll die."

Mommy smiled sadly.

"Oh, Riley, I'm dead already. I've been dead for a long time. Why are you always trying to fix things that can't be fixed?"

Riley's mind boggled at the question.

She felt as if it was one of the most important questions in the world.

"How am I supposed to know the difference?" she asked.

Mommy shook her head.

"Just walk away, Riley," she said.

"But I don't know where to go," Riley said.

Mommy turned away from her.

"Just walk away," she said again.

Then she disappeared into the mist.

A lurch of turbulence shook Riley awake. She could feel the plane descending. They'd be landing any minute now.

She remembered her dream vividly, and its message was painfully clear. Her mother was trying to tell her that she was trying to do too many things, trying to solve problems that she couldn't possibly fix.

But how could she pick and choose?

Should she give up on the case?

Or should she give up on Jilly?

Or was it something else altogether that she needed to give up?

"Just walk away," her mother had said.

"Walk away from what?" Riley murmured to the window.

She heard Bill's voice right next to her.

"Did you say something?"

"No," Riley said.

She kept staring out the window, wondering where Jilly could be.

CHAPTER THIRTY ONE

By the time Riley pulled her car up to her townhouse, she could barely breathe from sheer anxiety. It was late and dark now, after nine o'clock. She hadn't heard anything from home since her brief exchange of texts with Ryan on the plane.

When she turned the knob and opened the door, the first thing she saw was Ryan rushing to meet her.

"Jilly's home," he said. "She just got here moments ago."

Riley gasped from sheer relief. Her legs almost gave out from under her.

"I've got to sit down," she said.

Gabriela and April were waiting for her in the living room and Riley plopped down on the couch to talk with them.

"What happened?" she asked. "Where did Jilly go?"

"The *policía* brought her home," Gabriela said.

"The police?" Riley asked.

"They picked her up at a truck stop," April said.

Riley's heart sank. She remembered the truck stop where she'd first found Jilly.

Ryan sat down on the couch beside Riley.

He said, "A woman at a truck stop—a hooker, I'm pretty sure—phoned the police and said an underage girl was wandering around there. She apparently talked to Jilly and then called the cops. They picked Jilly up, and she finally gave them your phone number. The cops called, and Gabriela answered. Then they brought her home."

Riley sat silently for a moment, trying to grasp what she'd just heard. What did the girl think she was doing? Was she trying to sell her body again? Riley had hoped that she'd put such horrible ideas behind her.

"Where is she?" Riley asked.

"Up in her room," April said.

Riley got up and walked toward the stairs.

"Go easy on her, OK?" April said. "She's pretty upset."

Riley was starting to feel angry as she walked up the stairs. But she was in no mood to scold anybody.

She knocked on Jilly's door.

"Come in," Jilly said.

Riley opened the door and saw Jilly sitting on the edge of her bed. She had a box of tissues next to her. She'd obviously been crying.

"I'm sorry," Jilly said.

Riley just stood there for a few seconds.

Finally she said, "What happened, Jilly? Why did you do that?"

"I said I'm sorry."

"You're not answering my question."

Riley sat down on the bed beside Jilly.

"April and I had a fight," Jilly said.

"What about?"

"It doesn't matter. I was wrong."

"What was it about, Jilly?"

Jilly pulled a tissue out of the box and blew her nose. She let out a couple of sobs before she spoke.

"This morning before school, I ate some yogurt that belonged to her. It was in the refrigerator and it had her name on it, but I ate it anyway. She got kind of mad—not real mad, just kind of mad. And I got mad back and said some things I shouldn't have. I kept thinking about it at school, and I knew I was wrong, and that was why I—"

Jilly broke down in sobs, and Riley put her arm around her.

She couldn't get her mind around what Jilly had just said.

All this on account of some yogurt?

"But why did you go to a truck stop?" Riley asked. "What did you think you were doing?

"The only thing I'll ever be any good at."

Riley was quietly stunned. Did this child really think she'd never be any good at anything except selling her body?

"Don't say that," Riley said. "Don't ever say that. You're good at all kinds of things. You just haven't found out what they are yet. You're smart, and you can learn. And we're all here to help you."

"I'm nobody," Jilly said.

Riley lifted Jilly's chin and looked her in the eyes.

"You're not nobody. If you were nobody, nobody would worry about you. But Ryan and April and Gabriela were all worried sick about you. And I was so worried about you that I came flying all the way across the country. I'd say you're a pretty important person to get so many people so worked up about you."

Jilly laughed through her sobs. Riley hugged her tight.

"No more of this running away stuff, OK?" Riley said.

"OK."

"Now why don't you come downstairs and spend some time with everybody."

Jilly shook her head.

"Huh-uh," she said. "I've got to get some homework done."

Riley smiled. She was pretty sure that Jilly's real reason for not wanting to come downstairs was embarrassment.

She patted Jilly on the shoulder and left the room. She saw that the door to April's room was open, and April was sitting on her own bed. She'd been waiting to find out what had happened.

"How's she doing?" April asked in a quiet voice.

Riley walked into the room and sat in a chair facing April.

"I wish I knew," Riley said. "This whole thing is new to me."

"Not so new," April said. "I've been an even bigger pain over the years."

Riley chuckled sadly and shook her head.

"No, this is new—and different."

Riley and April looked at each other for a few seconds.

"It was just some stupid yogurt," April said. "I shouldn't have yelled at her about it."

"Maybe not," Riley said. "But she's got to learn to live with us. And we've all got to learn how to deal with her."

Riley looked around at April's room, which was surprisingly neat and orderly. Maybe Gabriela had helped with that, but April must have been doing her share.

"Just tell me that *you're* not getting into any trouble," Riley said.

April laughed.

"Not unless doing my homework and getting good grades and not having a boyfriend and hanging out with Crystal is trouble."

Riley chuckled.

"That's what I want to hear. How is Crystal?"

"She's fine. She says her dad asks about you a lot."

Riley remembered that text message she had gotten from Blaine a couple of days ago.

"Hope all is going well. When do you think you'll be getting back? I'll make dinner."

She hadn't answered it. Perhaps it had been rude of her, but she just hadn't felt like it. Besides, a family dinner at Blaine's restaurant would probably have to include Ryan now. Surely that would be awkward.

Riley said, "Well, I guess you can tell Crystal to tell her dad … I'm fine."

April looked at her with a quizzical smile.

"You're still mad at him, aren't you? About moving away, I

153

mean."

Riley was surprised. She hadn't realized her feelings were so transparent.

"I'm not mad at him," she said, not sure that she was being truthful. "But I'm disappointed, I guess. I thought he'd still be around."

"Well, *I'm* kind of mad at him," April said. "I mean, moving away like that, on account of a silly little thing like getting beaten up by a psychopath right here in our house."

It was a joke, of course, but Riley didn't laugh. It cut too close to home. Riley worried that her own dangerous life was toxic to anyone and everyone she loved and cared about. She often wondered if she had any right to a family and to anything like a normal life.

"Anyway," April added, "I think you're better off with Dad. You *are* getting back together with Dad, aren't you?"

Riley let out a burst of startled laughter.

"Don't be nosy," she said.

"Hey, it's my family too."

Riley and April sat looking at each other for a moment.

"I don't know, April. Let's just give things some time."

Riley turned her head and looked toward Jilly's room. She wondered if maybe she should knock on her door again and see if she was OK. But no, it didn't seem like a good idea. If Jilly was ever going to feel at home here, she was going to have to be allowed some privacy.

April asked, "Are we going to adopt Jilly?"

Riley looked at April and saw that her expression was worried. Did April feel threatened by the possibility of having a younger sibling in her life?

"I don't know yet, April."

April's eyes widened.

"Mom, we've *got* to adopt her! We're all she's got now! We can't send her back to her old life. She's told me such horrible things, and—"

April stopped short, as if she'd said something she shouldn't have said. Riley felt oddly pleased. It seemed that Jilly had been confiding in April, like a real sister would. And that was a good thing, even if it meant that the two girls had secrets that Riley couldn't know.

"I worry, April. And I'm not sure it's fair. I'm gone a lot of the time, and I know that Jilly's a lot of responsibility for you, too."

"I'm OK with it. Really."

Riley gazed at April in quiet amazement. Not long ago, April had been impossible to deal with. She had gotten involved with a vicious punk who had drugged her up and tried to turn her into a sex slave. She'd grown up so much in such a short time.

Thank God, Riley thought.

"We'll see, April," Riley said, stroking her daughter's hair. "It's going to take some time. Anyway, it's late, and I'm sure you've got homework to do."

"I guess," April said with a make-believe teenage whine.

"Goodnight. I love you."

"I love you too."

Riley left April's room and went back downstairs.

*

A short time later, the house was quiet and peaceful. Riley and Ryan were sitting in the living room having a drink together. They didn't say much for a little while. Riley appreciated the quiet, and she sensed that Ryan did as well. After all, his day hadn't been a whole lot easier than hers.

"How did things go in Seattle?" Ryan finally asked.

Riley sighed. She hadn't thought much about the case since she'd been home. "The case is closed," she said.

Ryan tilted his head and looked at her curiously.

"You don't sound very convinced."

Riley was surprised that Ryan had picked up on her misgivings. *He knows me better than I realize,* she thought.

"No, I'm not," she said. "But it's not up to me."

She took a long sip from her drink.

"How are you feeling about this thing with Jilly?" Riley asked.

Ryan thought for a moment.

"Scared," he said. "But kind of—well, exhilarated, I guess."

He looked into Riley's eyes.

"I've screwed up a lot over the years, and I'm sorry. And I feel like I'm getting a second chance. I'm exhilarated … and I'm grateful."

Riley smiled.

"April thinks we should adopt her," she said.

Ryan threw back his head and laughed.

"Well, I guess it's decided, then."

Riley laughed too, then said, "Let's take things a few steps at a time."

"Yes, let's."

Another silence fell, and this time it seemed to be full of all kinds of unasked and unanswered questions. Life was changing so much and so fast. Riley didn't know what to do next, and she knew that Ryan felt the same way.

Finally, he said, "I've been staying in your room since you went to Seattle, and I've got a few things up there. I'll go get them. It's about time for me to go home."

Riley felt a pang of sadness at his words. But she didn't argue. *Yes, that's best,* she thought.

Ryan got up and walked toward the stairs. Without quite knowing why, Riley followed him. Then she stood watching him in the bedroom as he gathered his things together.

"Thank you for being here through all this," she said, her voice catching with emotion.

He looked up from his belongings and smiled. Then he walked over to her and hugged her.

Riley felt as if she were melting as a world of worries and anxieties slipped away. She'd forgotten what it was like to feel this way. When she felt him start to draw out of their embrace, she held him tighter and put her head on his shoulder. Her body was warming with an old, familiar passion.

Riley felt tingles of pleasure as he stroked her back with his fingers. She slid her hand up under his pullover shirt. When she touched his bare skin, familiar electricity shot through her body.

She felt herself smile. Ryan was definitely not going home tonight.

CHAPTER THIRTY TWO

When Riley woke up the next morning, she groggily became aware that something was different from her usual rising time. She wasn't alone in bed.

She rolled over and saw Ryan's naked back as he slept beside her.

She smiled at the pleasant memory of what had happened last night.

It was enough to make her forget all that had gone wrong in Seattle. Well, not forget it, maybe, but enough to make her feel quite a bit better.

She got out of bed and put on her robe. As she walked downstairs, she heard the clatter of someone making breakfast in the kitchen.

Oh, dear, she thought.

She'd almost forgotten that there were three other people in the house. And pretty soon, all of them were going to know that Ryan had spent the night with her. The thought made her blush.

I guess I'll have some explaining to do, she thought.

When Riley got to the bottom of the stairs, she heard singing and whistling coming from the kitchen. She went into the kitchen and found April and Gabriela fixing breakfast together. Gabriela was singing a song in Spanish and April was whistling along.

They both looked at Riley with broad smiles.

"Well," Riley said, "the two of you look very happy."

Gabriela's smile widened.

"Y tú también," she said.

April giggled.

"That means you do too," April said.

"I know what it means," Riley said.

They know! she realized.

But how? Riley remembered how passionate things had gotten with Ryan last night.

Had everyone in the house heard what was going on?

Riley's blush deepened considerably.

Seeming to sense Riley's embarrassment, April said, "We saw Daddy's car out front."

Riley breathed a sigh of relief.

At that moment, Jilly came bounding into the kitchen.

"Hey, I just ran into Ryan upstairs," she said.

Then looking at Riley, she added with a mischievous grin, "Way to go!"

Riley blushed all over again.

Well, at least it seems to be OK with everybody, she thought.

Her cell phone buzzed in her bathrobe pocket. She saw that the call was from Bill. She stepped out of the kitchen and answered it.

Bill's voice sounded worried.

"Riley. How is everything there?"

Riley gasped slightly. She realized that she hadn't called Bill last night to tell him that Jilly was home safe and sound.

"Oh, Bill, I'm sorry, I should have let you know. She's OK. She's home. I'll tell you what happened later."

"I'm glad to hear it. So I take it you'll be able to make it to that meeting with Meredith this morning."

"Absolutely."

A brief silence fell.

Then Bill said, "Riley, I think this Seattle thing is working out for the best. Our coming back, I mean. We made a good arrest, and Solange Landis is probably guilty. If not … well, it's a local thing and we should stay out of it."

There was something forced in Bill's voice. Riley knew that tone. Bill sounded like that when he was trying to talk himself into something without quite succeeding.

He doesn't believe that for a second, Riley thought.

She also knew that his conscience was nagging him about it. Still, there was nothing they could do about it now. With some luck, Meredith would assign them to a new case this morning and they could leave Seattle behind them and forget all about it.

"I'll see you in a little while," Riley said.

"Right."

They ended the call. Riley realized that Ryan had come downstairs while she'd been talking to Bill. There was a burst of delighted laughter and conversation as he joined the others in the kitchen. He was getting a hearty welcome from Gabriela, April, and Jilly.

Riley smiled.

Maybe Bill was right after all. Maybe things really were working out for the best.

She went into the kitchen to join her family for breakfast.

*

After breakfast, Ryan left to drive the girls to school on his way to work. Gabriela went out to buy groceries. Riley got dressed and readied herself for her meeting with Bill and Meredith.

Then she sat alone in the living room. She had a few minutes to spare before she had to leave. Try as she might to keep the case out of her mind, it started to nag at her again. She hated leaving things so unfinished.

And she felt a growing doubt that Solange Landis was the serial poisoner.

I could be wrong, she told herself. *Maybe she's guilty.*

Besides, she reminded herself, *there's nothing you can do.*

She was all the way across the country now, under orders to stay away from Seattle. She couldn't affect the outcome of the investigation one way or the other.

Worst of all, Riley felt alone with her questions. Even Bill was trying to put the case behind him. Was there anybody in the world she could talk to right now?

She felt something pulling at her inside—something dark, something she knew she should put out of her mind.

Even so, she walked up the stairs into her bedroom. She took a box down from a closet shelf and opened it. Inside was a heavy letter-sized envelope with her name written on it.

She shivered as she took the envelope out of the box.

Put it back, she tried to tell herself. *Better yet, throw it away.*

But she knew she couldn't do that.

The envelope was heavy and bulky. And of course, Riley knew exactly what was inside. She'd opened it right away after it had been thrown against her front door not long ago.

And now she opened it again.

It contained a gold bracelet chain folded in a piece of paper. She unfolded the paper and read the message again.

Just a little gift in honor of our new partnership. It's been a pleasure working together.

I bought another bracelet that matches this one.

I'm going to wear mine all the time.

Will you wear yours?

Both the letter and the chain were from Shane Hatcher.

And no, she hadn't worn it. She hadn't even shown it to anyone else.

But she hadn't thrown it away either.

"Shane the Chain," she murmured aloud, remembering his nickname.

The bracelet was a grim reminder of Hatcher's fascination with chains of all kinds.

He was obsessed with chains and the pain they could inflict. As soon as he'd escaped from prison, he'd tracked down a nemesis from his gangbanger days, beaten him to death with tire chains, and duct-taped his mangled body to a post in an abandoned warehouse.

It was the last murder he had committed—and the last one Riley expected him to commit.

But he was still at large, and in a disturbing sense he was still Riley's responsibility.

She looked at the bracelet closely. It was nicely wrought with a fancy clasp. She figured it was an expensive piece—the kind of thing sold at high-end department stores and jewelry shops.

Turning it over in her hands, she saw something she hadn't noticed before.

Something seemed to be engraved in tiny letters on one of the links.

She hurried to a drawer and took out a magnifying glass. She peered through the lens at the tiny engraved writing. She wrote it down on a piece of paper. Then she studied it closely.

"face8ecaf"

What did it mean?

Because it had to mean something.

After all, Hatcher typically communicated with her in riddles. Sometimes it was hard to figure out the answers to those riddles. But she had a feeling that this one would be easy. Hatcher really wanted her to figure it out.

For one thing, she had a hunch about what the "8" meant.

It was a symbol.

It represented a chain.

And of course, the first four letters were a simple word "face."

And the last four letters—"ecaf"?

"Face" spelled backwards, Riley realized.

But what did that signify?

Riley thought for a moment. The word followed by the reversed letters suggested a mirror.

She felt a chill at the thought.

For as long as she'd known Hatcher, she'd bitterly told him that she wasn't like him, that they had nothing in common. He'd always smiled as if he knew better. And deep down, Riley also suspected the same.

Sometimes looking into Hatcher's face was like looking into a mirror—a mirror that displayed her darkest self, her own cruelest demons. And right now, she felt that darkness rising inside of her …

The darkness she'd known when she'd caved in a killer's face with a rock.

The darkness she'd known when she'd been tempted to hack another killer limb from limb with a butcher knife.

The darkness she'd known when she'd tracked down the young man who had drugged April, smashed his hand with a baseball bat, then further crushed that hand under her heel until he screamed for mercy.

Of all the people Riley had ever known, only Hatcher fully understood the darkness that lurked within her.

Her hand shook as she held the bracelet.

No, she told herself.

Put it away.

Throw it away.

But she couldn't.

And now she knew the answer to the riddle.

"Face to face," she murmured aloud. "That's what he wants."

She opened up her laptop and logged on to her chat service.

She typed in the cryptic characters and waited, holding her breath.

Just a few quick seconds passed.

And then there he was, his dark visage facing hers—Shane Hatcher.

She exhaled sharply and couldn't breathe for a moment.

Hatcher was sitting in front of a gray background that offered no hint of his location. His intense dusky features looked amused as he gazed at her over the tops of his reading glasses.

It was exactly as if he'd been expecting Riley's call that very moment.

And maybe he was, Riley thought, trying to regain her breath.

Maybe he knows me exactly that well.

"It's good to see you, Riley," he said, leaning back in his chair and putting his hands behind his head. "We've got some catching up to do."

CHAPTER THIRTY THREE

Riley was speechless. Hatcher appeared to be relishing her astonishment.

"Are you tracing this call?" he asked.

"I might be."

He let out a sardonic growl of laughter.

"I know you're not," he said.

Riley felt her resistance to him wither. There was no point in trying to persuade him otherwise. He knew her too well. She simply couldn't lie to him.

"If you know, why did you ask?" she said.

"I just wanted to hear you answer the question."

He was toying with her, as always.

The game is on, Riley thought bitterly.

Dealing with Shane Hatcher was always a game. And it was a game he would always win—not just because Riley didn't know the rules, but she didn't even know what game he was really playing.

"So how can I help you?" Hatcher said, lowering his glasses a little to look at her more closely.

"I don't need your help," Riley said.

"Then why did you call?"

Riley's lip was twitching with exasperation and anger.

"I sure as hell don't know," she said. "I'm hanging up right now."

Hatcher rolled his eyes and shook his head.

"No, you're not, Riley."

Riley looked down at the keyboard. All she had to do was end the call, then hit a simple command and log off. Then she could cancel her account so that they'd never connect like this again. But Hatcher was right, as always. She simply couldn't bring herself to do it.

"You need my help, Riley. We both know that. And I'm glad to oblige. But of course, I expect a little favor in return."

Riley gulped hard. He always expected a little favor. And his favors could be extremely troubling.

"And what's that?" she asked.

"The pleasure of working with you. In person, I mean."

Riley felt a little sick at the thought of meeting him in the real world. She didn't want to do that again—ever. She had no idea where he might be right now. But she wasn't going to travel there just at his whim.

"We're not going to do that," she said. "I'd rather stay far away."

"What makes you think you haven't been nearby already?"

Riley's heart jumped up in her throat.

Has he been stalking me? she wondered.

Might he even be near her house right now?

All she knew for sure was that he wasn't bluffing.

Somehow, he'd been close to her recently. And that could very well mean that he'd also been close to April, Ryan, Gabriela, and Jilly.

Perhaps he was nearby at that very moment.

Now she was afraid she was going to be sick.

"Tell me about the case you're working on," Hatcher said.

"I'm not working on a case," Riley said. "I'm between cases."

And that's the truth, after all, she thought.

A look of surprise crossed Hatcher's face. Whether it was feigned or real, Riley couldn't tell.

"Really?" he said. "Then have you given up the hunt for the woman who poisoned Cody Woods and Margaret Jewell? To say nothing of your favorite author, Amanda Somers? And God knows who else. That's not like you. That's not like you at all."

Riley's chest tensed uncomfortably. He not only knew about the case—he somehow knew of her fondness for Somers' novel. He also knew that she was sure that the killer was a woman. His grip upon her was tightening.

"I hear the FBI has got a suspect in custody," Hatcher said. "But I know that you doubt that Solange Landis is guilty of anything worse than forging records."

"I don't know that for sure."

"But you doubt it. And so do I. Isn't it about time we found out for sure?"

Riley felt dizzy now. She remembered something he had once said to her.

"We're joined at the brain, Riley Paige."

Riley fought down her panic.

No, he wasn't actually reading her mind.

But he had money and resources and a network of minions.

He could get information about anything that took his interest.

And nothing in the world seemed to interest him more than Riley.

Hatcher steepled his fingers together and looked upward

thoughtfully.

"Let's review where we are, shall we?" he said. "All three of your known victims were recently under medical care, but in different hospitals for different treatments. Did they have any healthcare workers or basic staff in common?"

Riley felt a strange shift in her emotions. Like it or not, Hatcher was the sole human being in the world who was on her wavelength right now. And she'd learned from experience that he could be extremely helpful.

"Not that we've been able to find," Riley said.

"Perhaps you haven't looked hard enough. We do know that all three of your victims spent some time in rehab clinics."

Riley was startled.

He's wrong, she thought.

She'd never known him to be wrong before.

"Cody Woods was never in rehab," she said.

Hatcher's eyes widened.

"Oh, but he was," he said.

"How do you know?"

Hatcher laughed.

"How do you think I know?"

Then he just sat there smiling, waiting for Riley to connect the dots.

Riley felt a jolt of understanding.

"You talked to some workers at the South Hills Hospital," she said.

He nodded. "A couple of orderlies. Very friendly chaps."

Riley shuddered as she realized …

He was in Seattle.

Now she understood what he meant a little while ago when he'd said …

"What makes you think you haven't been nearby already?"

He had seen her.

Just how much he'd seen of her she couldn't guess.

Seeming to pick up on her thoughts, Hatcher said, "That was some crazy meeting at Parnassus Heights Hospital that morning, wasn't it? You weren't ready for a full-throttle press conference, were you? You looked like you wanted to throttle Rigby and Sanders and that hospital director. I couldn't blame you. You seemed to hit it off with Prisha Shankar, though. I can understand why. That woman knows her business."

He was there! Riley thought.

It seemed impossible. Riley prided herself on her keen powers of observation. She thought she had taken note of every single person in that crowded room. But she had underestimated Shane Hatcher. Doubtless he had disguised himself as a reporter—cleverly enough so that even Riley hadn't recognized him.

"How did you get the orderlies to talk to you about Cody Woods?" Riley asked.

"Well, they didn't know who I was, of course. I'm not *that* famous. So I just asked. It's interesting the things people will tell you when you just buy them a beer. Told them I'd read about Cody Woods' death, and thought it was a shame, and wondered what they might know about it. They said that he went to a rehab clinic soon after he got out of South Hills Hospital."

Riley's mind rushed frantically as she took all this in.

"So all three victims were probably poisoned at rehab centers," she said.

"So it would seem."

Riley struggled with this information.

"But that doesn't make sense," she said. "We checked the records at South Hills. There was nothing about Cody Woods going from there to a rehab center. He went straight home."

"The records were wrong, I guess. Now how could that have happened?"

Riley's mouth dropped open.

"The records were altered," she said.

"Guess so."

Riley thought for a moment.

"But forged records take us right back to Solange Landis as a suspect."

Hatcher laughed again.

"Come on, Riley," he said. "In a big city like Seattle, Landis isn't the only healthcare worker who ever forged any records."

Riley leaned toward the screen.

"You've got to tell me everything you know," she said.

Hatcher smirked.

"Sorry, that's all I've got for now," he said.

"But didn't you get the name of the rehab center where Cody Woods wound up?"

"Maybe I did, and maybe I didn't. You don't know, do you?"

Riley was furious now. This was just like Shane Hatcher. He just loved to tease her with information.

Hatcher shrugged.

165

"But I keep forgetting—you're off the case, aren't you? And nobody else in the FBI even wants to talk to you about it. You don't have any allies there. You're completely on your own."

He squinted and peered at her closely.

"But you've never let that stop you before," he said. "And I don't figure you'll let it stop you now. And I think you know who to talk to at the FBI when you're *persona non grata.* It's somebody else who doesn't give a damn about the rules."

Riley's head was crowded with questions. But before she could say another word, Hatcher said, "Let's talk again soon."

And he ended the call.

Riley sat staring at the computer screen in a state of shock. The whole conversation now seemed like a dream. But it hadn't been a dream. And now what was she going to do?

Riley looked at her watch. She knew she needed to leave right now if she wanted to get to the meeting with Meredith this morning.

She also knew that she wasn't going to go.

As for now, she needed someone's help, and she needed it in a hurry.

But who could she turn to when everybody at the FBI was against her?

She remembered what Hatcher had said …

… somebody else who doesn't give a damn about the rules.

She had a pretty good idea of the kind of person Hatcher meant.

She got out her cell phone and dialed a number.

CHAPTER THIRTY FOUR

A gruff, husky voice quickly answered the phone.

"Van Roff here. And you, I presume, are Special Agent Riley Paige. Or at least my caller ID presumes it."

Riley smiled as she pictured the overweight technical analyst sitting at a huge assortment of computer screens.

"Your caller ID presumes correctly," Riley said.

"And you're calling me from Virginia," Roff said.

"Correct."

"And you're calling me because you don't think the poisoning case is really closed."

Riley was startled.

"Uh, how do you know?" she asked.

"Because you're calling *me*, that's why."

He was exactly right, of course. Hatcher had told her she needed to talk to "somebody who doesn't give a damn about the rules." And Riley knew that nobody in the FBI cared less about the rules than technical analysts. As a breed, they were always looking for an excuse to color outside the lines.

And they were extremely smart.

"You're right," Riley said. "I should warn you, though—I'm likely to ask you to do some things that aren't exactly, well, officially sanctioned. Let's just keep all this between ourselves."

Riley heard a peal of happy laughter. Apparently her words were music to his ears.

"Be still my beating heart!" he said. "And oh, just so's you know—this call may be recorded for my future entertainment. Don't worry, it'll be for my ears only. What have you got in mind?"

Riley thought for a moment.

"Something's off about what we know about Cody Woods' death. Let's review for a minute. He was admitted to South Hills Hospital for surgery, then he went home. Soon after that he checked back into South Hills because he was ill. And he died there. Now, both Margaret Jewell and Amanda Somers stayed in rehab clinics shortly before they died."

"Right. But not Cody Woods."

"Wrong," Riley said. "I'm pretty sure Cody Woods went to a clinic too."

"Did not. I checked."

"I think you got tricked, Mr. Roff."

She heard Roff let out a grunt of annoyed surprise.

"No!"

"I'm afraid so. The murderer tricked you."

Riley knew she was waving the perfect bait to get Roff fully on board.

"How do you know?" Roff asked.

"I've got a source."

"Who?"

"I'm not at liberty to say."

Roff audibly growled.

"Then this means war. Lemme think for a second."

A short silence fell.

"I'm going to try something," Roff said. "You stay right where you are, I'll call back in a few minutes. Let's make that a video chat."

Riley agreed and gave Roff her video address. Then they ended the call.

Riley looked at her watch and sighed. If she left the house right now, she'd still be late for her meeting with Bill and Meredith. She was definitely going to miss it. Should she call and explain?

Explain what? she asked herself. *That I'm disobeying orders?*

It wasn't an option. She was just going to have to live with the consequences of whatever she was about to do. She folded up her laptop computer, tucked it under her arm, and went downstairs and to the kitchen. She heated up a cup of coffee, flipped open the computer, and waited for Roff's call.

She worried as she waited.

Was she really willing to put her job in jeopardy again?

She reminded herself that she now had two kids to take care of. And one of them was very troubled. This wasn't a good time to get fired.

Maybe I shouldn't do this, she thought.

She could call Bill or Meredith right now, make up some excuse for being late for the meeting, then get there as soon as she could.

There was just one problem. She'd gotten Roff involved, and there was no way that he was going to back away from this.

Just as she finished drinking her cup of coffee, the video call came through, and she found herself facing the large, socially awkward technician. He was red-faced and sweating, apparently from the exertion of whatever he'd been doing.

"Bingo," he said. "I've got something."

"That was quick," Riley said.

"I've been busy. Real busy."

"What have you got?"

Roff's eyes darted back and forth, as if he wanted to make sure no one was listening.

"I still couldn't find any computer record of Cody Woods going to a rehab clinic. But I tried a different approach."

"How?" Riley asked.

Roff snorted with gleeful laughter.

"There's a new high-tech gimmick these days. Maybe you haven't heard of it. It's called a goddamn *phone call*."

Riley smiled. Roff's enthusiasm was truly contagious.

Roff continued, "So I found out which rehab centers a patient might go to from South Hills Hospital. I found three. I decided to call them all, see what their staffs could tell me. The very first one I called was Signet Rehabilitation Center—and *voilà!* I hit the jackpot right off the bat."

"Tell me what you found out," Riley said breathlessly.

"The head nurse there told me that she remembered Cody Woods. He'd come there after surgery at South Hills. But when she checked the records she didn't find anything about him. So somebody had definitely been tampering with records—both at South Hills Hospital and Signet Rehab. It's not wizard hacker work, but whoever did it is pretty slick."

Roff huffed and puffed as he clattered away at his keyboard.

He said, "As you know, I've been trying to find personnel that all the facilities might have in common. I couldn't find any for the other two clinics, and I came up empty when I checked Signet just now. *But ...*"

Three women's faces appeared on Riley's screen.

"At each of the three facilities, a freelance female therapist disappeared soon after the patients were treated. Here are their photos from employment records."

An arrow fell on the face to the left. She was a black-haired woman with enormous glasses.

"This is Lisa Tucci, who worked with Margaret Jewell at Natrona Physical Rehab. Right after Jewell was released, Lisa left word that she'd eloped and was flying east and wouldn't be available for work anymore."

The arrow moved to the face in the middle. The woman had curly, auburn hair.

"This is Judy Brubaker," Roff said. "She worked with Amanda

Somers at Stark Rehab Center. Soon after Somers was released, the clinic called Judy to find out if she was available. She said that she had to leave town for a family emergency."

The arrow moved to the face on the right. The woman had a kindly expression and short, blonde hair.

"And now we get to Hallie Stillians, who worked with Cody Woods at Signet Rehab. Hallie told the staff at Signet that she and her husband were moving to Mexico to live there for good."

As Riley scanned the three faces carefully, Roff said, "I've still got more work to do. For example, try to find any record of Hallie and her husband getting visas or crossing the Mexican border. And looking for official records of Lisa Tucci getting married. That's going to take awhile. And what do you think are the chances that I'll find anything at all?"

Pretty small, I expect, Riley thought without saying so aloud.

"So all of them went away," Riley said. "What else did they have in common?"

"None of their cell phones are in service anymore. And all three of the home addresses they gave were actually mail services—the kind where individuals rent mailboxes and come to pick up their mail."

Riley's mind was clicking away, putting together this new information.

"What do you think of all this, Mr. Roff?" she asked.

Roff sounded pleased that she'd asked for his opinion.

"Well, I guess it's just *possible* that you've stumbled across a whole different series of murders. I mean, serial killers usually pick a type of victim, right? So maybe this is a killer who picks off women who use mail services. Or who kills therapists whose patients have died."

Roff was thinking things through thoroughly, and Riley liked that.

She took a screen shot of the photos so she could refer to them on her own.

"Good work, Mr. Roff," she said.

Roff's face appeared again.

"What do you want me to do next?" Roff asked. "I'm between jobs, and things are as boring as hell around here."

"You can start by picking up where you left off—checking for plane tickets, marriage licenses, visas, and such."

"What else?"

Riley thought for a moment. Should Roff run searches over a

longer time span to see whether any similar women had turned up dead or missing? No, she had a hunch that he could make better use of his efforts.

"Just concentrate on these three therapists. Find out every single thing you possibly can about them. I'll be in touch soon. Thanks for your help, Roff."

She paused for a moment and added, "Oh, and I don't need to tell you …"

Roff finished her thought for her.

"Don't worry. This conversation didn't take place. And no such subsequent conversations are ever going to take place."

They ended the call, and Riley opened the screen shot showing the three workers.

Riley noticed something odd about the photographs themselves.

They weren't very sharp. They were all blurred slightly. But it didn't seem to be a photographic problem.

Instead, it looked as though all three women had deliberately moved a little at the very moment when the pictures had been snapped.

It was as if they didn't want to leave a clear record of what they looked like.

She also noticed that the women resembled one another—all of them middle-aged, with similarly shaped faces.

The same woman? she wondered.

There were obvious differences, of course, especially in hairstyle and color. And Stillians and Brubaker had blue eyes while Tucci's eyes were brown.

But she remembered that the gatekeeper at Amanda Somers' said that her caller might have been wearing a wig. And contact lenses could explain a difference in eye color.

Riley felt a prickle of excitement. The case had suddenly taken a new turn. She grabbed her cell phone and dialed Bill's number.

He was almost yelling when he answered.

"Riley! Where the hell were you? The meeting's over, and Meredith is pissed."

Riley paced back and forth and spoke nervously.

"Bill, listen. We've got to go back to Seattle. I think I've got something."

"What have you got?"

Riley stopped short. She suddenly realized that she had to be careful what she said.

"I can't talk about it on the phone," she said.

A short silence fell.

"Have you got anything absolutely solid?"

Riley's heart sank.

"No," she said.

Bill groaned with exasperation.

"Then I'm sure as hell not going back to Seattle. And you're not either."

"Bill, listen to me—"

"No, *you* listen. I can't do this. I can't blow off my orders and go back to Seattle with you. I can't afford to lose my job. And neither can you. Walk away from it, Riley. Whatever it is, just walk away."

Before Riley could protest further, Bill said, "Riley, we're not going to talk about this right now. Believe me, you've got other things to worry about. You've got to focus on keeping your job. Do you understand?"

Riley sighed.

"Yeah, I understand. Goodbye."

She ended the call and sat down. She was so agitated now that she couldn't think clearly. And in a matter of seconds, her phone buzzed again.

This time it was Meredith.

"You'd better have a damn good excuse, Agent Paige," he growled.

"Sir, I think I'm just about to get a break in the Seattle poisoning case. If I can just—"

Meredith interrupted.

"What were you doing when you were supposed to be at this meeting?"

Riley gulped. She knew that Meredith wasn't going to let her evade anything.

"I was checking some new information," she said.

"And how did you come by this information?"

"I've got a—source."

Riley didn't reply.

"Tell me you haven't been in touch with Shane Hatcher."

It's as if he can see right through me, Riley thought with despair.

But she also knew that she'd probably make the same guess if she were in his place.

She still said nothing.

172

And of course, she knew that her very silence was an admission.

When Meredith spoke again, it was with an even grimmer tone.

"Agent Paige, you can't work with an escaped prisoner who is on the FBI's most wanted list. Now tell me where he is, so I can send agents to apprehend him."

Riley replied in a low, shaky voice.

"I won't help you set a trap for him," she said.

A long silence fell.

"Agent Paige, I'm putting you on leave," Meredith said at last. "And it really could become permanent this time. That's all I've got to say for now."

Meredith abruptly ended the call.

Riley sat staring into space for a moment.

Alone again, she thought.

The situation was all too familiar.

But she had a job to do, and if she didn't do it, others might be killed.

As she started looking for commercial flights on her computer, she thought through all that she was going to have to do next.

She had to call Ryan and tell him she was leaving town.

She had to tell Gabriela too.

But what about April—and especially Jilly?

Would Jilly be all right during her absence?

She booked her flight with a heavy heart. She felt as if she were abandoning everyone she loved—and all because of a feeling in her gut.

What if I'm wrong?

CHAPTER THIRTY FIVE

Riley was walking toward her gate at Dulles International Airport to catch her flight to Seattle when her cell phone buzzed. She grew excited when she saw that the call was from Van Roff.

"Tell me you've got something, Mr. Roff," Riley said.

"I might. Maybe not what we expected, but maybe something."

Riley kept on walking as she listened.

"I've been looking for patients who were cared for by our three workers—Lisa Tucci, Judy Brubaker, and Hallie Stillians. Mostly I didn't find anything sinister. No deaths even, except for the last patients they treated. In fact, they generally seemed to do excellent work. Patients came in sick or hurt, and the women helped them get better, and they went they went on with their lives. Except ..."

Riley had arrived at her gate and sat down in the waiting area.

"Except what?"

"Well, there's this one guy. Lance Miller. He'd had a heart attack about a year and a half ago at the age of forty-five. Hallie Stillians was treating him at Reliance Rehabilitation Center in Seattle. He took sick while he was under her care and complained to the staff about it. He got better, but it sounded kind of suspicious to me."

Riley's interest was piqued. It certainly sounded suspicious to her as well.

"Could you give him a call and get some specifics?" she asked.

Roff grunted a little.

"Well, I'm afraid this interviewing-by-phone thing might be a little beyond my capacities. Those other calls I made earlier were just for cold hard information. Asking this guy questions about his illness would involve actually relating to another human being. I just don't deal with people well. I might mess that up really bad."

Riley laughed.

"I see your point," she said. "I'll be in Seattle this afternoon. Could you just call him and set up an appointment for me to visit him?"

"Sure. Should I have someone meet you at the airport?"

"No, I'll rent a car. I'm not going to contact any other local FBI personnel just yet."

Roff let out an approving chuckle.

"Say no more. If anybody asks, I don't even know you're there. In fact, I've never even heard of you. I'll just say, 'Agent Riley

Who'?"

They ended the call just in time for Riley to board her plane.

*

Six hours later, Riley got off the plane in Seattle and rented a car. As she drove, she listened to GPS directions to Lance Miller's house. It was early afternoon in Seattle, but it seemed much later, because the jet lag was hitting Riley harder than usual.

Riley wondered why she felt that way as she neared Miller's neighborhood. She traveled almost constantly and normally had little trouble adjusting. What was different about today?

It was only partially cloudy today, and the sun was shining. She drove by a public park where people were walking and children were playing, taking eager advantage of the break in the rainy weather. The sight of people enjoying themselves together seemed to answer her question.

I'm lonely, she thought.

Her family was all the way on the other side of the country, and she seemed unable to devote herself to them as she should. Her usual colleagues had turned their backs on her—including Bill. And now she had exactly two allies left in the world.

One was a geek who'd simply told her outright ...

"I just don't deal with people well."

And the other was a vicious killer obsessed with chains.

What did that say about her?

She still wasn't wearing the gold chain that Shane Hatcher had given her. But she was carrying it in her bag. She wasn't sure just why, except that there seemed to be little else in the world to make her feel grounded among her fellow human beings.

It seemed appropriate that she was now taking directions from a computerized female voice.

Lance Miller's house was in an upper-middle-class neighborhood bordering on Seattle's University District. She parked in front of a large but cozy craftsman bungalow that was painted an attractive shade of blue. It was surrounded on all sides by well-kept plants and bushes. She climbed the steep stone steps up to the porch and rang the doorbell.

A handsome man with sandy hair and a freckled complexion answered the door. Riley showed him her badge, introduced herself, and asked if she was speaking with Lance Miller.

"Oh, no, I'm Gary," the man said, shaking Riley's hand with a smile. "But Lance is expecting you."

Gary led Riley into the living room, where a lean, scholarly-looking man with round glasses and a closely-cropped beard rose up from his chair.

"I'm Lance," he said. "Please have a seat. Make yourself comfortable."

Riley sat down and quickly scanned the house and its two occupants. The men both wore wedding rings and were obviously married to each other. The living room was tastefully decorated without being the least bit ostentatious. Riley guessed that both men were reasonably successful professionals, perhaps university professors.

"I'll leave you two to talk," Gary said, then went upstairs.

Lance sat down and leaned toward Riley.

"The man who called me said you were investigating some poisonings," he said. "Does this have anything to do with the awful thing that happened to Amanda Somers? There seems to be some confusion about how she died—whether it was suicide or murder. It was very sad."

"Yes, it was," Riley said. She decided not to say that Somers' death was most definitely a murder and not a suicide.

She said, "I understand that you spent some time at Reliance Rehabilitation Center about a year and a half ago."

Lance shuddered.

"That was a strange experience."

"You complained to the staff, I'm told."

"Oh, yes. I was being poisoned. I'm still quite sure of it."

Riley took out her notepad and started to take notes.

"I hear that you were in the care of a freelance healthcare worker named Hallie Stillians."

Riley was a bit surprised by the smile that crossed Lance's face.

"Yes, Hallie. Have you met her? An odd creature, not quite of this world, but so very sweet. I don't know how I would have pulled through it all without her."

It was hardly the response that Riley had expected—not if she was right about Hallie Stillians being one of the poisoner's identities.

"Tell me all about what happened," Riley said.

Lance stroked his beard as he remembered.

"Well, I had a heart attack. I was only forty-six, but I ought to have seen it coming. My father died from heart disease at an early age, and so did his father. It was a genetic thing, and I was just a ticking bomb. I should have taken better precautions. I don't feel quite so—invincible anymore."

He stopped to think for a moment.

"I had surgery at South Hills Hospital, and it left me terribly weak and feeble. So I went to Reliance Rehab, and Hallie started working with me right away, doing physical rehab. We took an immediate liking to one another. She was so—quaint, I guess. Not really old, but somehow she seemed to belong to an earlier time. And she made the most delicious tea."

Lance winced sharply.

"But after little more than a day, I got awfully sick—nausea and vomiting, terrible pain in the palms of my hand and the soles of my feet. And I got ... well, very confused and disoriented. To tell the truth, I don't think I was quite in my right mind. I babbled a lot. I'm afraid I might have said some rather embarrassing things."

Thallium poisoning, Riley realized.

So far, what Lance was telling her was consistent with the other killings.

"How did Hallie deal with all this?" Riley asked.

"Oh, I don't think I've ever known a more empathetic or caring human being in my life. I swear, she was so concerned about me, she seemed to get sick herself. She actually said she was sick. And she said some rather odd things ..."

His voice drifted off.

"What did she say?" Riley said.

"She kept saying, 'It's this world. It's this awful world. It makes us all sick. It makes me sick too.' Well, I suppose that's true in a way. Most of us are pretty hardened and cynical, and we don't really think about what a hard world this is for so many people. Hallie was especially sensitive that way."

He paused again.

"Anyway, I was sure that I was being poisoned. And Hallie seemed to be sure of it too. I tried to complain to the staff about it. But they wouldn't believe it. I swear, they were some of the iciest people I ever met. Especially the head nurse, Edith Cooper. 'Nurse Ratched,' I used to call her, but Hallie didn't get it. *One Flew Over the Cuckoo's Nest,* you know."

Riley had caught the reference to the cold-hearted nurse of literary and movie fame.

Lance continued his story.

"After about a day and a half of this, I told Hallie I was afraid I was going to die. Hallie squeezed my hand and said, 'You don't deserve this. This is all a mistake. You don't deserve to suffer and die. You're special. I'm going to make sure you get through this. You just wait and see.'"

"What did she do then?" Riley asked.

"Well, it was less *what* she did than *how* she did it. She was just so gentle and caring. She rubbed the places where I hurt most, my feet and my hands. And she kept making more tea—a different recipe from before, something really delicious and soothing. She'd even sing to me—a really pretty lullaby, I can remember just a bit of it …"

Lance closed his eyes and sang in a pleasant voice.

You pine away
From day to day
Too sad to laugh, too sad to play.

He opened his eyes again.

"I got better pretty quickly, and Hallie said she felt better too. She said something I didn't really understand. 'It was an angel who made us both sick, but she changed her mind, because we're both good. And now we're going to be fine.'"

He smiled and added, "The truth is, I more than half think that Hallie's a bit of an angel herself."

Then he shrugged slightly.

"She finished my rehab work and I came home, perfectly healthy."

Lance stared off into space for a moment, lost in memory. Then he looked at Riley again.

"Is there anything else I can tell you?"

Riley felt a confusing surge of emotions. She couldn't bring himself to tell Lance that the woman he'd liked so much had almost certainly tried to kill him.

"No, you've been a great help," Riley said. "Thank you for your time."

When she left the house, she knew where she had to go next. Surely somebody else at that clinic had their own stories to tell about the woman who called herself Hallie Stillians.

Maybe I'll find out the truth at last, she thought as she started to drive.

CHAPTER THIRTY SIX

Riley was overcome by an eerie feeling the moment she walked into Reliance Rehab. There was something positively inhospitable about the place. For one thing, the temperature seemed unusually chilly.

But Riley sensed that there was something else in the air.

It's more than the temperature that's cold in here, she thought.

She showed her badge to a frowning and sullen receptionist and asked to see the head nurse.

As the receptionist led Riley through the clinic, Riley's discomfort grew. Nobody in the building was smiling. Everyone looked grim, and whenever someone glanced at Riley, she felt positively unwelcome.

She remembered something that Lance had said.

"I swear, they were some of the iciest people I ever met."

When they got to the head nurse's office, the receptionist knocked on the door.

A voice inside called out, "Who is it?"

"An FBI agent," the receptionist called back. "She's here to ask some questions."

Riley heard some scuffling inside the office. Then the door opened, and a rather agitated-looking woman appeared. She had a tight, pinched-looking face, and her smile seemed forced.

"Can I help you?" she said, sounding a little breathless.

Riley showed her badge again.

"Special Agent Riley Paige, FBI," she said.

"Well, this must be something serious, indeed," the woman said uneasily. "Come on in."

Riley went into the office and sat down. The woman sat down at her desk.

"I'm Edith Cooper, and I run things around here. What can I do for you? What do you want to know?"

Riley immediately noticed something odd about the woman's speech. She was talking very fast. And her eyes seemed rather glazed.

"I'm here about a series of poisonings," Riley said. "Perhaps you've read about them."

Words came tumbling out of the woman's mouth nervously.

"Oh, yes, absolutely. I'm so glad nothing like that ever happened here. But why are you interested in talking to me?"

Riley studied Edith Cooper's face for a moment, trying to make out what might be wrong with her.

"I'd like to ask you a few questions about a freelance healthcare worker who worked here. Hallie Stillians is her name."

"Oh, yes, Hallie. The patients liked her, but I'm afraid the staff didn't. We stopped hiring her about a year and a half ago."

Riley was taking notes now.

"Was that about the time she treated a patient named Lance Miller?" she asked.

Cooper's faced twitched.

"Yes, I believe it was," she said. "That man needed help—the kind we couldn't give him here."

"What do you mean?"

Cooper drummed her fingers on the desk.

"Well, he kept saying he was being poisoned, and he wasn't, it was simply impossible. It was a classic case of paranoid schizophrenia."

Riley was startled. After her visit to Lance Miller, she was sure of one thing—he wasn't the least bit paranoid.

Cooper continued, "I think Hallie was encouraging his delusions. We can't have that kind of behavior, not in this kind of place. We never had her back to work here again."

Cooper stared at Riley for a moment.

"But what does that have to do with—?"

Then her beady eyes sharpened.

"Do you suspect Hallie Stillians? Well, I wouldn't be surprised. I knew there was something wrong with that woman from the start. But how did she do it?"

"We haven't come to any conclusions yet," Riley said.

"Haven't you? Well, I hope you come to some conclusions soon. I think you'd better. There's a killer still out there, and someone else might die, it's almost certain. Haven't you arrested Hallie Stillians?"

Riley said nothing, just held Cooper's gaze.

Cooper said, "From what I've read, it sounds as if the poison that was used was thallium. Is that right?"

Riley still said nothing.

Cooper was certainly behaving in a suspicious manner.

There's something very strange about her, she kept thinking.

Cooper kept right on talking.

"I'm asking if it's thallium because, you know, it's called 'the poisoner's poison,' but of course I have no way of knowing. Was it thallium? And how was it administered? Was it pure thallium? Well, if I were a killer, I don't suppose I would use pure thallium. I'd mix it up with something, partly to avoid detection, partly to disguise the symptoms. I'm no expert, of course. I have no idea."

She stopped talking and stared back at Riley.

"Agent Paige, I get the feeling there's something you're not telling me," she said.

Her tone was defensive now, and just a bit angry.

"Am I a suspect? Because that would be perfectly absurd."

Again, Riley said nothing.

Cooper scowled, and her eyebrows tightened together.

"I think this interview is over," she said. "If you have any other questions, I'd suggest you ask my lawyer."

She handed Riley her lawyer's business card.

"Of course," Riley said. "Thank you for your time. I'll show myself out."

When Riley stepped outside into the cool fresh air, she almost gasped with relief. The atmosphere inside the clinic had felt positively suffocating.

She got into her car. Before she started the engine, she called Van Roff.

"Mr. Roff, I'd like you to find anything you can about the head nurse at Reliance Rehab. Her name is Edith Cooper."

Riley heard a clattering of keys.

After a few seconds, Roff said, "Wow. That clinic sure has a colorful reputation. I'm talking about malpractice suits all over the place. It's almost as if—"

Riley heard the sound of a door shutting.

"Oh, shit," Roff whispered. "We're busted."

She heard a familiar voice ask, "Is that Agent Paige?"

Riley felt a jolt of alarm. The voice was Sean Rigby's. He had obviously walked into Roff's office unannounced. Roff had probably put their call on speakerphone, so Rigby had immediately recognized her voice.

Rigby said, "Agent Paige, this is an interesting surprise. How are things back at Quantico?"

Riley gulped. She had to be careful what to say. She wasn't concerned about herself so much as Roff. She knew it wouldn't do to lie about her whereabouts.

"Actually, I'm in Seattle," she said.

"Seattle! I don't remember receiving any notice about that."

"This isn't an official trip."

Rigby let out an ironic chuckle.

"Oh. A pleasure trip, eh? Well. I'm glad you like our city so much. Enjoy your stay."

The call ended. Riley sat in the car and stared ahead.

He didn't believe me for a second, Riley thought.

And now Van Roff was likely to get the worst of it.

But then, Rigby hadn't seemed to mind that she was back on his turf again. She wondered if Rigby wasn't completely sure that the poisoning case was closed.

After a few minutes, her phone rang again. It was Van Roff, speaking in an agitated whisper. He obviously wasn't on speakerphone this time.

"Hey, I'm sorry about that. He just walked in."

"It's OK," Riley said. "I just hope you're not in trouble."

"I hope not too. With Rigby, it's sometimes hard to tell. Anyway, as soon as you left, he asked me what I was doing, and I said I was looking into Reliance Rehab and its director. He seemed interested. I guess he wants to follow up on it. That's a good thing, right?"

Riley didn't reply. The truth was, she didn't know. Edith Cooper certainly needed to be investigated. But could Riley trust the local field office to handle it properly? She had her doubts.

"I'll try to keep you in the loop," Roff said.

"Maybe it's best if you don't. For your sake, I mean."

"Well, let's just see how things work out."

They ended the call. Riley drove to the hotel where she and Bill had been staying and checked back in.

*

Later that evening, Riley was sitting in the hotel bar drinking alone. If Bill had come with her, she wouldn't feel so terribly isolated.

She turned the day's events over in her mind, trying to make sense of them.

Before her visit to Reliance Rehab, it had seemed perfectly obvious that a woman who'd called herself Hallie Stillians had killed Cody Woods. But after her weird interview with Edith Cooper, Riley didn't know what to think.

Cooper was certainly hiding something, but what?

Was it possible that she was at least linked to the killer in some way?

Riley had spent part of the afternoon doing research of her own online. Roff was right, Edith Cooper and her center had been sued for malpractice multiple times. Reliance Rehab had almost been shut down for good late last year.

But did that make Edith Cooper a murderer—or even an accomplice to murder?

She finished her drink and was about to go to the bar to get another when her phone buzzed. She shuddered when she saw the name of the caller. But she answered anyway.

"Agent Paige? Chief Rigby here. I thought you'd be interested in hearing some good news. We apprehended our poisoner just a little while ago. She's a clinic director named Edith Cooper."

Then he added in a knowing tone, "Perhaps you've heard of her."

Riley stifled a sigh. Of course he'd figured out right away that Riley was behind Roff's research on Cooper.

"What about Solange Landis?" Riley asked.

"She's still in custody. We've still got her dead to rights for forging documents. But she's not our killer, after all. Edith Cooper definitely looks guilty. We got a warrant to search her clinic, and Havens and Wingert found some suspicious white powder in her desk drawer. Our lab people haven't reported what it is yet, but it's surely poison of some kind."

Riley felt a jolt of realization.

Oh my God! Cocaine!

A poison of a different kind, but not what they had been looking for.

Cocaine use would explain everything that was strange about Edith Cooper. And judging from the weird behavior of her staff, the whole clinic was probably riddled with drug users. It was no wonder that Reliance Rehab had been sued for multiple cases of malpractice. The medical care they gave was probably barely competent at best.

Riley said, "Chief Rigby, I'm not sure that—"

She stopped in mid-sentence.

"Not sure that what, Agent Paige?"

Riley again reminded herself to be careful what she said, for Van Roff's sake. The lab would find out soon enough that Cooper's powder wasn't thallium. Meanwhile it was just as well that Cooper was in custody.

"Nothing," she said. "Congratulations."

Rigby laughed cryptically.

"I've got a funny feeling that congratulations are due to you as well. No need to be modest, I know you had something to do with this. And I'll put in a good word for you at Quantico. We'll be popping champagne bottles here pretty soon. I'll let you know when, and I hope you'll join us in celebrating. Meanwhile, you deserve a little R&R. Enjoy our lovely city."

He abruptly ended the call.

Riley felt despair creeping up inside her.

I've accomplished precisely nothing today, she thought.

A murderer was still at large, and she was powerless to do anything about it.

She wanted another drink—wanted it too badly.

She decided against it.

She left the bar and walked out into the dim, gray evening, surrounded by the thick Seattle mist. Even out of doors, she felt strangely claustrophobic, as if the world was closing in around her.

As if I were bound hand and foot, she thought.

One thing seemed certain—it was time to give up and go home.

There was simply nothing more she could do.

But just as she turned to walk back to the hotel, she saw a familiar figure approaching her through the mist.

CHAPTER THIRTY SEVEN

Riley felt a rush of adrenaline as the man came toward her.

She knew that it was a fight-or-flight response. Her every animal instinct told her that danger was nearing and her body should prepare for combat.

Or run away.

And yet she stood frozen in her spot, unable to even breathe.

In another moment, Shane Hatcher stood within arm's length, fully visible in the swirling mist. This was just the second time she had seen him in person since his escape from Sing Sing. His presence here was much more intimidating than it had been when they met within the prison walls.

Riley tried to remind herself that she was in no physical danger from this man. But deep down, her whole body knew that Shane Hatcher was the most dangerous man she'd ever met—and possibly the most brilliant.

Shane looked her up and down, as if sniffing out her alarm.

"Relax," he said with a sinister smile. "If I wanted to kill you, you'd be dead already. I'm just making good on that little favor we discussed."

His words weren't the least bit comforting. Even so, Riley started to breathe again.

Hatcher held out his hand. He had a gold chain bracelet on his wrist.

"You're not wearing yours," he said.

"I'll never wear it."

He smiled knowingly.

"You've got it with you."

Riley didn't reply. She knew it was pointless to lie.

"Walk with me," Hatcher said.

Neither of them spoke for a few moments as they walked along the street together. Riley heard footsteps and then braced herself as another pedestrian passed by them.

Could that person see them clearly? If so, did it matter?

Who could possibly guess that one was a renegade FBI agent and the other a criminal mastermind who had escaped from a maximum security prison?

The passerby went on his way, apparently oblivious to anything odd about the other pedestrians out in the fog.

"I hear there's been another arrest," Hatcher said.

Riley nodded silently.

"And you still don't think they've got the real Angel of Death."

Riley was startled that he used that term.

"I *know* it," Riley said. "I interviewed that woman. She's a mess and probably deserves being charged and locked up. But she's definitely not the poisoner that I'm looking for.

"And so the real assassin will surely strike again."

"Yes. She won't stop until I stop her."

They were both quiet again for a moment, then Hatcher said, "You've been working with Van Roff, haven't you?"

"How do you know?"

Shane let out a purr of a chuckle.

"I've done my research. Roff seems to be the smartest guy in the Seattle field office. And he doesn't give a damn about the rules. I knew that you'd just naturally hook up with him sooner or later. It was inevitable. I'd like to meet him one of these days. Perhaps I will."

Once again, Riley felt herself being drawn into an alliance with Hatcher. But she knew from experience that he really could help her.

She said, "Van Roff found that three therapists disappeared, one after each of the victims died. They had different names and different addresses, but the addresses were all mail services."

Hatcher nodded as he walked.

"So they're all the same person," he said.

"I'm sure of it," Riley said. "But after every disappearance, she comes back as someone else. We have no way to identify whoever she's masquerading as now. I've seen photos of women that could be her, but she's something of a chameleon."

Hatcher stood thinking for a moment.

"Tell Roff to search to find out how often that has happened— Angels of Death who've struck over the years. We're looking for nurses who disappeared suddenly when a patient died. Just before or after."

"That's a complicated search," Riley said.

"Not for Van Roff. And remind him to look for addresses that are mail services rather than houses or apartments. Tell him to follow the trail back to the beginning. He'll know when he's really found her."

They walked together in silence for a moment.

"You're closer than you think," Hatcher finally said. "And she knows it."

There was something different about his tone now.

Did Riley detect a trace of worry?

Then he said, "When it comes time to make an arrest, send someone else. Don't go yourself."

"Why not?"

Hatcher said nothing for a few seconds.

"Consider the most terrible Angel of Death of them all—Josef Mengele."

Riley shuddered. Did Hatcher know that she and Solange Landis had discussed Mengele?

No, he couldn't possibly, Riley thought.

It was simply another uncanny, uncomfortable example of Hatcher thinking along lines that she'd been considering too.

"What about him?" Riley asked.

"He was still doing his horrible work at Auschwitz in 1944 when he knew for certain that Germany was losing the war, that the Red Army was on its way. What did he do then? Did he slacken in his atrocities? No, he accelerated them, became more vicious and sadistic than ever. Angels of Death are like that. When they feel threatened, they become all the more determined. They change their methods, become more deadly. They want to make sure the job gets done. This woman is no different."

They walked in silence for a moment.

"Send someone else," Hatcher said again. "Whoever makes that arrest isn't likely to survive."

Their footsteps continued to echo through the mist.

"Just keep walking," Hatcher finally said. "Don't bother to look back."

Hatcher stopped and Riley continued on.

After she'd gone about ten more feet, she couldn't resist anymore.

She turned to look.

She saw absolutely no one in the mist.

But she heard Hatcher's voice echoing, seemingly from nowhere.

"Just keep one thing in mind. Everything happens for no reason."

Then she heard a burst of vanishing laughter.

*

As Riley came through the entrance into the lobby, she spotted a familiar figure standing at the desk talking to the clerk.

This one didn't give her chills.

"Bill!" she called out with a gasp.

Bill turned to see her and smiled.

Riley rushed toward him and threw her arms around him, almost weeping for joy.

They were back.

CHAPTER THIRTY EIGHT

It was night now in Seattle, and Riley knew they needed to enlist Van Roff's help again. She and Bill went up to her hotel room to call the technical wizard, and a few minutes later they had him on the speakerphone.

"I'm at home," Roff said. "So it's easier to talk now."

"But I need you to do a pretty complicated search right now," Riley replied. She felt an urgency about catching up with this killer before someone else died.

He laughed. "That's not a problem. I'm well connected right here."

"Agent Jeffreys is here with me. We need you to track a new lead."

Roff greeted Bill cheerfully, then added, "I heard the office gang brought in Edith Cooper. She wasn't the one?"

"Edith Cooper was a good catch. Just not the one we're looking for."

"Damn. I thought we had your villain. But I'm always intrigued by a new hunt. So what do we do now?"

Riley gave him the new instructions that she and Hatcher had discussed.

"Very interesting. I'll get right on this. But how will I know when I've found what I'm looking for?"

Riley remembered what Hatcher had said.

"He'll know when he's really found her."

"Don't worry," Riley said. "You'll know."

The call ended, and Riley and Bill just looked at each other for a moment. Riley could hardly get over her relief at seeing him.

"What made you decide to come?" Riley asked.

Bill looked away from her.

"Meredith told me you'd been in touch with Hatcher. I figured he must be here in Seattle. Is he?"

Riley didn't reply.

"OK, so you can't talk about it. But I knew I'd better get here right away."

Riley smiled.

"So you could rescue me from Hatcher?" she said.

Bill smiled back.

"You never need rescuing," he said. "But it really hit me—you had nobody on your side at all except an escaped convict. Not to

189

mention, I'm the one that dragged you into this case to begin with. You did it for me. So, it wasn't right. I couldn't let that slide. I'm your partner. I'm supposed to stick by you."

Riley squeezed his hand.

"Thanks," she said. "But I'm afraid *you'll* be in trouble now."

Bill squeezed her hand back and smiled.

"Trouble is what we do—and we'll always do it together."

They sat in comfortable silence for a few minutes. Then something started to nag at Riley's mind.

"Bill, Hatcher said something to me that I don't understand. He said, 'Everything happens for no reason.' What do you think he meant?"

Bill shook his head. "If you don't know, I sure don't."

Riley sat thinking about it. It was obvious play on that old clichéd saying …

"Everything happens for a reason."

Riley winced. She hated that saying. People always said it when something terrible had happened, and it was supposed to give comfort, but it never did. Riley always thought it was glib and shallow—and even downright insensitive.

But Riley had never told anyone that she felt that way.

She felt an uncanny shiver.

Once again, Hatcher seemed to have touched a uniquely personal chord.

But why had he said that just now?

For no reason, I guess, she thought with an ironic smile.

Riley's phone buzzed. It was Van Roff again. Riley put him on speakerphone.

"Bingo," Van Roff said. "I've *really* got something this time."

Riley and Bill glanced at each other in expectation.

"What is it?" Riley asked breathlessly.

"I've got a trail of names—all female healthcare workers who used mail service addresses, and who disappeared shortly after a patient died. They all paid for their mail services in cash—except for the very first one, whose name was Alicia Carswell."

Riley felt a tingle of excitement.

Her real name! she realized.

Roff continued, "She used a credit card, so it was easy to find out more about her. I was able to bring up her Social Security number and a driver's license. Her picture looks a lot like the others."

"What's the address on the license?" Bill asked.

Roff recited the address and Bill jotted it down.

"I'm not sure it's current, though," Roff said. "It's an old license, expired for years. It looks like she's been off the grid for a long time."

"It's all we've got," Bill said.

"Thanks," Riley said.

They ended the call, and Riley and Bill headed straight for her rented car.

*

Riley and Bill drove through the dark, mist-shrouded city to the address that Roff had given them. It was a small attractive, old-fashioned house in a working-class neighborhood. The yard was overgrown, and the white picket fence was in disrepair. There wasn't a single light on inside.

"Does anybody still live here?" Riley said as she parked the car.

"Let's go see," Bill said.

They got out of the car, walked up to the front door, and knocked.

No one answered.

Riley looked at Bill for an indecisive moment.

Then she turned the doorknob.

The door swung open easily and they walked on in. Riley found a light switch near the door and flipped it on.

It was as though she'd stepped into a living room from an earlier time.

"It looks like the fifties in here," Bill commented.

The furniture was colorful, early modern, and very clean, although it looked well used. Family portraits and images of cheerful scenes hung on the walls. Unlike the outside of the house, everything here was in good repair and in its proper place.

Somebody still lived here, all right.

Riley and Bill split up. Bill headed for a bedroom and Riley to the kitchen. The kitchen was even more picturesque than the living room. Whoever lived here had gone to a great deal of trouble to keep this place frozen in time.

Perhaps it was a happier time, Riley thought.

But in her gut, Riley sensed that things weren't at all what they seemed. As she glanced around, her eyes fell on a row of colorful, old-fashioned kitchen canisters that were labeled with fancy lettering—coffee, tea, sugar, flour …

Riley opened up the tin that was labeled coffee.

It contained a white crystalline substance.

"Bill, you'd better get in here," Riley called out.

Bill was with her in a second. Riley showed him the contents of the canister.

"This isn't coffee," Riley said. "I've got a hunch it's thallium."

"Jesus," Bill murmured. "This kitchen doubles as a lab for preparing poisons."

Riley turned and saw a notepad on the Formica table. The sheets of paper were prettily decorated with images of flowers. Neatly written on the top sheet was "Brio 15."

Riley showed it to Bill.

"What do you think this is?" she said.

"An address, maybe?" Bill replied.

Riley whipped out her cell phone and called Van Roff.

"Hey, where are you?" he asked.

"We're at Alicia Carswell's house," Riley said. "She lives here, all right. We found a note in her kitchen. Does 'Brio 15' sound like an address to you?"

"I know my city well," Roff said. "I don't think that's a public street. Lemme check."

Riley heard a flurry of computer keys.

"Brio 15 is a cottage on a private road in a retirement community. And it's really close to where you are. I'll send directions to your phone."

"And send a backup team to the address," Bill said. "We don't want to take any chances with this one."

Riley looked out the kitchen door and noticed the front door still standing open.

It hadn't been locked when they'd come in.

She left in a hurry, Riley realized.

"Hurry up," she told Roff. "I've got a feeling we don't have a minute to lose."

CHAPTER THIRTY NINE

The lane called Brio wound among a scattering of small attractive cottages. The street was quiet, with lights on in most of the cottages along the way but no outside activity. In spite of the peaceful scene, Riley was sure that one of these picturesque little places was hiding a deadly killer.

Bill pulled the car up to number 15 and parked. When he turned off the engine, everything around them was quiet. But Riley felt a renewed surge of alarm. She remembered the haste with which the woman seemed to have left her home.

Something bad is going on in there, she thought.

She was glad that an FBI backup team was on its way, but she didn't have time to wait for them. She and Bill got out of the car and trotted toward the cottage. When they reached the front door, Bill was about to knock and call out.

Riley stopped his hand and held her finger to her lips, silencing him.

Signaling Bill to follow her, she moved to the right and peeked in a wide window. She saw a well-lighted living room, but no one inside. Then they moved toward the windows on the other side of the door. When they looked through those, Bill let out an audible gasp.

"What the hell!" he whispered.

Riley couldn't believe her eyes.

A nightmarish, bug-like figure was lurking near an elderly man who lay unconscious on a bed. It was a woman wearing a white laboratory coat, heavy elbow-length gloves, goggles, and a mask with an oxygen canister. She was taking a glass vial out of a small portable safe.

"We're out of time," Riley said. "Let's get in there."

They tried the front door and found it locked. Riley moved out of Bill's way as he stepped back and got into position to open it. He brought his foot up, throwing his weight into a kick just below the lock.

That's all it took. The door flew open and Riley darted inside.

The figure was now hovering over the unconscious man.

She was holding an upturned eyedropper over him.

She turned and looked at Riley and Bill, barely seeming surprised.

Muffled sounds came through the mask, and Riley realized that the ghastly creature was singing. She remembered the tune and the words from her visit to Lance Miller ...

You pine away
From day to day
Too sad to laugh, too sad to play.

Riley drew her weapon.
"Stop right there," she ordered.
The woman just stared at her through those goggles, still singing in that muffled voice.

No need to weep,
Dream long and deep.
Give yourself to slumber's sweep.

Ignoring Riley and Bill, the woman lowered the eyedropper toward the man's face.

With a cry of fury, Bill charged the killer. He grabbed the wrist of the hand that held the eyedropper. The woman let out a screech and fought him.

As they thrashed back and forth, Riley holstered her weapon and looked for an opening to help Bill subdue the madwoman.

The woman's mask and goggles flew off in the struggle, and she staggered backward. Suddenly, liquid spurted from the eyedropper.

Grinning horribly, the woman turned toward Riley.

She held up the eyedropper.

"Empty!" she cried. "And I'd gone to so much trouble! And I had Mr. Auslander all tucked in and sedated and ready. Such a shame."

Still smiling, she pointed to Bill's hand.

"There's no saving you, though," she said.

Bill looked at his hand, glistening with drops of the clear liquid that had spurted from the eyedropper. He was about to brush it off with his other hand.

"Don't touch it!" Riley said.

Bill looked at her with surprise.

"What is it?" Bill said.

"I've got no idea. Just don't touch it."

The woman sat down in a chair and laughed quietly. She touched her own face and felt the liquid that had splashed there too.

Riley recognized her face from the photos she'd seen of the poisoner's aliases.

Yes, this was the one. This was the healthcare worker responsible for her patients' deaths.

"But what about me?" she said in a strange, delirious voice. "I'm poisoned too. Oh, but don't worry. *I* can't die. Esther Thornton—the woman you see—*she'll* pass away. So did Judy Brubaker and Hallie Stillians and a half dozen others. But not *me*. Don't you know what I am? Can't you see my black wings?"

She sang some more.

Far from home,
So far from home—
This little baby's far from home.

She touched her arms, gazing at them sadly.

"But these wings are withering. I must cocoon myself, spin black silk, grow new wings. I'll return. Angels never die."

She sat humming and swaying now.

She closed her eyes and seemed to drift out of consciousness.

Then she held completely still and fell silent.

Catatonic, Riley realized.

In her escalating madness, the woman had put herself in a catatonic state.

The man in the bed was groaning now. Although he'd obviously been sedated, the uproar had wakened him. He sat up slowly and rubbed his eyes.

"Esther?" he said in a weak voice.

Then he saw Riley and Bill.

"What's going on?"

"Stay right where you are," Riley said sharply. "Don't move. Don't anybody move."

Everybody in the room was frozen for a moment.

"What do we do?" Bill asked.

"I know who we need to ask," Riley said.

She got out her cell phone and dialed Prisha Shankar's home number. She got a machine message. Riley's voice was shaking.

"Dr. Shankar, please pick up. This is Agent Riley Paige. This is an emergency. This is a real life and death—"

She heard Prisha Shankar's voice.

"Hello."

Relieved, Riley put the phone on speakerphone.

"Dr. Shankar, my partner and I have just found the murderer. We stopped her in the act. She's dressed in goggles and a mask and has huge gloves on. She had a vial and an eyedropper. We kept her from dropping the liquid on her intended victim, but some splashed on her face and my partner's hand. What should we do?"

There was a moment of silence.

"Goggles, mask, gloves?" Shankar finally said.

"That's right."

"Good God," Shankar said.

Riley heard the sound of vehicles approaching.

"Our backup agents have arrived," Riley said.

"Don't let them in!" Shankar shouted. "Don't let anybody in!"

"Why not?" Riley asked.

Shankar sounded breathless with alarm.

"Keep them out. It's not safe in there."

"But my partner and I—"

"Your *partner's* not safe. He's dangerous. To *them*."

CHAPTER FORTY

A car screeched to a halt outside and footsteps approached the broken cottage door. Riley rushed to the door and pulled it shut. She shoved a chair under the door handle.

"This is the FBI," called a voice from outside. "Open up."

"Listen to me!" Riley screamed. "Don't come in! This is Riley Paige, FBI from Quantico. We have been exposed to a toxic substance here. My partner and I are handling the situation. You must not come inside."

A short silence fell.

"What should we do?" the voice outside asked.

"Just wait," Riley said.

Riley and Bill stared at the telephone.

"Talk to us," Riley said.

"Agents Paige and Jeffreys, I want you to listen to me carefully. I believe that the chemical your partner was exposed to is dimethylmercury. It is extremely, unspeakably dangerous, and it can even pass through most protective clothing. By now there might be vapor in the air, and even that can be deadly."

Bill's eyes widened with horror and disbelief.

"But I feel OK," Bill said. "I don't feel any pain or—"

Shankar interrupted. "Symptoms don't occur for months. But if it has enough time to really get into one's system, death is inevitable."

Riley and Bill stared at each other in shock.

"What now?" Riley asked.

"I'm sending a hazmat team. They'll be there in minutes. When they get there, let them inside."

Hazmat—hazardous materials, Riley realized.

She had never been involved in a hazmat situation before.

"Now follow my directions," Shankar said. "Take Bill to the bathroom, and wash his exposed hand with soap and water for fifteen solid minutes. Make sure to use plenty of water."

Riley was struggling against panic now.

"But if it's as dangerous as you say—"

"This is just to get started. Begin doing this right now. Keep the phone with you on speakerphone. I'll stay on the line."

With the phone in hand, Riley led Bill to the bathroom and started the faucet. Bill put his shaking hands under the water and started to scrub the exposed area. Riley stood by his side, feeling utterly helpless.

"Isn't there anything I can do?" she asked Shankar.

"Just wait."

After a couple of minutes, Riley heard a loud pounding on the front door.

"Someone's outside," Riley told Shankar.

"It's the hazmat team," Shankar said. "Go let them in."

Riley hurried to the front door and removed the chair that was blocking it. The door opened to reveal five hazmat workers, all of them grotesquely clad in bulky bodysuits with huge clear plastic masks. Two of them had yellow tanks on their backs.

The sight was spine-chilling, but she knew that these grotesque figures were on her side.

With a deep sense of gratitude, Riley stepped aside and the figures lumbered inside.

"Where is the substance?" one worker asked in a muffled voice.

Riley pointed to the bottle and dropper that had fallen on the floor.

One of the workers gingerly picked up the bottle and the dropper and put it into a silvery bag. Two of others began to spray the room with the contents of the yellow tanks.

"What should I do?" Riley said.

"Go into the bathroom. Undress. Shower. Keep showering and scrubbing yourself all over until we tell you to stop."

Riley went into the bathroom, took off her clothes, got into the shower, and turned on the water. As she turned around, she saw the silhouette of one of the workers standing on the other side of the shower curtain.

She had no idea whether the figure was a man or a woman. But she knew better than to worry about a thing like that now.

She scrubbed herself all over for what seemed like forever, all the while wondering what was going on just outside.

Finally the figure on the other side of the curtain said, "That's enough. Come on out."

Riley turned off the shower and stepped naked out of the stall. Bill was still there, turned away from her. Another worker was standing beside him.

The worker who had been just outside the curtain was holding gray pajamas and a pair of slippers.

"Get into these," the worker told Riley.

The voice sounded like a woman.

Riley dried herself and put on the pajamas and slippers.

"Your turn," the other worker said to Bill, holding out another set of pajamas.

Bill began to disrobe as the worker led Riley out of the bathroom.

The poisoner was still sitting there, completely unresponsive. The elderly man was sitting on the edge of the bed, looking almost equally stunned.

"What about them?" Riley asked the worker.

"They'll get showers too," the worker said. "Come with me."

The figure led Riley outside toward a waiting emergency vehicle.

"But what about my partner?" Riley asked. "Is he going to be all right?"

The woman didn't reply as Riley climbed into the back of the vehicle.

"What about my partner?" Riley asked again.

"I don't know," the woman said.

She climbed in beside Riley and closed the door.

CHAPTER FORTY ONE

Later that night, Riley sat in her hospital bed for what seemed like forever. A nurse had drawn blood quite some time ago, and Riley was waiting for lab results.

She had frantically asked about Bill over and over again, but no one would tell her anything. The only thing she knew for certain was that Dr. Prisha Shankar had taken charge of both her and Bill. At least that offered Riley some comfort. She felt sure that both of them were in good hands.

At last, a hand pushed aside the curtain beside Riley's. Dr. Shankar was holding a clipboard.

"I've got good news," she said. "We just did a complete heavy metals panel, and you don't have any dimethylmercury in your system. You can go home now."

"But what about my partner?" Riley asked.

Shankar smiled.

"You can ask him."

Bill stepped through the curtain, smiling rather weakly.

Riley gasped from sheer relief.

"Bill! Are you all right?"

Bill shrugged.

"It looks like I'm going to be," he said.

Dr. Shankar explained.

"He was contaminated, and he does have dimethylmercury in his system. Like I told you, symptoms don't appear for months. That was probably one of the reasons the poisoner finally decided to use dimethylmercury. The time gap would have made it almost impossible to trace the poisonings back to her."

Shankar patted Bill on the back.

"He'll need regular chelation therapy until we're sure that his system is clear. We caught it in plenty of time, don't worry."

"Chelation therapy?" Riley asked.

"It's a way of clearing heavy metals out of the body," Shankar said.

Bill pointed to a bandage in the crook of his arm.

"I'll get it intravenously on an outpatient basis. I can get it done back at home, too."

He rubbed the bandage.

"I've got to say, it burns quite a bit," he said.

"With some luck, that will be the only side effect," Shankar said.

Then she laughed.

"Now I suggest that the two of you get out of here," she said.

"Good idea," Riley said, getting out of bed.

"And Agent Paige?" she added.

Riley turned.

"Damn good work."

EPILOGUE

The following night, Riley was back in Fredericksburg sitting in the living room, telling Ryan all that had happened. She had arrived very late, after all the flight delays, and Gabriella, April, and Jilly were all fast asleep. She didn't want to wake them.

Besides, she enjoyed having this quiet time alone, just with Ryan.

The house was still, and they sat beside each other on the couch, each enjoying their second glass of wine.

Riley took a deep breath as she finished her story.

In the silence that followed, Riley closed her eyes and remembered her day in flashes: the long flight home with Bill; his gratitude at her help and her relief that he would be OK; Meredith's call, his reluctant congratulations and reinstating her, with a warning that they'd need to meet when she got back; even Rigby called and congratulated her in his own awkward way. None would come and admit she had cracked it, yet she could hear it all in their voices, the awkward silence that signaled respect—and that meant more to her than she could say.

"Thank God you're safe," Ryan finally said, breaking the silence, hugging her.

Ryan was now speechless.

While they sat there in silence, Riley kept remembering what Shane Hatcher had said to her ...

"Everything happens for no reason."

Today for some reason, Riley felt almost as if she were starting to understand what that meant.

Finally Ryan said, "But what about that crazy woman killer? She was contaminated too, wasn't she?"

"That's right," Riley said. "She'll get the same chelation treatment as Bill."

"But how many people did she kill?"

Riley sighed tiredly.

"We're still trying to find out. A half dozen at least, over a period of years."

Ryan scratched his chin.

"And yet she's going to get full medical treatment. That doesn't seem fair."

"You're a lawyer, you should understand," Riley said. "The law doesn't deal in *poetic* justice—just plain old ordinary legal justice. And it remains to be seen whether she'll be competent to stand trial. The last I heard, she's still slipping in and out of lucidity. I'm sure her lawyer will put up an insanity defense."

Ryan shook his head.

"Don't you just hate that?"

Riley didn't reply. Until now, she'd always loathed insanity defenses. But Alicia Carswell was one of the strangest criminals she'd ever apprehended.

What was the diagnosis the psychiatrist had given early this morning?

Oh, yes, Riley remembered. *"Organic delusional disorder."*

Alicia Carswell suffered from a grandiose belief that she was some kind of angel.

Riley was struck by something especially strange. She had tracked a good many insane killers over the years. But in the past, all that insanity had always had a cause, some roots in childhood or heredity.

But Amanda Carswell's madness seemed to have no cause whatsoever.

So far, the authorities had found no sign that Carswell had lived anything other than a perfectly happy childhood, nor was there any history of insanity in her family. Prisha Shankar had explained to Riley and Bill that this was typical of organic delusional disorder. Its cause was often impossible to determine. It seemed to arise out of nowhere.

Again Hatcher's words rang in Riley's head.

"Everything happens for no reason."

It was all very unsettling. Somehow, blind chance had turned this woman into an insane murderer.

The thought made her shiver.

The world seemed to make a little less sense today than it had before.

Riley stood then and walked over to her windows. The blackness of the night, seeping into her living room, had never bothered her before.

But tonight, it did.

She reached up and pulled the string, closing the blinds right.

The world was darker, indeed.

Filled, she knew, with an endless sea of serial killers.

And as much as she tried to run from them, tomorrow, she knew, or perhaps the day after, she'd get another call.

And another.

And another.

One day, she knew, she'd reach a tipping point and stop taking that call.

But for now?

She had no idea.

Coming Soon!

Book #7 in the Riley Paige mystery series

Blake Pierce

Blake Pierce is author of the bestselling RILEY PAGE mystery series, which includes six books (and counting). Blake Pierce is also the author of the MACKENZIE WHITE mystery series, comprising three books (and counting); of the AVERY BLACK mystery series, comprising three books (and counting); and of the new KERI LOCKE mystery series.

An avid reader and lifelong fan of the mystery and thriller genres, Blake loves to hear from you, so please feel free to visit www.blakepierceauthor.com to learn more and stay in touch.

BOOKS BY BLAKE PIERCE

RILEY PAIGE MYSTERY SERIES
ONCE GONE (Book #1)
ONCE TAKEN (Book #2)
ONCE CRAVED (Book #3)
ONCE LURED (Book #4)
ONCE HUNTED (Book #5)
ONCE PINED (Book #6)

MACKENZIE WHITE MYSTERY SERIES
BEFORE HE KILLS (Book #1)
BEFORE HE SEES (Book #2)
BEFORE HE COVETS (Book #3)

AVERY BLACK MYSTERY SERIES
CAUSE TO KILL (Book #1)
CAUSE TO RUN (Book #2)
CAUSE TO HIDE (Book #3)

KERI LOCKE MYSTERY SERIES
A TRACE OF DEATH (Book #1)

CPSIA information can be obtained
at www.ICGtesting.com
Printed in the USA
BVOW05s1006020117
472335BV00023B/575/P